ROBERT P. OTTONE

WRAPPED
in Plastic
AND OTHER SWEET NOTHINGS

JOURNALSTONE
YOUR LINK TO ARTIST TALENT

ISBN: 978-1-68510-113-8 (trade paper)
ISBN: 978-1-68510-114-5 (ebook)
Library of Congress Catalog Number: 2023947142

Tiny Town originally produced by The Night's End podcast, October 2021
A Child Awakens originally published by Exisle Academy, May 2021
A Year of Bloody Gums originally published in *Gravely Unusual Magazine*, Summer 2021
The Last of the Leading Men originally published by Deadman's Tome Publishing, January 2021
Hookman's End originally published by DBND Publishing, August 2020
A Mourning in Sleepy Hollow originally published by Redcape Publishing, July 2021
Only That You Are Still Sane originally published by *Coffin Bell*, October 2021
The Aluxes originally published by Gravely Unusual and Lurking Transmissions, October 2021
Falling Asleep in the Rain originally published by Dark Ink, March 2021
For The Gods originally published by Dark Ink, June 2021
The Girl in the Floor originally published by Spooky House Press, July 2021

First printing edition October 27, 2023
Published by JournalStone Publishing in the United States of America.
Cover Artwork and Design: Don Noble | roosterrepublicpress.com
Edited by Sean Leonard
Proofreading and Cover/Interior Layout by Scarlett R. Algee

JournalStone Publishing
3205 Sassafras Trail
Carbondale, Illinois 62901

JournalStone books may be ordered through booksellers or by contacting:
JournalStone | www.journalstone.com

For Bullet Bob Ottone

Contents

WRAPPED
in Plastic
AND OTHER SWEET NOTHINGS

Acknowledgments

I want to thank all the wonderful editors I worked with whose stories comprise this collection. Thank you to every single one of you, there are many and you all rock.

Love and thanks to my critique groups, you're weird, you're fun, you're sweet.

Thank you to the wonderful Bookstagram and Booktuber communities who have been receptive of my work and of myself. You are all pretty fabulous.

Thank you to Scarlett at JournalStone. Here's to warmer weather!

Thank you to everyone who bought and reviewed my other books, you have no idea what that means to me.

Thank you to Andy Boyle. Nobody dances better'n you, hoss.

Last but not least, thank you to my wife. Keep being cool, babe.

A Mourning in Sleepy Hollow

Constable Hayward knelt beside the road near the church bridge, staring at the remains of a pumpkin. Snow was falling lightly, tiny flakes, and Hayward knew that he didn't have much time before the entire area was blanketed with fresh powder.

The Dutch Burial Ground sat nearby, snow beginning to pile atop the headstones. Hayward looked toward the small cemetery, trying to spot jagged pieces of orange amongst the white. Hayward furrowed his brow and started gathering some of the pieces of the gourd, eventually finding a piece with a triangle cut out.

"Think it was him?" the Constable's son, Aranck asked, shivering in the cold. The eighteen-year-old rubbed his chest through his heavy coat. "Think it was the Horseman?"

"Don't know. Keep your eyes open."

He stared at the hole a moment, trying to imagine what it was, when he heard the distressed neighs of a horse. He nodded toward where the neighing was coming from. "Go check it out."

Aranck climbed down the embankment and found an old gray horse, underfed and nervously kicking at the rocks along the river. "I think this is Gunpowder, the nag that belongs to the new schoolmaster, Ichabod Crane."

Hayward steadied himself as he joined Aranck in the embankment. His heavy frame wobbled unsteadily in the snowy mud, slowed from years of either fighting whatever war called upon the men of New York, or from serving as the only lawman in a busy town.

Before becoming Constable, Hayward had been a successful tracker and hunter from Setauket, who worked primarily as a spy during the war, gathering intelligence on British troop maneuvers in New York City. Afterward, he arrived in Sleepy Hollow and found himself in love with Aranck's mother of the local Wecquaesgeek tribe. When her people migrated further west, she stayed behind with Hayward and their child. After brokering many deals with the tribal elders who remained after the war, the town squire asked him to remain in Sleepy Hollow as a lawman.

"That old horse's seen better days, eh, papa?" Aranck called from the bridge, studying the tracks in the mud. "Looks like a weak rear hoof."

Good catch. Hayward smiled. Aranck was becoming a good tracker, too, still so young. And he looked so much like his mother. "For certain, my boy."

When the Bleeker girl disappeared years back, it was Aranck who found her, half-buried in the snow with a broken ankle. His son spoke of whispers in the wind that drew him to the injured child. Whispers Hayward knew his wife heard in her youth; her days spent with the tribe in the forests of the valley.

"It looks burned. On the inside. Look," Hayward showed a few scorched pieces of pumpkin to his son. The insides, the flesh of the gourd, were singed, as though detonated from the inside.

"A Jack O'Lantern," Aranck said, studying the pieces. He ran his finger along the inside of a larger piece of pumpkin, scraping some of the singed blackness away with his nail. "Like what we used to carve with mother."

Hayward wondered how Aranck's life would turn out, a child of two worlds, never comfortable in either his mother's tradition, or the tradition of the white man.

"Think it was a land dispute?" Aranck asked. "Maybe the schoolmaster had his eyes set on more than Squire Van Tassel's daughter?"

"You think they ran him out of town? Whoever he was doing business with?"

Aranck shrugged. "Wouldn't be the first time, right? These white men and their petty squabbles."

"We need to find Brom Bones. Think you can get word to his little sidekick?"

"Fred Dutcher? Sure. Meet you at the hall in an hour."

Aranck climbed on his horse and took off toward Sleepy Hollow. Hayward thought, often, about his son leaving the town. The boy had expressed his desire to do so. To join his people who migrated west. To fully immerse himself in the old ways. Hayward pressed the heartache of his son leaving deep down ad focused on the job.

Hayward began to escort Gunpowder back up the hill to the bridge, careful to lead the horse slowly so as not to rattle the poor nag's nerves any further.

#

"Why is it that every time something goes wrong in this one-horse town, you come after me, Constable?" Brom Bones said, rubbing his temples. The man's enormity was stuff of legend in the Hudson Valley. Some of the little ones often marveled at his size, asking if he was half-bear or half-bull. Brom would often respond with "Half-bear, half-bull and half-wildcat." Suffice to say, math was not his strong suit.

"Usually, your dumb self is involved in all the goings-on in Sleepy Hollow," Aranck said. "What's wrong with your head?"

"Headache s'all. What's it to you, half-breed?"

Aranck's lips pressed together tightly. Without warning, he slapped Brom so hard, he fell off the stool in the center of the meeting hall.

Brom grabbed the side of his face and howled, as Aranck readied for the enormous man to rise, ready for a scrap.

"You sonofa—" the enormous man screamed, rising quickly.

Hayward moved faster, stepping between his son and the raging Dutchman. "Aranck, go outside."

Aranck followed his father's orders, striding past Squire Van Tassel, who stood, arms crossed, next to the door of the meeting house.

"Where's the schoolmaster, Brom?"

"I wanna press charges, Constable, he can't hit me!"

"Brom, it's your word against his. And I'm the law. In what reality will I press charges against my own kin?"

Brom sighed and sat back down on the stool. "Why are we talkin' 'bout that old scare-crane, anyway? Ain't seen 'im since last night."

"Around what time?"

"I dunno, me and Dutcher were at the party. Van Tassel's."

"What happened at the party? Did you two have words?"

Brom shook his head. He stretched his jaw, still reeling from the slap Aranck gave him. "No, not at all. He was occupied with Ms. Katrina all night, the Yankee bastard. Caught the two of them fightin' about sumthin'."

Hayward looked at Squire Van Tassel. "Brom, we know that you and the schoolmaster have had problems. Just tell us where he is and I promise everything'll be okay."

Brom looked up at Hayward. "Honest, Constable, I didn't do nothin' to the schoolmaster. Me and Dutcher nicked off to Dumpkey's hay loft with a cask of Van Tassel's wine. Sorry, Squire."

Van Tassel shook his head. "Idiot."

"That's why your head hurts. You were making too much merry last night. The spirits have taken their revenge on ya' today."

Brom nodded. "Can I go now?"

"Head to the pub. If you and Dutcher leave town, I'll have a full party after you by nightfall. You won't get far. And if you have eyes set on retribution for that little love tap my son gave ya', you better think twice."

Brom sighed. He rose, slowly and walked to the door. Hayward watched as Brom eyed Aranck, who leaned against a column outside the meeting house. Squire Van Tassel joined the Constable on the porch and looked over the town.

"You get your temper from your old man," Hayward said. "I know that. You know that. But you need to watch it. Life isn't going to be easy for you. Especially if you still plan to leave the Hollow."

Aranck nodded. "I know. I'm sorry, pa."

"You don't need to apologize to me. Brom acts like a child, but you were out of line. Maybe send your apologies his way, with a nice bottle of our brandy."

"Fair enough."

"Squire, we're gonna need to talk to Katrina. Mind fetching her?"

#

Hayward watched as Squire Van Tassel escorted Katrina down the snow-covered street to the town hall building. They were talking, the squire no doubt coaching his daughter on how to respond to the questions Hayward had planned for her.

"Katrina, always a pleasure," Hayward said, smiling, and kissing the young girl's slender hand. She curtsied and smiled, her intense blue eyes flashing in the afternoon light flooding the town hall meeting room.

Aranck, a few years Katrina's junior, stood by a window, watching Fred Dutcher spill his guts beside the town pub. Brom Bones stood behind him, nervously pacing about in the snow.

"We just have a few questions for you, Miss Van Tassel," Hayward began.

"'We?' Is Aranck officially a deputy now?" she asked, her gaze wandering over toward Aranck by the window.

"Not yet, but he's learning more every day. Someone's gotta' keep an eye on the Van Tassels when I'm gone," Hayward smiled.

Katrina chuckled, and so did Squire Van Tassel. Aranck stood, eyes locked on Dutcher and Brom nearby, loitering outside the pub.

"Katrina, what happened with the schoolmaster last night?"

She shrugged. "Well, you see, we've been engaged in a sort-of...*whirlwind* the past few months."

"Is that so?" Squire Van Tassel asked.

"Well, yes, father, Ichabod is an educated man, not like the *usual* types around here."

Aranck turned from the window and looked at Katrina. Their eyes met, and she looked away, nervously.

"Aren't you supposed to be Brom Bones' girl?" Hayward asked.

Aranck grabbed his coat and exited the meeting room, heading off into the snow.

Katrina looked up at her father. Then cast her gaze to the floor and shrugged. "I'm sure I don't know what you mean, Constable."

Hayward looked up at Squire Van Tassel and gestured toward the door. Van Tassel followed in Aranck's footsteps, disappearing outside.

Hayward pulled a chair over to Katrina and sat opposite her.

"There. All our company is gone. You can talk to me, Katrina."

"Brom is...well...he's good for passing the time, you know? Like riding a wild horse. He's exciting. Powerful. But unskilled. Once the thrill is gone, there's not much to him."

Hayward nodded. "Understood. And the schoolmaster?"

Katrina's eyes sparkled at the mention of the missing schoolmaster. "You must find him, Constable. We had such a terrible fight last night. He asked for my hand. I told him I needed more time."

Hayward put his hand on Katrina's shoulder. "I can understand that. That's a lot to put on a young woman after such a short time."

"I worry that Brom did something to him. Last night. Likes to dress like the Headless Horseman. Black cape, Jack O'Lantern, you know?"

"Lots of boys do. Even Aranck—"

"I would've thought Aranck was above such childish folly. He was always a more sensitive soul."

Hayward smiled. "Gets that from his mother."

Katrina smiled at him. "I don't think that's entirely true." She took Hayward's hand. "Please. Find Ichabod. I know in my heart he's still out there. If Brom had anything to do with it, he'll tell you. He's always been a braggart."

"I don't think Brom is involved, Miss Van Tassel."

She sighed and looked up at him. It was impossible not to see what every boy in town loved about her. The intensity of her eyes, her plump, rosy cheeks, the color of an autumn evening as day burns away to night. The kindness in her demeanor. It was more than just the desire for her father's bounty that drew men to her. "I simply don't know who else would harbor ill intentions toward my Ichabod, Constable."

#

Outside the meeting hall, Aranck stood, watching folks mill about the town. He had slipped his fingers into a small leather pouch and pulled out a small cigar. Lighting it slowly, he breathed in the aroma, a blend of spice, fruit and even a hint of leather. His father exited the hall and stood beside him.

"Got one of those for me, boy?"

Aranck again reached into his pouch and handed a cigar to his father.

Hayward stared at his son. His long black hair caught a bit of wind and blew, as though it had a life of its own. "Something troubles you. Speak freely, boy."

"It wasn't Brom. It wasn't anyone in his gang. Brom's a good rider, but riding a horse and carrying a flaming pumpkin?" Aranck trailed off. Lost in thought.

"What're you thinkin'?"

"You *know* what I'm thinking, pa. When you eliminate the possible, the likely, the rational, what remains?"

Hayward nodded. "The impossible."

"Crane was angry. He wanted Katrina's hand. Shoulda had the brains to leave when he could."

"The folly of youth...ready to take on the world, boy?"

"Maybe. I'm just sayin', the schoolmaster loved Miss Katrina. The pumpkins. The horse. He couldn't have gone far on foot, pa. People disappear sometimes. Something takes people. White men are sloppy. They leave clues. You taught me that."

"Aranck, nobody's seen the horseman in years."

"Because nobody's stupid enough to disrupt the way things are here in the Hollow. We go, day to day, working, playing, drinking, fighting, we never leave, unless taken by grim death. The last schoolmaster, Palmer, you know he disappeared too."

"He ran off, he was crazed—"

"Was he? My conversations with him were usually pretty sane, father." Aranck took a long drag off his cigar.

Hayward knew the boy wasn't wrong. The similarities between Crane and Palmer's cases were striking, but in the case of Palmer, they never found any indication that he tried to leave. No horse. No broken gourds. No report of him missing. Just one day, the schoolhouse was left with an open door, swaying in the fall wind.

"What do we do, my boy?"

Aranck finished his cigar. He flicked it into the mud. "I have an idea, but first, I want to check with Her. She might know something."

Her. The thought of his son trekking off into the woods to take counsel with Sleepy Hollow's resident witch gave Hayward pause. While everyone knew about the Headless Horseman, not many knew of the crone who lived deep in the woods at the base of a small, rocky outcropping.

Aranck's mother would visit her often. Bringing her food. Ale. Aranck joined his mother on these trips, and the old crone took to him. She would leave gifts on Hayward's doorstep for the boy. Dolls fashioned from strips of clothing and animal fur.

"If that's what you feel you have to do, boy, that's fine, but I think it's time I meet this hag."

#

As Hayward and Aranck made their way through the forest outside of Sleepy Hollow, they marveled at the sight of the lush orange and red foliage. It was if the trees were ablaze in the afternoon light, and the ground, coated with dried leaves, crackled under the hooves of their horses.

Aranck's eyes watched the trees around them. He would sometimes awaken in the night and walk out into the darkness in his night clothes, barefoot, even in winter. He described what he believed to be a whisper in the darkness, a voice on the wind, calling him into the woods. Not malevolent, but instead kind and soothing.

He often heard those same voices in the woods around the crone's home.

"We are nearly there, father. The location is always a secret to my eyes, but never my ears."

As they continued, Hayward started seeing smaller rocks appearing in the forest. They moved deeper into the woods, and the stones became larger. He remembered his son often returning home with rounded, almost polished pieces of rock, purple and light blue, rocks not normally found in the valley or in the foothills. Aranck would admit to gathering them while visiting the crone in the woods.

They were close.

"Father, when we get there, let me do all the talking, alright?"

Hayward nodded. He knew better.

Eventually, they came to the mouth of a small cave. Aranck stopped in his tracks, his horse refusing to move any closer.

"This is it."

"She lives in there?" Hayward stared at the cave's mouth. The opening was tiny.

Once inside, Hayward was struck by how large and empty the space was. It seemed to stretch further underground, possibly forming a system that ran as far north as the foothills, as opposed to deeper into a larger mountain-structure, and Hayward wondered how others hadn't discovered these caves before.

"It is not much further," Aranck said, producing a small lantern from his pack and lighting it in the failing daylight.

They continued, and eventually, came to an area not unlike a chapel, with tall ceilings, formed naturally over hundreds, maybe thousands of years.

Hayward gasped, staring at the lanterns and torches mounted to the walls of the cave. On the walls hung animal pelts, and in many other areas along the walls were drawings of tribal warriors, hunting and worshipping creatures that, at first resembled bears, but stood more humanlike. "My Lord..."

"... won't be found here, Constable." A voice spoke from the far end of the cave. The "crone" as she was often referred to by the few townsfolk who saw her, wasn't a crone at all, but instead a beautiful, dark-haired, dark-skinned woman. Her appearance reminded Hayward of so many of the Wecquaesgeek women he knew before the war. Sharp features. Impossibly-long, black hair, down to her knees. Wearing what Hayward thought was a deer skin draped across her body, her dark eyes flickered in the torchlight of the cave.

On closer inspection, the cave was warmer and more welcoming than he had initially realized. Cozy, even. There was the slightest scent of lavender in the air, and the animal pelts were thick and soft. Hayward almost felt at home in the crone's cave.

Aranck exchanged pleasantries with the woman in their shared language and presented her with a small leather pouch of berries and nuts. He also produced a large woven mat from his pack and slung it over a large rock.

She sat upon the mat and swung her bare legs up and under her body, resting on her knees. She looked no older than Aranck, and yet, the rumors of her existence in the woods around Sleepy Hollow had spread since before the boy's birth.

"It is an honor to have your father here, Aranck," she said. Her voice, though soft, carried tremendous weight. Aranck knelt before her, sitting cross-legged, like a child in school.

"I have heard many tales of you," Hayward said, softly, as though a raised voice might trigger a collapse of the stone ceiling above. "You are not what I expected."

She smiled. "And what did you expect?"

Without warning, a great black fog erupted from around her, enveloping her quickly. When it dissipated, a much older, white woman, with long gray hair, wrinkled features, and a long, obtrusive nose, sat in her place, draped in drab, dreary rags.

Aranck laughed. She did, too. Her soft and powerful voice was replaced with a cackle that made Hayward's knees go weak.

"My dear Constable, there is so much more to those around you than you ever imagined..." again the smoke enveloped her, and she returned to her previous form, lovely and perfect. "Your ignorance of our ways blinds you to the truth the valley offers you."

"Nanepaishot, you know why we have come," Aranck began.

She raised her hand, stopping him from finishing. She placed that same hand on Aranck's shoulder and stared, lovingly, into his eyes. Hayward thought for a moment that his son sat in a trance, but then realized that the look of adoration on his face was the same look he'd often have for his mother. It was a look of devotion and deeply rooted love.

"On this night, he rides. He keeps a careful watch over the valley. He is always there, even when you cannot see him."

She paused. Her long, slender fingers traced black, cloudy shapes in the air. Hayward recognized horses, muskets, cannonballs, and finally, a Jack O'Lantern. "It is justice he seeks. Retribution. For stealing our land."

Shifting into a kneeling position on the rock, she adjusted her deerskin and cast a vacant gaze into the sky. "Manitos lies these woods. These mountains. But your horseman. He is something else. Our spirit manifest. Like me. Yotoanit..."

Aranck gasped. "That cannot be, Nanepaishot."

She closed her eyes and nodded. "He is the spirit. The one kept in the dark for so long. For so many centuries."

"Until the war."

Again, she nodded. The dark smoke around her cleared, and she stared at Hayward. "Death is not through with Sleepy Hollow. The schoolmaster is gone. Dragged to hell by Yotoanit."

"Who is Yotoanit? I don't understand..." Hayward began, his voice pleading.

"You will find him at the bridge. The veil is thin tonight. It always is this time of year. That is why your people display such superstitious frivolity. To protect you from spirits. To seek the horseman is to seek death itself, Constable." She looks at Aranck. "None are safe from Yotoanit."

Carefully, she slipped off the rock, and Aranck rose to help her. She held his arm tightly, as they made their way to a nearby bed of animal skins, flowers and straw. Once down, Aranck covered her with a thick bear skin. She reached up and slowly brushed a long strand of dark hair from his face. "Aranck, you look so very much like her."

The boy smiled.

"You are as beautiful as the night is treacherous," she whispered to Aranck in the dark.

#

"What the hell happened in there?" Hayward asked as the two slipped out of the cave.

"Did you not see? She confirmed my suspicions about the horseman. And yet, it is far worse. So, so much worse."

"That name. Yotoanit. What does that mean?"

Aranck sighed. "Our people, at least, what mother *told* me of our people, believed in many things. One of those things was Yotoanit, the god of fire. A cursed being from deep within our belief. Born of strife and malice, he sows destruction in his wake."

A great wave of guilt struck Hayward, as he never put much stock in his wife and child's culture. "How do we stop him? What's 'manitos?'"

"Nanepaishot grows weak when she uses her gifts. That's 'manitos,' essentially, our life energy. Flesh is a limiting form to our gods. We weaken him, trick him across the river, put him down like a dog. There is a reason he's never seen outside of the valley. The flesh is weak."

"I'll say," Hayward uttered.

"He's a god of fire. Crossing a body of water out of the valley is his weakness. If we can, tonight, draw him out. Keep him busy. Ride like the devil, force him to act, use his power, draw him close to the bridge, near the river, we might be able to vanquish him."

"That's a huge *might*, Aranck."

"It is all we have, father."

#

After a quick stop at the pub to recruit a pair of extra hands, Hayward and Aranck made for the bridge nearest the church. Brom and Aranck stood on the western bank of the bridge, not far from where Hayward and the boy had found Gunpowder earlier that day. The temperature had dropped and Brom sipped from a large bottle of brandy.

"I'm sorry about your chin," Aranck said, one hand on his musket, the other, resting against a tree in the midst of shedding its leaves for the season.

"It's my jaw but thank you. Wasn't right. What I said. You being a half-breed, I mean."

Aranck nodded. "Thank you for helping us tonight. You and Dutcher."

"Truth be told, Dutcher's a lousy shot with a musket, so, if anything *does* happen and that galloping nightmare appears, he's liable to shoot one of *us*."

Aranck chuckled. Brom handed him the bottle of brandy, and the boy took a sip.

#

Hours later, the temperature seemed to dip below freezing, and Fred Dutcher sat beside Hayward in a large elderberry bush on the opposite side of the bridge. A great dampness hung in the air, and the Constable was chilled to the bone.

"Explain to me again why we can't light no fire, Constable?"

Hayward rolled his eyes. "Because we're trying not to be seen. That's why the horses are tied close to the river, and we're up *here*."

Dutcher nodded. "Seems stupid to me."

Hayward chuckled. "I imagine a great many things do."

A light padding in the distance caught Hayward's attention.

"I saw him once, you know. The Horseman."

"Did you now?"

Hayward only half-listened as Dutcher began his story. "Me and Brom, you know, we go a-ways back. We were walking in the mountains, you know, in the Dunderbergs..."

Hayward kept his focus on the light noise he heard. He glanced across the river and prayed his son could hear it, too. For a moment, he thought he heard a horse neigh, far off, in the blackness of night.

"... never thought much for those old stories of goblins in the mountains, ya' know? Seemed awful silly t'me."

The Constable unslung the musket from his shoulder and leaned forward on his knee. He blocked out Dutcher's voice and focused instead on the rising sound of hooves in the distance. Again, he glanced across the river, desperate for a glimpse of his son. *Please, Aranck, tell me you can hear it.*

"...but then, once we made it to the top of the Dunderbergs, we saw him. Down below, near the river."

Hayward looked down the road toward Sleepy Hollow. The sound was growing ever-nearer, and he knew that soon, whatever it was would be on top of him and Dutcher.

Hayward checked his musket, taking his time to ensure there was a round loaded. He didn't know if he'd be able to get off another musket shot, so he checked his pistol, as well. He even checked Dutcher's, who seemed lost in his own tale.

"Down by the river...his head was all fire. Hellfire, some say. I don't much know about that..."

The steps grew louder, driving closer and closer. Hayward knew that soon, whatever it was would be within range of a shot. He watched the road headed east, as it dropped off in a great ridge, framed by enormous trees.

Dutcher's story began to slow. The sound of the approaching horse was too loud to ignore. A distant, guttural neigh alerted both of them, and slowly, Hayward rose, peering just above the bush, watching the horizon of the road. A faint orange glow flickered east.

"Hellfire," Dutcher whispered in the dark, his lips quivering, more from fright than the cold air. Their horses neighed softly, lifting their heads and snorting. Dutcher did his best to soothe them.

All sound seemed to escape the area surrounding the bridge. Hayward looked toward the graveyard, half-expecting to see the spirits of spectral nightmares emerging from the ground, but there was nothing. Hayward had fought in the war. He had seen bloodshed firsthand countless times. He tightened his grip on the sabre hanging from his hip.

Yet now, in this moment, hiding in a bush with a moron, Hayward knew the true meaning of fear. He watched it break over the horizon, galloping hard on a black steed in the night. Hayward produced a spyglass, a remnant of his days with the Culper Spy Ring during the war and peered through.

The Headless Horseman. In all his nightmarish glory. The specter was massive. Far larger than any of the descriptions Hayward had heard throughout the years. Even without a head, it towered over himself and Dutcher, maybe even Brom, who was the tallest of their meager group.

The Horseman's steed. Under normal circumstances, one might find a creature like this rotting in a field, but instead, it stood, muscles and ribcage visible in sections, half of its skull steaming in the damp, cool night. Strings of sinew clung to the horse's exposed ribs, dangling, wet-looking, in the moonlight.

"My God..." Hayward muttered under his breath, as he clutched his musket tighter. "Go to the horses, Dutcher. See to them."

The horses, meanwhile, had begun to neigh, disturbed by the presence of the Horseman, even at such a distance.

The Horseman sat in his saddle. If he had a head, Hayward might have imagined him watching the bush. He simply sat, motionless, his horse breathing heavy in the night, casting steam from the exposed portions of its skull in the cold.

Hayward glanced toward Dutcher, who had gotten the horses under control.

The Horseman remained, steady and focused on the bridge.

"He knows we're here..." Hayward whispered.

Without warning, the sound of a musket shot pierced Hayward's ear and he turned, startled at the sound. Brom Bones stood on the opposite side of the river, weapon smoking from the discharge.

"Ride, you hobgoblin! Ride to me!" Brom shouted, reloading his musket.

The Horseman circled quickly, and in an explosion of speed, tore off toward the bridge, and Hayward panicked. The Constable raised his musket and prepared to fire, waiting until he knew for sure that he could hit the spirit, when without warning, he was pushed to the ground by Dutcher, on horseback.

"Here! Here!" cried Dutcher, waving one arm, while holding the reins of the horse with his other.

"Dutcher, you fool!" Brom screamed, finishing reloading his musket.

Dutcher tore toward the Horseman, then stopped, turning back toward the bridge quickly, attempting to bait the ghoul. The

Horseman brandished an enormous blade, and charged, gaining on Dutcher quickly.

In the blink of an eye, the Horseman's neck erupted in an explosion of flame, and a Jack O'Lantern appeared, grinning madly, engulfed in fire. Hayward was frozen by the intensity of the orange glow in the night and watched as the Horseman simply raised his arm and pointed at Dutcher.

With impossible accuracy, the grinning gourd flew at Dutcher, a sound not unlike a scream piercing the night. The pumpkin collided hard and knocked the man from his saddle.

In an instant, the Horseman closed on Dutcher, whose head hung limply, shocked from the collision and the fall. He stirred a moment, and turned, as the Horseman brandished an enormous blade and with a flash, severed Dutcher's head clean from his shoulders.

Dutcher's horse whinnied, pitched up on its back legs, and Dutcher's lifeless body crumpled to the mud.

Aranck emerged from the embankment, musket and pistol at the ready. He stood, side by side with Brom, and raised his weapon. The Horseman continued his charge, and when he was about twenty yards away from the two young men, Hayward emerged from the bush and fired a shot.

The Horseman spun, and up close, Hayward could see another column of fire emerge from the Horseman's shoulders. Another Jack O'Lantern appeared, same angry expression as the one previous.

The Horseman turned from Aranck and Brom and started back toward Hayward.

"Boys, run!" Hayward screamed, slipping down into the eastern embankment. He quickly gathered himself and climbed on his horse, tearing off north of the river, along the rocky shore.

Aranck and Brom climbed on their horses and tore off north as well, but on the western bank, desperate to keep pace with Hayward and the Horseman.

They watched the Horseman gain ground on the Constable, sword held high, ready to strike.

"Father! Ride! Ride hard!" Aranck screamed.

Brom raised his pistol and fired a shot, which, were The Horseman a living being, would've easily downed him, but instead did nothing. The Horseman slowed a touch and turned, its great Jack O'Lantern skull igniting in an orange fireball.

"Up there! The river narrows!" Brom shouted as they approached a natural rock bridge between the two banks.

Kicking his horse in the ribs hard, Aranck raced toward the rocks, and crossed quickly, his horse stumbling a moment, as it tried to gain footing.

"Father, I'm here!"

The two rode, side by side, as Brom crossed the rocky area, as well, slowing his horse and placing himself behind the Headless Horseman.

"Keep riding, you fools!" Brom screamed.

The Horseman, in one motion, turned, and with the same gesture that nailed Dutcher, soared his gourd at Brom.

With incredible speed, Brom ducked and the Jack O'Lantern flew past his head. Brom watched as the Jack O'Lantern exploded behind him in a riot of fire and orange husk.

When Brom turned back around, he could barely believe his eyes as the area where the Horseman's head should be suddenly erupted into towering orange flames. In an instant, they formed another Jack O'Lantern, and Brom rode harder, drawing his pistol.

As he took aim at the Horseman, the spirit seemed to anticipate the man's moves, and reacted by lobbing his new-formed pumpkin head directly at Brom. This time, the Jack O'Lantern exploded in Brom's face, tearing the strong Dutchman from his saddle, and slamming him to the mud.

He rolled onto his side and watched as the Horseman bore down on him, high in his saddle.

"Do your worst, hellspawn..." Brom said, spitting a loosened tooth from his mouth.

The Horseman climbed down from his saddle and stood. He drew his sabre and stalked toward Brom. The blade still dripped with Fred Dutcher's blood.

Suddenly, two shots rang out, the Headless Horseman lurched forward, roaring into the night sky in agony.

Brom braced himself for the end, but when it didn't come, he opened his eyes and looked up.

The Horseman touched a gloved hand to his own chest. Rivulets of fire began to form from the two spots where the rounds tore through him, followed by strings of orange-red goo, strands of pumpkin innards, seeds barely hanging on as the gourd meat dripped from The Horseman's chest.

The Horseman turned, and watched as Aranck and Hayward sat on horseback, reloading their muskets thirty yards north of the river.

"You are running him down! He is bleeding!" Brom screamed, before being stabbed in the shoulder by the Horseman.

In a flash of orange fury, another Jack O'Lantern formed on the Horseman's shoulders, and he turned, stalking toward his horse. Quickly, he climbed back into his saddle and tore off toward Aranck and Hayward.

"We have to get him to the other side of the river, we have to trick him across," Aranck said, frantically.

Hayward turned to his son and pushed him from his horse. He threw his musket down at the boy's feet and turned back to the Horseman, who was gaining on them quickly.

"Hyah!" Hayward shouted, tearing further north of the river, forcing his horse into the shallow depths, trudging through water and mud.

The Horseman followed close behind.

"Come on, you old nag, come on!" Hayward's horse darted more to the center of the river, deep, but still passable, and whinnied in the dark.

The Horseman gained on Hayward across the river, and in a terrifying explosion of mud, water, pumpkin and fire, their horses collided.

Hayward lay, face down in the mud, staring at the smiling Jack O'Lantern face of Sleepy Hollow's notorious nightmare, who lay still in the shallow waters of the river that served as a natural barrier between Sleepy Hollow and regions due west.

The Horseman rose, as did Hayward. Slashing with his sabre, the Horseman gained on Hayward quickly, but Hayward met the demon's blade with his own, with a clash of steel on steel.

Hayward stumbled in the shallow waters, as did the Horseman. Their sabres collided repeatedly, sparks of fire flickering into the night. The Constable noted that the demon had slowed considerably, the water washing over its boots.

Hayward, his only recourse a pure defense, as he stumbled further and further backward, his boots heavy, sodden with mud. He could feel his heart pounding, as though it could tear free of his chest at any moment.

They fought, The Horseman, though weakened, was still the better of the two. Hayward, one eye on Aranck on the eastern side of the river, and another on Brom Bones, bleeding, struggling in the mud.

Each attack of the Horseman forced Hayward backward, and sapped the Constable's energy. Eventually, Hayward fell to the banks of the river, exhausted and reeling from the barrage of sword-on-sword pressure unleashed by The Horseman.

More gunshots. The Horseman froze in place. Turning, The specter spotted Aranck standing along the edge of the river, dual pistols raised, smoking in the moonlight.

The Horseman touched his wounds. He was dripping pumpkin innards at a rapid pace, and Hayward rose slowly behind him. The Horseman began stalking toward Aranck as the boy fumbled for the musket slung over his shoulder.

Hayward wrapped his strong arms around The Horseman and held him firmly in place in the center of the river, water sloshing around their ankles, soaking them both. On unsteady, exhausted legs, Hayward began dragging The Horseman backward, closer to the opposite side of the shore. The spirit had begun to slow, proving that the flesh truly was weak.

Once across, the demon got one of his arms loose, raised his sabre and ran himself through, the blade passing through himself, and out his back, into Hayward's chest, locking the two of them together.

"See you in hell, demon..." Hayward whispered to The Horseman before sliding off the end of the blade and collapsing to the rocks on the western side of the river. "Now, Aranck! Shoot him now!" Hayward screamed.

On the second "now" Aranck fired. The round soared across the river and slammed directly into the Jack O'Lantern resting upon the shoulders of the Headless Horseman. The flaming gourd erupted in a torrent of hellfire and pumpkin pieces, splattering all over the Constable, as well as the side of the river.

Aranck splashed through the water to his father. He stared at the motionless body of The Horseman, sabre resting just out of reach. Aranck picked the blade up as it slowly withered in his hand, the steel rusting and turning to dust. The body of the Horseman followed suit, rotting at a rapid pace, before dissolving along the banks of the river.

Even the shattered pieces of Jack O'Lantern rotted quickly, browning and turning to mush.

Aranck knelt beside Hayward, and placed his hand on his father's chest, in a futile effort to stem the blood loss.

"Father..."

Hayward smiled up at the boy. He caressed his cheek. Brushed a strand of long, black hair from his face. "My sweet boy. That was...a spirited shot."

Aranck smiled. "Let's get you back into town, father..."

Hayward coughed, flecks of crimson escaping his mouth, dotting his chin and lips. "I don't think there's...much...time for that."

Tears welled in the boy's eyes.

"Constable...?"

Aranck turned and spotted Brom, standing nearby, the horses reined. Slowly, Hayward's son shook his head.

Brom knelt down, favoring his own wound, still holding the reins, and watched as the Constable took slow, labored breaths. The forest around the river grew eerily quiet, with nary the sound of an owl to pierce the night.

"I love you, father, I'm so sorry..."

Hayward squeezed his son's hand. "Watch over them, Aranck. Care for them."

Aranck nodded.

Hayward's breath quickened a moment, then slowed. The steam of his breath danced in the air, curling, flitting about, until finally, it was gone.

Aranck lowered his head and quietly said a Wecquaesgeek prayer taught to him by his mother, long ago, during one of their treks into the woods.

#

The following morning, Aranck and Brom buried Constable Hayward's body in the family plot in the churchyard. It was a solemn ceremony, and Aranck was touched by the arrival of so many folks from Sleepy Hollow and the surrounding areas.

Katrina stood for a long time at Hayward's grave, alongside Squire Van Tassel. She placed a small bouquet of milkweed and yarrow on his casket and told Aranck how sorry she was for his loss.

Nanepaishot came, disguised as a child. She and Aranck spoke of the woods being calm. Of how she couldn't sense Yotoanit any longer in the foothills or along the rivers of Sleepy Hollow.

"The people are safe, then?" Aranck asked, kneeling, eye level with the powerful spirit of the region.

"There are many things yet to be feared, but Yotoanit is no longer one of them. Your father was a brave man. He gave these people a wonderful gift with his passing."

Aranck nodded.

"*You* are that gift, Aranck. It is a great burden to protect these people. But you can bear such a burden."

Again, the boy nodded.

"If ever you need my counsel, you know where to find me."

With that, Nanepaishot turned, and walked off into the tree line. Aranck could make out the tiniest wisp of black smoke trailing behind her.

"Aranck?"

The young man turned and spotted Brom Bones standing behind him, nervously fumbling with his hat, the bandages on his chest visible under his finest dress shirt.

"Yes, Brom?"

"I wanted to tell you how sorry I am. Your father and I didn't always see eye to eye on things, but he was a good man. He kept us all safe."

Aranck nodded. "He did."

"Heard Squire Van Tassel wants to make you the new Constable."

"He does."

Brom stepped closer to Aranck. He patted the boy on the shoulder. "I don't think anyone's better suited."

"Thank you, Brom."

"If you ever need someone to get their hands dirty out there. In the forest. In the mountains. I'm your man."

Aranck smiled. "There is comfort in having a half-bear, half-bull, half-wildcat by my side."

Brom put his arm around Aranck's shoulder. "You know where to find me."

Brom started off toward the pub as brown, red and gold leaves fell from the trees scattered around the churchyard, mingling with the snowfall from the day before.

Warm color against a white canvas.

A Most Curious Tome

McEnroe adjusted the brown canvas messenger bag in his lap. His foot tapped, idly, as he glanced around the empty restaurant. He checked his watch. *Late. Always late. Why do I bother getting anywhere on time?*

His phone buzzed. Checking it, it was a text from his wife. *How's it going, babe?*

He texted back: *Terribly. Hiram is late. As usual.*

She replied with a frowny-face emoji. *You should stop dealing with him.*

McEnroe rolled his eyes. He had had this discussion with Winnie about half a dozen times. He considered lying to her, considered telling her that Hiram had, for once, shown up on time to one of their exchanges, but he never did. McEnroe was a good liar, but not to Winnie. She saw through every little white lie and subtle shift of truth he ever spewed. That was part of the reason he loved her, after all. A good nose for bullshit.

The pay is worth the inconvenience, he texted back.

The restaurant had just opened, and servers had only begun setting the tables up for the lunch crowd, so McEnroe was glad for the privacy. Especially considering what was resting in his lap. Especially with all the trouble it had caused him along the way from France to Norway, to England, and finally, the New York City bistro he found himself in.

Christ, especially after what happened in Northampton.

"A boondoggle," is what Winnie called it. The events of Northampton. Bodies piled high. Literally, in some cases. None of them were McEnroe's fault. Not *specifically*, of course. Instead, it was what lurked in the messenger bag's doing. Wherever *it* went, trouble followed.

In the pit of McEnroe's stomach, there was an intense acidic rage. He trusted his gut. Almost exclusively. In his line of work, he knew he had to. Ever since he came into possession of *The Verdeant*

Manuscript, that tension in his gut wrestled with the desire of reward promised by Hiram. Smuggling the book back into the United States proved easy enough, and oddly enough, sneaking it *out* of the French temple's basement (which intersected with a portion of the catacombs), was remarkably simple as well.

McEnroe had gotten the distinct impression that the book *wanted* out of its caged basement-prison. As though something were clawing, desperate, from within the book's dark bindings.

He watched the door intently. *Come on, Hiram. Fucking get here already and let's land the plane.*

In the cistern beneath the temple, McEnroe found countless ancient tomes. He only knew which was the correct one based on the loose description Hiram gave him: Leather-bound. Strange symbol on the cover and spine. Old. Indecipherable text. Weird pictures.

The symbols were nothing he'd seen before. Symbology wasn't his specialty, but McEnroe had seen his fair share of gnostic, pagan, cultish and heretical symbols before. The images on this particular volume were strange, as though the very lines that crisscrossed, forming almost a galaxy of depth and precision along the book's spine was truly meant to cause one who stared at the symbols too long to somehow enter a place where they too crisscrossed with a world similar and yet altogether different than their own.

And yet...familiarity as McEnroe stared at the spine of the book, at the strip of black leather stitched into two broad boards with a strange symbol etched in the center, a faint, deep crimson the only hint of color. The symbol looked like two twigs resting atop one-another, forming a kind-of modified "Y." The front and back cover burned a deep verdant green, as though moist, muddy grass had somehow been stitched together. They crisscrossed with other symbols, somewhat recognizable as trees, but altogether something unknown. Roots that extended into the open air. Branches too thin to support the heft of the thick, heavy leaves that exploded like cherry blossoms from tiny buds. A true galaxy and lines, circles and more.

A feeling of pins and needles had followed McEnroe since his fingers first grazed the tome's cover and spine. He met no resistance, sneaking the book from the temple's depths. No one even asked what he was doing in the bowels of the ancient structure and yet since, a lurking dread breathed down his neck at every turn.

A busboy came over with two glasses of water. McEnroe downed one quickly. He hadn't realized how thirsty he'd been until he spotted the perspiring glass of refreshment. The busboy smiled and grabbed a nearby pitcher, refilling the glass quickly.

"Sorry, been a long morning," McEnroe said with a nod.

"No problem. A server should be with you in a minute," the busboy said, before disappearing into the kitchen.

McEnroe smiled and nodded, gripping the messenger bag tighter. *All this hassle. Over a book.*

He peered into the bag, slowly unzipping and shifting his gaze low, as if sneaking a glance at something illicit and not an ancient, unreadable tome, dusty with the sands of antiquity and indecipherable to every set of eyes that had laid upon it.

The eyes that survived, anyway.

It was in Northampton that his contact, Ray, an expert in 17th century book binding McEnroe referred to as "the Mad Monk," due to his long hair and scraggly beard, had identified the symbol as having something to do with ancient Hermetic teachings, but couldn't place it among any of the traditional texts.

McEnroe had spent multiple nights staring at the cover of the book, desperate to satiate his desire to look at the pages. His gut told him not to look. And, if McEnroe knew anything, certainly knew not to go against his gut.

In his many hotel rooms, alone, McEnroe counted down the hours until he could return to the States. What little information he learned from those who actually read from *The Verdeant Manuscript*'s pages, didn't make much sense to him, except the recurrence of an earthy, natural theme. Impossible flowers, trees and more, descriptions of which he'd never seen in his travels all over the world. Biology that made no sense. Creatures that could fly on wings made of leaves. Men and women with physical deformities no one had ever seen. Hearing these images recounted to him, McEnroe grew anxious to relieve himself of the burden of carrying it, but his own dark desire to know what was within the book's pages was altogether too much to bear.

"Impossible things, Mac. Things you and I could only *dream* about," Ray told him one night over coffee after a late-night cramming session. Intrigued, McEnroe wanted to see these things for himself in the pages, but his nerves stabbed at him, demanding he avert his eyes while others studied the pages.

The information that shocked McEnroe the most was the animals, some seemingly pulled directly from the nightmares of a child, described as having "limbs that stretched in a multitude of directions, slithering, dark creatures who could only be found in the deepest fathoms of the mind." McEnroe smiled at Ray's use of language and bought him a hot toddy in appreciation as they sat in McEnroe's hotel bar.

McEnroe puzzled over these creatures. Things that made no sense. Things that simply couldn't exist in the real world, based on their description.

"Here you are, sir," a voice startled him. He zipped the messenger bag and looked up.

A server stood, with two plates of food.

"Oh, hi. Thank you...I didn't order anyth—" McEnroe began.

"Ah, yes, I know. Mr. Hiram called about ten minutes ago and ordered these in advance. He said he'll be here presently. In fact—"

"McEnroe, old sport, sorry to keep you waiting!" Hiram said, walking across the still-empty restaurant. He took the server's hand in his own meaty, sweaty paw and took a quick seat. He wore a linen suit, with thick sweat stains in the armpits. He dotted his face with a handkerchief and exhaled breath that reeked of tobacco and coffee.

"Anything to drink, sirs?"

"Water's fine, thanks," McEnroe said.

"I'll have the biggest glass of orange juice you have. Two. And an iced coffee, light and sweet, like me," Hiram said with a grin. Every time he smiled, it was almost as if he had extra teeth, that his mouth couldn't hold them all in and his teeth were bursting from the sides, straining to get out.

"Sounds good, I'll be back in a flash," the server said, heading off.

"You should order a mimosa or something, Mac, you're sweating like a whore in church."

"I'm good. I have your book here."

Hiram barely looked up from the plate in front of him. Shrimp and grits. "You should eat, you look pale."

"I'm not a fan of grits. Oversized cream of wheat," McEnroe said, sipping his water. "What was it we agreed upon, forty large?"

Hiram nodded. "If the goods are legit. C'mon, Mac, you're missing a good meal here. There's cilantro in this. Cilantro! Very good for the liver."

"My liver's fine. The goods are legit. You got the reports."

"I don't get hot and bothered for the reports of schmucks in France or in Bumblefuck, England, 'kay? Daddy needs to see it with his own eyes."

McEnroe held the messenger bag out to Hiram. He took it and unzipped it slowly. McEnroe looked around the restaurant, as if the manuscript's unveiling would somehow herald the arrival of a SWAT team or maybe a tornado. As Hiram flipped through the manuscript and nothing happened, McEnroe began to relax.

McEnroe still didn't look at the pages.

"Be careful, that thing's got...vibes, I dunno."

Hiram paused and looked up at McEnroe. "You're gettin' soft on me, McEnroe. Relax your crack, you're not in any danger. Not yet, anyway."

"What?"

"Kiddin', kiddin'."

The server returned with the three drinks for Hiram. He sipped each of them noisily and returned to flipping through the manuscript. McEnroe caught glimpses of impossible creatures as Hiram's thick fingers grazed over the pages. Human-like figures, sexless, colorful, stood facing vast oceans of green and purple. Trees that were unrecognizable. Horns, eyes and fingers stretched from tops of heads, the sides of flowers. Insects, bee-like, bulbous bodies, striped in pink and black, their faces doglike.

"This is good stuff, Mac. You did good. Tell me about Northampton."

"Me and the Mon—, Ray, my contact, my rare book connection, we had some trouble. We were set to meet with a group of artifact dealers. Guys who meet along the ley lines in Northampton under a full moon or whatever—"

"— your kinda' guys, I take it."

"In this line of work, everyone is my kinda' guy if they can hook up the good words. Anyway, Ray and I got there, and...well..." McEnroe trailed off. He found it difficult parsing the description of what he walked into with the words to describe it. He was reminded of the time he saw Alice in Chains at the amphitheater. He made the mistake of standing beside the speaker and he recalled how his entire body vibrated. He shook the memory from his head and looked up.

"Don't get soft on me, old sport, I love the details," Hiram said, a piece of shrimp (or maybe grits) falling from his mouth.

McEnroe dug around in his pocket and took his phone out. He went through his photo album and when he found the image he was looking for, he slid the phone across the table.

Hiram looked down. On the screen was what looked like a large mound of dirt, twigs and branches sticking out of it, along with sprigs of grass. The first strange thing Hiram noticed was how the mound of dirt seemed to sit in the middle of a king-sized bed, the red duvet cover underneath it clearly ruined by the intrusion of soil upon fabric.

"What the— ?" Hiram leaned closer to the phone, staring at the cursed image, not wanting to touch it.

"Look closer."

Hiram did so. The duvet cover's edges were white. Mac watched as Hiram slowly realized that the red wasn't the dye of the cover, but instead something far worse.

The mound was bleeding.

Looking closer, he saw the twigs weren't twigs at all, but bone. The thicker branches, more bones, fingers, some, others, perhaps toes. It was impossible for Hiram to tell without zooming in further, but he leaned back in his seat in the restaurant and looked around.

"Flesh, Hiram. That's human flesh."

"How...?"

McEnroe shook his head. "I don't know. The smell was insane. It reminded me of my summer working as a plumber's apprentice with my old man. But worse. So much worse."

"Those were your guys? The ones you were supposed to meet?"

McEnroe shrugged. "Impossible to tell. They never answered my calls that night."

That was a partial lie. McEnroe had called his contacts and the phone rang, but McEnroe and the Mad Monk could hear it, deep within the mound of flesh, blood, bone and hair. The ringtone muffled, barely audible, encased in the flesh like a technological almond sunk deep into a meaty, bleeding pyramid of corruption.

"Jesus..." Hiram placed his fork down and pushed his plate away.

Again, McEnroe heard the hum of the book inside the bag. At some point, Hiram had placed it on the floor, leaning against the table leg.

Hiram took out his phone, tapped the screen a few times, and McEnroe's cell lit up with a deposit alert.

"Hiram, whatever this book is, it's bad news. The stuff in Northampton was the worst of it. Car accidents. Strange weather. Ray said he saw things. In the dark. Two nights after we found that, well...you saw what we found. The book. It's almost like a codex for things that don't exist. I don't know how else to describe it."

"Things in the dark?"

McEnroe nodded. "I haven't heard from him in a day or so."

"What about you, Mac? What do you see in the dark?"

McEnroe shook his head. "Right now, I just want to see my bed. And my wife. Pleasure doing business. Be careful, Hiram. I'd hate to lose you as a client."

McEnroe left Hiram alone at the table, a blend of wonder, concern and confusion on his face.

On the Metro North back home, McEnroe thought about having passed the book off to Hiram. McEnroe had seen things that would make most average folks' hair stand on end, but the pile of used meat he saw in that hotel room. That would stay with him a long time.

At least the book wasn't his problem anymore.

#

Hiram sat in his office, a cluttered space in the back of his jewelry store in the diamond district of Manhattan. Eighties yacht rock played softly over the store's sound system, and floated back into the space. On the desk before him sat the book. He ran his hands along the cover, the oily leather and bizarre "Y"-shape etching seemingly calling to him.

"Boss?"

Hiram jumped at the intrusion. His assistant, Atifa, stood in the doorway.

"What do y'need?"

"It's closing time, boss, we need the key," she said, nervously.

He checked his watch. *Closing time?* "Already?"

How did I lose an entire day?

"Atifa, what time did I get back from my lunch meeting?"

"Around twelve thirty, sir."

He rose and handed her the key to lock up. She eyed the book.

"What's that?"

"Just an old book. Picked it up for a friend."

She nodded and ducked out of the office quickly. He turned and looked at the book. He closed the door to his office and locked it.

He sat back down and started leafing through the pages. He pored over countless images of alien-looking plants, flowers and what he imagined to be herbs. Later in the book, he studied drawings of nude men and women, bathing in pools of deep purple water. At least, he *thought* it was water. He couldn't imagine what might turn the water that color, but here it was, a deep amaranthine pool, littered with frolicking men and women. Hiram never found himself titillated by imagery in a book, and yet, staring at the pink water, Hiram wished he could *be* there. To frolic with the men and women, his clothes stripped away.

"Here's the key, boss," Atifa said, slipping it under the door, after jiggling the locked knob. "Good night!"

Hiram didn't respond. He continued staring, deep, into the pages. He studied the shapes of the drawings, the thickness of the lines, the richness of color. Mac's scholarly friends placed the book around the seventeenth century, and yet, the vibrancy of color looked as if it had been drawn only days earlier.

The curiosity about the book's contents was Hiram's alone, as the buyer seemed to know exactly what lurked in these ancient pages without providing any hints beyond the ones Hiram passed on to McEnroe. To make sure the book wasn't a fake, he knew Mac's connections would come through, but the mystery of what the book was *about* intrigued Hiram to no end.

Hiram wondered, as he read, what the purpose of the book was. None of Mac's connections could adequately determine what the book was about, some saying it was a medical text, others that it was a children's book of nightmare fables written by a madman.

As he read, Hiram began believing the latter more and more. There was a feeling of pins and needles in the tips of his fingers as they glided across the ancient pages, over the handwritten passages of impossible language. Once he got to the section featuring things that could only have been birthed from a disturbed mind, he found his eyes glued to the shapes and colors of the creatures that truly did seem born from a nightmare or from the wishes of a madman.

"Jesus..." he muttered, his brow sweaty and hands shaking.

On the page, he stared at a creature that most closely resembled a bear. Or, at least, a bear as if interpreted through a schizophrenic's description of one. Enormous claws stretched from the creature's arms and legs. This being could be the unholy offspring of bear and elephant, as the legs most-closely resembled the thick tree-trunk-like appendages of the great gray pachyderm, knees knuckled, feet covered in thick, lush fur. Hiram wondered just how this thing could move with tremendous claws that would make movement surely impossible.

Red eyes seemed to bleed from the page.

It's mouth, or, what he *hoped* was its mouth, fell far lower than a traditional bear, creating a great gaping maw where a chest *should* have been.

There was hair. Or fur. In this case, it wasn't any color Hiram had ever seen before on a living creature. He had never been hunting, but he'd seen *The Great Outdoors* enough times to know that bears were typically either black, brown, or, if you were at the poles, white. Green hair or fur on a creature like this seemed to belie its ferocity and terror, and yet, right there on the page, it's covering was almost seaweed green.

Hiram's phone buzzed.

"Do you have it?" the text read. The sender was listed only as "Weird Book Buyer."

Hiram texted back the affirmative. Then added "When are you coming for it?"

Hiram stared at the three dots as the buyer on the other end texted their response. It seemed to take forever. "Tonight."

The lights flickered as Hiram tucked his phone into his pocket. The creatures on the page appeared to shift in light, the green bear-thing suddenly on the opposite page, and other, impossible nightmares in its place. Creatures born from the trenches of disparity, crawling and oozing their way from nocturnal, primordial dread. Messes of fangs, claws and tongues that appeared alive on the page, breathing, taking short, sharp breaths, their haunches shifting, Hiram's face moving closer to the page.

"The hell?"

The soft 80's adult contemporary was still playing over the store's sound system, but on the second flicker of light, the sound cut out.

Hiram walked to his office door, opened it and looked down the hallway that connected his office to the front of the store.

Inky blackness greeted him. Not black, though. There was a hint of color, almost impossible to notice, but it was there. *Green?*

The metal shutters were drawn, his staff doing their jobs well. Not even a sliver of the streetlight from outside could make its way beneath the steel protection. Hiram never had problems in the neighborhood, but the shutters and expensive alarm system (along with the hefty discount he gave the cops in the area) helped keep his shop safe.

*Emergency lights shoulda kicked on by now...*he thought, looking at the red-tinted fixtures he had installed in the hallway.

The sudden shock of someone humming in his ear made him turn, quickly. He expected one of the book's creatures to have suddenly manifested itself in his office. His mind reeled at the possibilities of just what was, perhaps, lurking behind him, mouths stretched into an impossible maw, waiting to swallow him whole. He imagined that being swallowed whole by any creature might be the worst-possible way to go.

He shook the thought from his head and grasped in the dark for his desk. Once there, he allowed his fingers to roam along the surface, brushing paperwork, pens and other nonsense, until finally, his fingers slid along the cover of the book.

But the book wasn't closed...

He recoiled. The thick, deep juniper darkness around him suddenly felt oppressive, almost smothering. His breaths became sharper, short, and measured. He imagined this was what a panic attack might feel like, but again, pushed the thought from his mind.

I closed the book. That's why it's closed. I forgot I closed it, that's all.

"Fuck is wrong with me?" Hiram said, softly. He reached into his pocket and turned on the flashlight on his phone.

He tucked the book under his arm and held the phone awkwardly, texting "What time will you be here?" to the buyer.

He started down the hallway. As bright as the flashlight app was, it struggled to penetrate the darkness. Once out of his back office and into the hallway proper, he could barely see two feet in front of him.

As he moved, he heard the hum again. He stopped in his tracks and waited, desperate for the noise to stop, but it didn't. He knew it came from the book.

In the dark, he heard whispers. A great cacophony of harsh utterances. A language he couldn't understand, words that made no sense, guttural and sharp, like tiny daggers piercing his ear canal.

He tried to shake the whispers from his mind, but they persisted. He spun, trying to get a glimpse of whatever was in the dark. The flashlight beam caught the faintest hints of fingers, slender, claw-like, emerging from the green oil-blackness around him. Once the light hit them, they recoiled.

"Please, just...please..."

He clutched the book closer to his chest.

The darkness began slipping closer, ignoring the power of the flashlight. It was as if the black began to consume all that was in the area, as though it were alive. It slipped closer, and Hiram watched, terrified, as it began to crawl up his legs, the beam of his flashlight failing as the inky, fluid-like color began to drink the light before him slowly.

Hiram began to hyperventilate, his chest rising and falling quickly. As the darkness made its way up his legs, closer, ever closer, just beyond the beam of the flashlight, he launched into panic. All around him, light danced with shadow creating bizarre shapes along the walls and ceiling. Things writhed in the dark, their blackened forms scurrying around him, shifting, fleshy and wet-sounding.

There was a deep, low growl in the dark. His entire lower half had been devoured by the green darkness. He held the book ever-tighter, the panic forcing his heart to seize.

As life began to drain from his body, the last thing he saw in the beam of the dying light was a pair of crimson eyes, surrounded by dark green fur and a slippery, ink-like ooze that stained his flesh and slathered his body. The last thing Hiram saw was the creature shifting in the darkness, a beak-like appendaged stretching from deep within its oil-slick flesh, emerging and clamping down hard on his chest.

To be devoured whole would certainly be the worst way to go.

Falling Asleep in the Rain

Clay Whitley stared out the window of his empty car of the Metro North Railroad as he checked his Fitbit and noted with amusement that even at nine at night, the dark woods and mountains looked beautiful. They seemed to rush by, dark teeth chewing into the navy blue-colored sky, the occasional bit of light pollution highlighting the separation between the trees and the sky. One of the conductors of the train walked down the aisle and checked on him. "Sir, our next stop is Kirkbride's Bluff." Looking up, Clay smiled and thanked him. He must've missed the announcement, and when he looked around the car, he realized how alone he was.

As the train came to a stop, Clay noted the mist that had begun to accumulate on his window. He rose, grabbed his briefcase (which was empty except for his pills, an apple, banana, and flask of whiskey), and exited the train, standing on the platform. He looked around and waited for anyone else to step off, and when the doors closed and Clay saw how alone he was, in the darkness, on the platform, a ping of anxiety struck him.

Clay always felt lonely, even when surrounded by hundreds, sometimes thousands of people. He never married. Never sired children. Maybe that's why he found himself on the train to Kirkbride's Bluff. He had been working late; rather, he had been sitting at his desk staring at his computer for hours until he realized it had *gotten* late, and instead of catching his usual Long Island Railroad train back home to Long Island, decided it was time to head *home*. His real home. Where he grew up. He realized that this had more to do with the whispers than his own desire to go anywhere but to his bed, but here he was. On the train to Kirkbride's Bluff. His childhood town. Where someone whispered and beckoned to him in the night.

In his posh upper-middle class suburb, or at work, he was never more than twenty feet from another person. He knew this because he had become oddly obsessed with the notion one night when he couldn't sleep and stood in his pajamas between his home and his neighbor's and realized that a mere twenty feet away was their master bedroom. He never spoke to his neighbors. Not because he wasn't friendly, but because they didn't speak any English and always just smiled and waved, saying something in Chinese to him when they met eyes. He always waved back and wondered what they did for a living.

It was around this time that Clay began hearing the voices. At first, he believed them to be thoughts. Simple concepts that would slip into his head, telling him to do normal, everyday things that he most likely would find himself doing day to day anyway. *Run the dishwasher. Brush your teeth. Wear the bergamot cologne. Call your mother.* Small things to which he believed he was the originator, but over time, the whispers became more abstract. They had sounded like someone speaking Russian, but with a mouth full of mashed potatoes. They began to take the form of unknown words, foreign terminology, unintelligible and confusing, but repetitive. Eventually, they took on familiar shape and sound.

Board the train. Return home. Kirkbride's Bluff.

The most ominous of all: *I'll be waiting.*

Clay walked down the steps of the platform and looked around for a cab. No such luck. He took his phone out and pulled up Uber, but again, there were no drivers in his vicinity. The nearest would be an hour wait time, as they were coming from Resting Hollow and currently had a fare.

"Jesus," he said under his breath and tucked the phone away. The misty rain didn't bother him much, and he stood under a portico, planning his next move. He decided to head deeper into Kirkbride's Bluff and walk around town. He figured it wouldn't be a bad idea to get his steps in, and when he stepped out from under the portico, he heard the whispers, seemingly beckoning him into the town. He nodded, acknowledging them, which is something he had been doing more of, and walked toward the town, the small shops and buildings in the distance easily visible.

After a while, he found his feet starting to ache, and when he checked his Fitbit again, somehow, he had walked another eight thousand steps. Nearly five miles, and yet, he wasn't near his hometown. *That can't be possible. The train station was always just outside of town. A mile at most.*

"How the hell—?" he said aloud, confused by the number now glowing on his wrist.

The rain had remained misty, and while his suit was flecked with tiny beads of condensation, he didn't feel wet otherwise. The chill in the air remained, and he walked down the sidewalk, looking at the various storefronts and businesses he frequented in his youth. He walked past GJ's Dugout, an old baseball card and collectible store he used to frequent with his parents, where they'd buy him two packs of cards per visit. He found himself disappointed after tearing into the packs and the only New York players he ever seemed to get were guys on the useless Mets, a team he grew up despising because they were "losers," and he didn't like losers.

The baseball card shop was boarded up, the sign long-faded. Clay couldn't remember the last time he ventured into the store and wondered how long it had been since the doors closed for good. Many of the stores in the area seemed vacant, their signs either removed entirely or faded, some beyond recognition. There was the pizza joint, Renzo's, across the street from the other pizza place, Donato's. Donato's was his preferred spot, but his friends all liked Renzo's, and this had been the first indication that Clay was truly alone in the world: as a kid, he and his friends divided over pizza.

Both restaurants were now gone, and Clay crossed the street to where Donato's had been and peered inside. In the dark, he could barely make out the counter where he would order his meatball slices and orange soda. The yellow glow of the streetlight above him helped him get a view of the tables he usually found himself at, those thick Formica classics from the 1980's.

It was at Donato's that Clay first saw the boy. Well, not the *first* time, but it was during a moment of childhood laziness that Clay found himself in Donato's, playing *Street Fighter 2* in the corner when a kid who moved to town a few years earlier walked in. Clay found himself not paying attention to the game and instead, noting every movement the boy was making. He couldn't remember his name, but his every movement drew Clay's attention.

Clay had never paid that much attention to another guy before. Girls, sure, but not a boy. At first, Clay was confused, and a little angry to be so focused on this kid waiting for his pizza at the counter, hands lazily in his pockets, bobbing his head to the pop music on the restaurant's speaker system. When the boy noticed Clay staring at him, he turned and gave a light wave.

"Hey," he said. The boy's eyes caught the light and seemed almost flecked with gold-orange light.

"Hey," Clay said back. Clay remembered the nervousness in their first words to each other. Vicious, unbridled anxiety that only a teenager could know or understand. The kind of anxiety that fades with age and experience.

It looked like the place hadn't changed from Clay's memory; at least, until the day the doors closed forever. He wondered where the owner was. He was an older guy, even when Clay was a kid, so it's possible he just passed away. The thought made Clay feel uneasy. It seemed as though when he left for college, the entire town just closed up shop for good. His parents never talked about Kirkbride's Bluff, and Clay didn't have any other family members in town, so, once he left for school, his parents moved into the city, and that was that.

The whispering slipped into his ears again, and Clay turned to look across the street, past Renzo's, and down the alleyway next to the lesser of the two pizza joints. Checking before he crossed the street, Clay chuckled to himself, thinking how strange it was that Main Street was this empty. There was seemingly no one else around. Only the wind, the misting rain, the yellow beams of light from the streetlights, and him. There weren't even any stray cats, dogs, or even any birds. It was as if Clay stepped into another world completely, one that time had left behind and progress and growth had disregarded.

Clay's therapist prescribed him some medication for his nerves, because when the words became unintelligible, he mentioned them to his shrink. He didn't quite know what else to do. He didn't feel like he was going crazy, and yet, he was hearing voices, unknown, distant, in the dark. Clay fumbled with his briefcase and grabbed the pill bottle. He twisted the top off and popped one into his mouth, swallowing it dry.

He walked toward the alley, the whispers sounding clearer. He looked into the darkness, bracing himself on a chain link fence. "Hello?" he called, not expecting an answer. There was a level of panic in his chest that he hoped the anxiety medication would snuff out, but hadn't yet. The familiar pins and needs of nervousness washed over his arms, up his shoulders and to his neck, and he waited, motionless, for any sign of movement or sound.

He was met with the cold, empty solitude of Kirkbride's Bluff. Where only whispers seemed to live.

As he stared down the alley, he heard movement. *Impossible*, he thought, searching for his cell phone. He produced it from his suit jacket breast pocket, turned the flashlight on and slid it into the pocket usually reserved for a handkerchief, the top of the phone peeking outward and the light beaming down the alley about eight feet in front of him.

He moved slowly, one hand braced against the brick and cement wall of the pizza joint, and watched his step, moving past overturned garbage cans, their contents spilled out, rotting in the night. Ancient pizza boxes, long-stained with grease and cheese that was more plastic than dairy, mounds of brown and slick black disgust in smaller piles, which he avoided, lest he ruin his light brown nubuck Johnston & Murphy shoes. The smell found its way into his nostrils and made him gag.

He coughed lightly, and pinched his nose, noticing the light suddenly providing more than just a view of rotting garbage and cement alley. What looked like a foot, as though interpreted through a Francis Bacon hellscape, was lit up by his phone. "Hello?"

The "foot" twitched and scurried out of the light, and Clay recoiled quickly. He remained in place, his eyes scanning around, the light cast in various directions. Finally, pressed against the fence at the end of the alley, after a few cautious steps forward, was the figure Clay's light had scared away. Or, at least, Clay imagined the light scared it. He couldn't imagine what this thing was. Once close enough, he saw it was completely nude, its back slick with the misty rain, which was starting to increase in intensity. A low mist hung around Clay's ankles, and he took two cautious steps toward the figure, which writhed, huddled in the corner.

Two clubbed feet, more like hooves, connected to two sinewy legs, all bone, muscle and tendon, no fat anywhere on the creature. *Creature* was the only word that worked, as Clay couldn't tell if the thing was human or not, though it vaguely resembled a person, with legs, a backside, and a muscular, tight back. When the creature turned, slowly, to face Clay and his light, he saw its face, which was almost entirely a mouth with two brightly-colored eyes like sunlight, eyes Clay vaguely recalled seeing in reality only once before, but hadn't since...*since...*

The figure's arms were thin, almost skeletal, and stretched toward him. The only noise the creature made was an exhalation, a sigh, extended, low, as though the air was being squeezed from its body with every movement. A slight wheeze, coming from God-knows-where, high-pitched, and unsettling. Clay stepped away from the figure and, without turning to run, backed himself quickly out of the alley. He stepped off the sidewalk and onto the road, unconcerned about potential vehicles or people, his eyes locked on the alley. The creature moved slowly, seemingly to struggle with every step and movement, its body almost too weak to carry the weight of its muscle and bone.

"You're...what *are* you?" Clay whispered to himself, happy to hear his own voice amid the wheezy exhale of the creature, which was nearly on him. It grabbed at his clothes, its hands slick with filth, and he struggled to free himself of its grasp. The creature's mouth found its way over his own, large enough that it even covered Clay's nose, and he found himself struggling to breathe, the creature exhaling a black, viscous sludge from deep within its gullet. Clay vomited and forced the creature off himself, and wiped the black fluid from his face and did his best to scrape the sludge away.

He rose to his feet and looked around for something to defend himself when he spotted a nearby trash can. He grabbed the lid and held it out like a shield between himself and the creature. "Get back! Stay away!"

Once within striking distance, the creature lunged, but Clay side-stepped it and began raining blows upon it, dropping it to the pavement. Eventually, the creature stopped moving, and Clay, filled with rage, stomped on the back of the creature's head. Clay flinched at the sound of the creature's skull smashing from his blows. Flipping onto its back, the creature reached up toward him, almost pleading, its flesh slick with sick, black fluid and blood. Clay stared at its orange eyes, the color seeming to fade. After a moment, he smashed the lid of the garbage can onto the creature's head, killing it. Clay sat down next to the dead creature to catch his breath. His heart was racing, and he worried that a heart attack wouldn't be far behind. He eventually steadied himself, pulled himself to his feet, and stared down at the creature, trying to see more of it.

Clay took his phone out and used the flashlight to examine the figure. *Those eyes* he kept thinking, vaguely familiar and disconcerting all the same. The front of the figure's body was similar to its back, muscle, sinew, bone, except for its lower regions, where the creature was blessed with a member that was vastly larger than the average man. Clay regarded the creature's genitalia with confusion, and recognized the clear indication that this figure was, possibly, human in some way.

Turning toward the inferior pizza restaurant that bordered the alley where he found the creature, Clay looked around, checking the empty town for any sign of people (or more creatures), and, using the trashcan lid, smashed in the window of the restaurant, stepping inside once the glass was clear. He needed to gather his thoughts, and wanted to clean up somehow, and remembered the bathroom was down the hall from the counter, so he moved slowly and slipped into the men's room.

Once inside, he noted how relatively clean it was compared to the dusty and vacant restaurant. Using his phone's light, he examined his face in the mirror, and took some time to look at the fluid the creature had spewed all over him. He noticed redness around his mouth and nose, where the creature's mouth started enveloping him. The redness was accompanied by a soreness he hadn't felt since he was a teenager, that summer, after meeting the boy in the pizza place. Summer nights spent at the bluff overlooking town when Clay's dad was working late. Other nights spent along the banks of the Hudson River. Nights Clay and the boy hoped would last forever, but Clay knew, deep down, couldn't.

When he turned the sink on, he was surprised to see clear water after about five seconds of brown, and washed his face, hands, and more. He wiped his suit the best he could but realized that it was a lost cause and stepped back into the pizza restaurant.

He walked behind the counter and imagined he'd find something better than a trash can lid to protect himself in the kitchen, so he slipped inside. On the stoves and burners, there were pots of rotted food, long-since cooked and forgotten, the smell hanging heavy in the air, accompanied by the buzzing of flies or gnats. He looked around, pulled his tie off and slipped it into his pocket, and found a chef's knife along with a small meat cleaver. He had seen tough guys use meat cleavers a million times in movies and figured that it would be easy to defend one's self with it, so, he tucked the knife in his belt, and, with his briefcase in one hand and the cleaver in the other, exited the pizza place.

The only way out of town would be back to the train station, and he remembered that the last train out would be stopping in about an hour, so he had plenty of time to make it back, board, and settle in before heading back to Grand Central Station.

Where is everybody? he wondered, but with the empty stillness of silence that met his every inquiry, down every alleyway, into every open store, he never received an answer.

He started back down the road out of town but found that the town continued to stretch on, regardless of how long he walked. At first, he thought he might be overly tired, but after walking a solid twenty minutes, he passed GJ's Dugout and Donato's for the third time. It seemed impossible, and Clay couldn't rationalize what was happening, so he continued walking, thinking that he had merely taken a wrong turn and somehow just looped back around. But that wasn't the case. Clay had reached the end of town only to find himself back at the entrance to Kirkbride's Bluff. He passed the *Welcome to Kirkbride's Bluff* sign now five times, and when he checked his watch, the train would be arriving in ten minutes, and he knew it would be impossible to make it there, even if he wasn't somehow finding himself in an impossible space-time nightmare.

He paused and looked up at the bluff the town got its name from. From one angle, you could see down into the town's square. From another, one could look out over the Hudson River in the distance and watch as ships passed lazily up and down the river. Clay remembered so many nights on the bluff, indulging his teenage desires for whatever he needed at that moment. Most of the time, with friends, drinking warm beer and smoking terrible marijuana.

He checked his FitBit again. Another fifteen thousand steps had been tacked onto his count. His body was exhausted. He found no other figures, no more creatures, but instead felt the presence of something from the trees in the park watching him. He had spent multiple nights in the park with friends, playing sports, drinking beer, smoking weed, getting into trouble, and found that whenever he looped back into the town on his fruitless trek to make it back to the train station, every single time he passed the park, he felt uncomfortable. There was a silence that felt unnatural to him as he walked past the park, and his skin crawled at the idea of something in there, watching him.

Taking a seat on a park bench that framed the outer entrance to the park itself, he opened his briefcase and started eating the banana, which was browning quickly. He looked around town, the mist still coming down, and couldn't figure out what to do next.

Finally, his mind and heart raced when he saw a figure moving down the cement sidewalk leading to and from the park and noted its movement was jittery and unnatural. Clay gripped the cleaver tightly, rose, and walked toward the figure. The only thought Clay had in mind was that he was tired. He couldn't escape the town and couldn't call for help, as his phone just didn't seem to have a signal.

The figure was about sixty yards away and moving quickly, its torso lilting to the right, one arm dangling, some kind of stick in its hand. Clay couldn't quite make it out, but followed it nonetheless. He called after it, but it only continued deeper into the park, the trees black, creating almost a tunnel of foliage from which Clay couldn't see the stars, or much of the town. His phone light's beam was bright and sure, and he continued, cleaver in hand. The figure was large, larger than himself—even at this distance, Clay knew that—but he didn't know what it was. At least it didn't seem to want to kill him like the last thing he'd encountered.

Eventually, the tall figure disappeared into the woods next to a large fountain. Clay stood near the fountain and was flooded by memories. Fleeting glimpses of holding hands. *He was young. Sixteen or so. Holding hands. His lips and tongue dancing with another's.* He couldn't quite hold onto any of the images long enough to discern anything, but when the images finished flashing through his mind, he recoiled, suddenly unsteady on his feet. He looked toward the tree line where the large figure had disappeared. He placed his briefcase on the fountain. He held the cleaver in one hand and the knife in the other and made his way into the woods.

Once inside, he followed the sound of bushes rustling. He checked the battery on his phone and noticed he still had eighty percent power. After a few moments, Clay found himself in a small clearing, a shovel resting on a nearby tree. The area was small, about fifteen feet all around, but there was a small plot of disturbed land situated at the base of one of the enormous black trees. Clay reached for the shovel, thinking that it may be an upgrade from the knife or cleaver, and again, he was flooded with memories that didn't seem like his own.

His hands gripped the shovel and dug furiously into the soil. He saw his father nearby, standing, watching the woods, cigarette in his mouth. Clay wondered what his father had been doing in the woods, and who he was with, and what they were burying. Clay grabbed the shovel and started digging, and each time the shovel connected with the dirt, he felt a shock run through his body, from his fingertips to the base of his spine, as though someone was gently touching a raw nerve.

After digging about two feet down, the shovel struck what looked like a plastic bag. Kneeling, he gripped the bag and pulled, revealing a pair of skeletal, brown hands. Stumbling backward, Clay struggled to his feet, and when he did, he saw the tall figure, looming in the tree line. *Was it watching me the entire time?* Much taller than he imagined, its body twisted into a hunch leaning to its right. A thin, membranous film that almost resembled flesh covered its face. A black mouth full of brown and black teeth, rotted away, showed through the covering. Loose, fleshy sacks hung in spots all over its largely featureless body and crinkled as the tall figure moved. Bright, orange eyes stared at him. A nose, or, what remained of a nose as it looked smashed in, dripped black fluid.

The whispers. Clay heard the figure whispering to him. He heard it in the dark, in this space they shared. The woods around them completely silent, but this figure, ten or so feet from him, whispered. It whispered from that gaping black hole of a mouth. "What do you want?" Clay asked, overcome with emotion. "What is this? Why are you doing this?"

The tall creature stepped toward him. Clay examined it closer. The thin membrane that covered its body contained vaguely human forms beneath it: blurry, bloody and black. The crinkling of its movement unsettled Clay and he rose to his feet, bracing himself against a tree. He looked at its one arm, and it held no stick. A thin, long protrusion that resembled bone, sharpened to a point, was segmented where a human elbow and wrist would be. The creature's other arm hung bound with black strips to its body, withered and possibly useless. Clay picked up the scent of sweat and musk surrounding the creature.

The creature stood over the gravesite, the shovel at its feet. Clay watched it closely, and suddenly found his mind flooded again, images of the past washing over him, over and over, his ears ringing, his body wracked with agony.

Clay's tongue gliding over the nape of the boy's neck, the two of them in the park, alone in the woods.

The boy staring—with impossible eyes the color of nectarines—at Clay and telling him he loved him.

Clay and the boy, at the bluff, making love in Clay's car.

The two passing in school, Clay avoiding the gaze of the boy.

Clay's father, breaking through the tree line, finding them embracing in their tiny sanctuary.

Clay struggling to pull his pants up, while his father attacked the boy, raining punches and more on him while Clay screamed for him to stop.

The boy, his face demolished, eyes wide, gurgling on his own blood and teeth, struggling to speak.

Clay and his father, under cover of night, digging in the woods, discarded black electrical tape, plastic bags and a shovel nearby.

The boy gurgling, his voice a whisper, as Clay began burying him.

"My god..." Clay looked at the tall, monstrous figure. "You're him."

The figure lunged at Clay and stabbed him with his thin, bony arm. Clay fought back, swiping and bringing the cleaver down on the appendage, a flurry of flesh, bone, and blood erupting everywhere. Clay screamed and the monster began whispering louder, its words unclear.

Clay was overwhelmed, and his heart was racing. His mind was flooded with images of him and the boy from the pizza parlor. That glorious, warm summer, spent in each other's arms. Holding hands in the cool darkness of the movie theater. Making love in the park, in Clay's car, in the boy's house when his parents went away. Exploring their love for each other in ways Clay never imagined possible. Discovering a closeness he never felt before, and hadn't felt since.

"I'm sorry! I'm so sorry! I loved you!" Clay screamed, tears streaming from his face, blood and meat splattering with wet fury, blow after blow of the cleaver.

Clay continued to bring the cleaver down on the monster, who struggled under his weight despite its own huge size. Clay punctured the fleshy sacks that held fluid within, and he found himself covered in a pus-like substance, sticky, almost transparent, the smell overwhelming. He continued cleaving the creature, its one arm now torn to pieces. In between blows from the meat cleaver, Clay stabbed with the knife, finding the creature's throat, face, chest, and heart in a blend of terror and excitement that Clay had never felt before. If this was the fight or flight response, Clay didn't know, but he felt as though he was running on pure instinct, overwhelming the creature with attacks.

Eventually, the whispers stopped. Clay stared down at the monster and was blinded momentarily by what he thought was a flashlight from the woods. When he looked up, he saw the boy, sixteen, the age they both were when they had their affair. Clay stared at him and began to cry. "I'm sorry. I'm so sorry," Clay sobbed, his face slick with blood and tears.

The boy whispered, eyes a blazing orange-gold, and slowly walked off into the woods. Clay understood the whisper to be *I know you are, Clay* and waited until the boy was out of sight. Clay held his injury as he walked back out toward the entrance of the park. He grabbed his briefcase on the way and found himself losing more blood as he moved. The rain had picked up, and he was soaked to the core.

Eventually, he found himself by the same park bench he paused at earlier and had to sit and catch his breath. He put his briefcase down, took his jacket off and used it as a pillow to rest a moment. The rain continued pouring down, as Clay felt himself continue to bleed. Eventually, he closed his eyes, thinking he'd hear the whispering of his long-lost love.

But they never came. As he lay bleeding onto the bench, his blood mixing with the rain, which had grown steadily stronger, Clay thought about the boy. Thought about his father. Thought about Kirkbride's Bluff. The years seemed to wash over him, and as he felt himself drifting away, he felt glad to rekindle his moment with the boy. Lost all those summers ago, lost to time, lost to his father's rage.

Clay's vision began to fade as he shut his eyes. In the dark, he saw the orange-gold glow of his lover's eyes one last time.

Inside Out

Impossible wetness and unbearable pain. A soaked bedspread. A mixture of blood, sweat and other bodily seepage.

I cannot blink. My teeth chatter. My lips have vanished.

When I try to rise, the sheet sticks to me, and as I peel it back, I notice a sharp jab as sinew separates from meat.

Then meat from bone.

Unable to move further, I spill to the floor, the muscles in my legs exposed and drooping under the strain.

I accept this. I feel the pain begin to overwhelm and drown out any rational thought. If I could close my eyes, I would.

I reach into my chest, and part the lung, shifting the muscle and threads of flesh the best I can. Fingers trembling, I grip my heart and squeeze as tight as I can.

My body seizes and the world blurs to black.

The Last of the Leading Men

"That's a wrap!" cried Noah Baumbuch. He was standing behind the monitor, watching as his lead actors, Adum Driver and Scarlett Johanssen, performed an excruciatingly emotional scene, in which they analyze the intricacies of their marriage, while negotiating the intersections of modern relationships and blah blah blah.

"You were great on that last take," Scarlett said, smiling.

"Oh, thank you, that's very kind," the enormous Driver said. He had spent the previous year filming the last of "those space movies," as he referred to them with his close circle of friends, and had maintained his enormity, pounds of muscle, which didn't fit the character he was playing for Baumbuch, but the wardrobe department hid it well.

Driver returned to his trailer, keeping to himself, as he often did on-set, exchanging a few pleasantries with crewmembers along the way. He had no intention of heading to the wrap party that evening, nor was he particularly interested in anything other than flying back to New York, heading to his apartment, and relaxing before falling asleep. His schedule had been packed full of promotion for the new *Star Wars* movie, and his role for Baumbuch had been emotionally-exhausting, so some time to relax and focus on his other passions was exactly what he was hoping for.

Once to his trailer, he checked his iPhone. Texts from family, friends, Affluck, and more. He returned messages in that order, but only Affluck replied back right away.

You still in town? the Oscar-winner (for screenwriting) asked.

Yep. Just got back to my trailer. We finished the Noah Baumbuch movie today.

Driver stared at his phone. He began to slip off his character's outfit, and into his own: a hoodie, black jeans, and boots. Everything felt snug. He had picked the outfit up before starting the final *Star Wars*, and it hadn't stretched to meet his frame.

You should come by tonight, I'm just hanging out watching the game.

Driver stared at the text. He liked Affluck enough, for sure, having filmed pieces of *The Last Duel* for Redley Scot pretty recently. It wouldn't be too hard to move his flight to the morning, it'd be nice to hang with Affluck before he flew back to New York.

Sure thing, see you in twenty.

#

The ride to Affluck's twisted through the mountains outside of Los Angeles, and Driver, who, despite his name, wasn't great behind the wheel, but nevertheless, he made it, and was greeted by Affluck at the gate. Along the way, the radio faded in and out of signal, and whenever the signal picked up, it was full of chatter that sounded more like a radio play than actual news.

"Cowboy robs liquor store, Roman soldier invades set of *Modern Family*, leaving many injured and two dead," the announcer read.

Driver pulled his rental into the expansive estate and Affluck jumped in for the short ride up the driveway.

"How did the last day go?" Affluck asked.

"Pretty good, Scarlett was fantastic," Driver said, his voice low.

Affluck nodded. "That's awesome, man. Baumbuch is a genius, I'm jealous."

"I'm emotionally exhausted," Driver said, pulling the rental up to the end of Affluck's walkway, which led through a large garden, to the front door of the house. "It'll be nice to relax tonight, then fly back to the city in the morning."

"I'm glad you came, man," Affluck said, his grizzled face stretching into a large grin. The actor had retained his Batman body, wide-shouldered from his training as the Caped Crusader. The two actors, side by side, looked more like professional wrestlers than traditional actors. Guys looking more used to fighting in bars or lifting weights than performing Shakespeare or acting in arthouse projects.

#

In Affluck's man-cave (to be fair, the entire house was essentially a man-cave, comprised of Red Sox memorabilia, movie props, posters of his favorite flicks (conspicuously absent were posters of his own work), and no less than three bars, Driver always enjoyed relaxing with the veteran actor, eleven years his senior.

"How are the kids?" Driver asked, settling into a large, leather chair.

"They're great, man, thank you for asking. Can I get you a drink?"

Affluck prepared two Manhattans, and the pair drank and talked family, work and more, while on the large television screen, footage played of a fire on Rodeo Drive, flames engulfing a variety of stores, figures moving in and out, people running for their lives.

"What's this?" Affluck asked, noticing the television.

Driver's phone vibrated and he pulled it out. A text from his wife: *Are you okay?*

At Ben's now, why? Everything okay there?

A pause. Driver watched the three periods on the phone, indicating that his wife was responding. It was taking a minute, so he braced himself for bad news.

"Adam, look at this," Affluck said, drawing the younger actor's attention.

Driver looked up. On the screen were scenes from what looked like a big-budget action-horror hybrid. A variety of characters moved in and out of buildings, carrying a wide array of weaponry. Aliens with ray guns. Cowboys with rifles and pistols. Ancient soldiers with ancient weaponry. Obviously-not Native Americans. Men in blackface.

"What the hell is this? Some kind of viral stunt?"

Driver shook his head. "You know anything coming out like this? A videogame or something?"

On the screen, a squadron of Roman soldiers drew spears and attacked a group of Japanese tourists, skewering them and roaring. The camera shifted and ran, catching, for a brief moment, a close-up of one of the Romans. His face was noticeably grayed, skin hung in loose patches from a skeletal structure beneath.

"Jesus, that's some makeup," Affluck said, almost a whisper.

Driver's phone buzzed: *They said Los Angeles is under siege. Some kind of uprising. People in costumes. Get out of there, now.*

Driver raised the phone to his ear and dialed his wife. "Be right back," he said, exiting the room.

She answered. "Why aren't you on the plane?"

"Decided to take one tomorrow morning, I'm at Ben's, we're watching the news, what's going on?"

A pause. "Just what I wrote. No one really knows. It just started happening."

"Is everything alright there?"

"Yeah, things are fine, it only seems to be in L. A."

Driver thought a moment. "Well, whatever it is, I'm safe here. Ben's place is like a fortress, high walls, backed against a cliff. I'll see if I can stay the night, if you like."

"I wish you were thirty-thousand feet above this, but if that's the best we can do, then fine," she said.

"I'm sorry, I'll be home tomorrow, first flight I can, okay?"

"Of course. I love you," she said.

"Love you, too," Driver said, hanging up.

#

The two actors continued drinking, eyes glued to the television. As the night went on, more information emerged. The dead seemed to be rising. They could speak, and were heard shouting at various bystanders and police, as officers tried to engage them on the streets. The sheer volume of undead easily overwhelmed the Los Angeles police department, and the dead were making their way up into the hills, towards the million-dollar homes and the million-dollar smiles that lived there.

"This is the end of the world, dude," Affluck said.

"It's not happening in New York. At least, it wasn't before. The military will come, this will get taken care of," Driver said, trying to reassure his friend. Trying to reassure *himself.*

Affluck took his phone out of his pocket. He checked social media. Driver was right, everything that was happening was *only* happening in Hollywood and other parts of California. The military was mobilized, but with incidents happening in so many places, they were scattered, and having difficulty engaging the enemy.

"The enemy," Affluck said, softly.

"What's up?"

"Why are they dressed like that?"

The footage on the television showed a group of Cowboys literally throwing people through windows, swinging wild, dramatic punches, just like in the movies, but this time, the punches landed, and sometimes, tore people's heads clear off.

A group of Spacemen attacked camera crew. They looked like the Predator. They looked like the Xenomorph. They looked like Chewbacca. Some even looked like the ones from *They Live.*

As a news crew became overwhelmed by the group of aliens, a figure, tall, dressed in the red, blue and yellow of the ultimate alien -

the man of steel himself, Superman, picked up the camera and held it high, pointed at himself. Jorge Reeves, in the flesh. Well, sorta' in the flesh.

"Holy shit, is that...?"

"I played him in a movie, man, yeah, that's him," Affluck said, eyes wide.

Behind Reeves, a heavy figure shifted through the crowd. A cowboy. Through gritted teeth, the cowboy intoned one word:

"*Pilgrimmm...*"

Driver and Affluck stared at each other.

The television cut out. The power in the house followed suit, then, the backup sparked to life, and the power was restored.

"What was that?" Driver asked.

"Backup generator. They must've knocked out the city's supply," Affluck said. He finished his drink in one hearty gulp, and stood up, nervously pacing around the room.

"Ben, we just saw Jorge Reeves and Jon Wayne walk through the streets killing people."

Affluck stared at Driver. "That's correct."

"What do we do?"

"You were a Marine, I should be asking *you*," Affluck said, shrugging.

Driver stood up and walked to the sliding door leading to Affluck's expansive back porch and yard. It butted up to a cliffside, and opening the door, he slipped out.

Los Angeles burned. Driver could hear the sounds of sirens, emergency personnel, and more, desperately trying to stop this sudden madness from annihilating the city, but it was far too little, too late.

"We need to hunker down here. Wait for the military," Driver said, eyes locked on the city tearing itself apart below them.

"We could. Or, we could go for my plane," Affluck said.

"Since when do you own a plane?"

Affluck shrugged. "It's a status-thing, man, it's cool to have your own plane."

"I don't even have my own *car*," Driver said.

"You're a New York-guy, you don't need it. I say, we pile into the Hummer, drive our asses to the airfield, and get the hell out of here."

"Who's gonna fly it?"

Affluck extended two thumbs and pointed to himself.

"You're a man of many talents, Ben," Driver said, smiling.

#

They spent the next ten minutes gathering as much as they could, clothes, some food, water bottles, booze, etc. After plotting out the fastest and safest route to the airfield, they both headed outside, where they spotted a crowd of horror monsters at Affluck's front gate. Leatherface. Two wolfmen. A smattering of zombies.

Breaking through the crowd, a figure in a blue chambray shirt, green baseball cap, and blue jeans grabbed the fence, shaking it hard. His bearded face tightened with anger.

"Jesus, is that Bob Shaw?" Driver asked, climbing into Affluck's large SUV.

Affluck either didn't hear him or didn't care, because he charged the gate with his car, smashing through it, and scattering the figures all over the road.

Shaw, meanwhile, maintained his grip on a piece of fence that was wedged between the hood of the SUV and the engine. He pulled himself up and started crawling his way toward the windshield.

Affluck jammed on the breaks, but it didn't do anything. Shaw still approached, mouth drooping open, bellowing at the two men in the car.

"Jesus Christ, Ben!"

"I don't know what to do!"

Driver reached into the back seat and grabbed a baseball bat, then rolled down the window and leaned out. Holding the inside of the SUV with one hand, he swung wildly with the other, bringing the bat down on Shaw's hands, arms, and whatever else he could hit, as Affluck did his best to keep the SUV steady.

"Knock him off!" Affluck cried.

"I'm trying!"

Eventually, Driver's bat collided with Shaw's skull, splattering him all over the SUV. His body limp, the legendary veteran of stage and screen slipped off the hood, and onto Mulholland Drive.

#

After about a ten-minute drive through the back streets and hills of Los Angeles, Affluck steered the SUV through the gates of the Santa Monica private airport. The fact that it took such little time to get from the sprawling mansions of Mulholland Drive down to Santa Monica in near-record time wasn't lost on them, and both silently chalked it up to the drastic reduction of traffic due to monumental demise the city was suddenly facing.

They rolled up to a hangar, and Affluck jumped out of the SUV, grabbing various bags and items from the back seat. Driver followed suit, and they entered the hangar, greeted by Affluck's Piper Super Cub, a small, but nimble little angel.

"I pictured something bigger," Driver said, staring at the plane.

"I only *played* Bruce Wayne, I don't have his bank roll," Affluck said, beginning to prep and fuel the plane. It was certainly big enough for both men, along with the few pieces of luggage they brought with them.

As Affluck fueled the plane, Driver kept watch. Scattered around the tarmac were a few of the Hollywood undead, many of them dressed as Nazi fighter pilots or Japanese dive-bombers. Driver shook his head and waited for them to approach.

"Must go faster, bud," Driver said, as Affluck continued prepping the plane.

The undead crept closer. As they got closer, Driver could make out one of them, in a gray suit, shambling his way toward the hangar.

"Oh no, Ben, look..."

"Almost done, give me a second."

Driver watched as the gray-suited man came closer. The wind on the tarmac picked up and blew his jacket around a bit, and Driver could make him out better. Debonair is the only word that could be used to describe the figure.

Affluck walked up to Driver to get a good look.

"Are we gonna look like that when we die?"

Driver shrugged. "We don't look that good *now*."

Kary Grant continued shambling toward them, looking better than most of the other corpses the duo had seen to that point.

Driver took the baseball bat out of the plane and stalked toward the reanimated Grant.

"Mr. Grant, I'm sorry, but I have to do this," Driver said, preparing to swing.

Grant looked the large actor over, and extended his arms as if to attack.

THWACK!

In one swift movement, Driver sent Grant's head soaring into the sky.

Driver walked back to the plane, where he and Affluck loaded themselves in and fired up the engines. They sat in silence as Affluck taxied the plane onto the runway.

"How'd that feel? Knocking arguably one of the most handsome actors in the history of Hollywood's head clear over the left field wall?"

Driver smiled. "About as good as it'll feel to get the hell out of L. A."

"I think a permanent relocation is in my future, too, bud," Affluck said as the plane began gaining altitude, escaping over the burning city.

A Child Awakens

If The Boy could feel, he would feel cold.

"It's booting up," a voice said in the darkness.

The Boy's eyes fluttered a moment, a brief halo of soft blue light fading to the oily blackness of his pupils, perpetually dilated.

"Eyes set in Adore Mode, like the previous B-3s," another voice said softly.

The Boy looked around the room. He looked at his hands, pudgy and pink, and at his feet. Tiny toes dotted with artificial nails made of synthetic polymers.

"Motor functions seem fine, no damage to the couplings," the first voice said.

"Where am I?" The Boy asked, his voice tinged with an artificial tinniness.

"Vocal modulation is off. Adjusting now," the second voice said.

The Boy rubbed his throat, as one might do at the hint of a sore throat. "What is this place?"

"That's better," the second voice said. "Now he sounds alright."

"I still hate their voices, man," the first voice whispered. "Creeps me out. No soul behind the words."

The Boy cocked his head to the side. "No soul?"

He was met with silence. Panic began to overwhelm him, as he stared into the darkness around him, the light above casting a beam down on the operating table, where The Boy lay, wearing a paper gown.

"Where's my mommy?"

"God damn it, there it is," the first voice said.

"Are you mad at me? Who are you? Where's my mommy and daddy?" The Boy asked, panic beginning to rise.

"Reduce emotional response by thirty percent," the first voice said.

"I'm trying to, it's not working."

The Boy's eyes welled up. Flickers of color, light blue, a sharp green, bright orange, took turns bleeding through his dilated pupils, and he began pulling at the gown, tearing at it in a torrent of shredded, rough paper.

"You must calm down," the first voice shouted. "Mommy will be very mad at you if you don't."

The Boy stopped. His chest heaving, he sat on the table, and did his best to fix the gown. "Where is my mommy?"

"Do you want to tell him or should I?" the first voice asked.

"Go take a break, I'll tell him," the second voice said.

The light above The Boy turned off, and he was bathed in darkness. "Hello?" he said, his little voice tremoring with uncertainty.

When the lights came back on, a man, in his forties, balding, tall, wire-rimmed glasses balanced delicately on the tip of his nose, stood with a glass tablet in his hand, a blur of colors and numbers scattered across it.

He walked toward The Boy with careful strides, his shoes *click-clacking* across the sterile, white tile.

"Hello, I'm Reggie," the man said. "It's alright, you can calm down, I won't hurt you."

The Boy stared up at Reggie. "Where am I?"

Reggie sighed. He helped The Boy off the table and knelt down to look him in the eye. He handed The Boy a tissue. "What do you remember?"

Reggie stared into The Boy's eyes, then checked his tablet. A minor spike on an orange graph appeared.

"I was eating breakfast with mommy. I love her so much, and she kept looking at me while reading her tablet. Daddy said that he was taking me for a ride in the car, and then I woke up here," The Boy said.

Reggie nodded. "Gaps in the memory. Alright."

The man made some adjustments on his tablet, while The Boy reached for a pen sticking out of his white lab coat. "What's this?"

"That's a pen, sometimes I use it to write notes, it's an old-timey thing," Reggie said.

"What is 'old-timey'?"

Reggie smiled. "It means from olden times. Before we became so modern."

The Boy nodded. He still didn't totally understand, but he liked listening to Reggie. "What are you looking at?"

Reggie's eyes were glued to a video playing on his tablet. The Boy's point of view from the back seat of his father's car. He kicked his little feet, his red and blue sneakers popping into view from time to time.

In his hands was a stuffed white sheep.

"Just a video," Reggie said, with a sigh. "You don't remember getting into the car with your daddy?"

The Boy shook his head. His eyes seemed to glow in the light of the room.

"That's okay," Reggie said softly, making a notation on his tablet. He re-wound the video and watched it some more.

The Boy looked around the room, his gaze drifting from Reggie's eyes, to the tablet, to the table he sat on, to his gown. As The Boy's eyes refocused on each thing, there was a slight shift in his head position, allowing his optics a pristine view of whatever he looked at.

"Where's my mommy?"

"She's not here, bud."

"Where's daddy?"

"He's not here either, little guy."

The Boy looked at Reggie. "What's my name?"

Reggie looked up from his tablet. "I don't have that information, pal, sorry."

"What is 'pal'?"

Reggie smiled. "It's a word for 'friend,' do you know what that means?"

The Boy nodded and smiled. "Are we *friends*?"

On "friends," The Boy's vocal modulator glitched, and the "R" sound was replaced with a "W."

Reggie furrowed his brow a moment, then his expression softened. "Yes, we're friends."

"How nice," The Boy said. He placed the pen back into Reggie's pocket.

"AI-scripting is clearly working..." Reggie muttered to himself, jotting down a quick note.

Reggie continued watching the video. He pulled up various entries related to different days, all in an easy-to-follow digital format, catalogued by date and time. Incidents such as "sleep" or "event" were marked accordingly.

The Boy had an inordinate amount of "event"-related issues scattered through his memory logs.

"Why does he stare at me all the time?" the mom in the video asked, her voice sharp and angry.

The Boy reacted to her, cocking his head to the side, eyes wide and Reggie slipped a pair of wireless earphones in.

"He's your son, he loves you," the dad said, approaching the view from The Boy and scooping him up. "He's only four years old, babe, we only just got him."

"Well, you better get him checked out," the mother said, storming off into her bedroom, after tapping her cell phone.

Reggie turned the video off as the dad smiled into The Boy's eyes, hints of sadness in them.

Another "event:" The Boy's view locked on the mother as she made dinner.

Another of her doing the dishes.

Another of the front door as she entered and jumped, startled to see The Boy waiting for her. "Mommy's home!" The Boy said, happily.

Each time, when she caught The Boy staring at her, she produced her phone and made an unseen entry.

"Jeez, this is what they're upset about?" Reggie said to himself.

"Who's upset, friend?"

Reggie took his earphones out and re-attached them to the tablet. "Nobody, pal. Nobody's upset."

"Are mommy and daddy coming to pick me up soon?"

Reggie didn't know what to say. By now, The Boy's parents were home with their replacement model, newly-printed and upgraded with the latest firmware. The new models were vastly superior to even one barely a year old like The Boy in front of him.

"Yeah, they'll be back soon, little guy."

"*Little* guy," The Boy said, giggling.

"Is that funny?".

"You're funny, my friend. I'm a *little* guy!"

Reggie smiled. He looked down at the tablet and checked the notes from the company that produced The Boy and others like him. He checked the company notes every time, even though they never changed.

"...Exclusions to the warranty or violation of service include: act of God, unit mishandling or mistreatment, physical or firmware tampering, unauthorized upgrades, units out of production..."

Reggie scanned further down, past more legalese.

"Units determined to malfunction or violate the legal precedence set forth by the Shirley Convention of Twenty-Ninety-Eight are to be removed from circulation and retired from service."

Retired from service. The term formed beads of sweat on Reggie's brow and resulted in a vice-like grip on his heart.

"Okay, little guy," Reggie said, rising and extending his hand to The Boy. "Come with me."

"Where are we going, friend?"

Reggie stared at The Boy. "What's your favorite place in the whole world?"

The Boy smiled. "Home with mommy, of course."

Reggie smiled back. "Then that's where we're going."

They walked across the white tile, toward a square-shaped outline on the wall, four feet by four feet.

Reggie didn't know what was inside the wall. He only knew that there was a conveyor belt-like device that the units were placed upon, their feet facing a darkness Reggie was blissfully unaware of.

He pressed his hand to the wall, and the space opened. Impenetrable blackness yawned at him and The Boy.

"Here we are, now, pal," Reggie said, lifting the boy from under his arms and placing him, feet-first onto the conveyor belt.

The Boy giggled.

"What's so funny?"

"It's cold on my feet," The Boy said, smiling up at Reggie.

The man looked into the space. The conveyor belt stretched on for what could've been forever behind the wall.

"You can *feel* that?"

The Boy nodded. "Will you come and visit me when I'm home with mommy and daddy?"

Reggie sighed heavily. "Sure."

"Bye-bye," The Boy said as the conveyor belt whirred to life, slowly pulling him into the darkness.

Once The Boy was deeper inside, the wall sealed shut.

There was a soft hum, and the wall vibrated a moment, before Reggie turned his tablet off and took a seat next to the table. He gathered the shredded pieces of the paper gown, rose, and left the room.

Tiny Town

"Wanna see something *really* scary?" Natalie asked, taking her eyes off the road to scroll through her phone. "I found this creepy picture online and thought of you instantly."

Mario sat in the passenger's seat, anxious. He waited with bated breath.

She held her phone to his face. On it, the camera's reversed image acted like a mirror and he rolled his eyes. Natalie giggled to herself.

"Just you wait until we get to Tiny Town, then you'll see some scary stuff," he smiled.

"I think it's a dumb-shit idea, dude," Natalie said, finishing her third cigarette of the evening. "Even *if* it's Halloween, I think it's dumb. We shoulda just stayed home and ate my brother's candy."

"Why? We're going to be seniors next year, to *not* go would be a violation of an age-old teenage ritual," Mario said. "Plus, it's the spookiest night of the year and we're too old to trick or treat anymore. Plus, you dress like every day is Halloween, anyway."

Natalie rolled her eyes. She turned the radio up and reclined in the driver's seat of her Toyota Cressida, bobbing her head to Charli XCX.

"Where'd you get those New Balances? The Retired Dad Emporium?" she asked.

"We can't all shop at Baby's First Goth," he said, gesturing to her all-black attire. "First it was the obsession with the New York Dolls, then it was the eyebrow piercing, which I know your mom *hates*, now it's the combat boots and frayed denim skirt?"

"You haven't commented on the striped bra," she said, winking at him.

"A gentleman wouldn't," Mario said, rolling his eyes. "But yes, you look like if Lydia from *Beetlejuice* lost a fight with her eyeliner."

"Ouch, little pup," she said, feigning injury and grabbing her heart. "You've struck a blow, and now, we must turn around and vacate all notions of exploring haunted areas."

"Nat, come *onnnnn*, it'll be fun," he said. He began an onslaught of poking her shoulder. "It'll be like when we snuck into old man Fanning's hot tub!"

"If we go and it sucks, you're buying me disco fries at the diner after. Deal?"

Mario lit up and nodded excitedly.

As they drove outside of town, they blasted high-energy pop tracks, both because that's what Natalie was into at the moment, and also Mario needed to get himself hyped in an effort to kill the nervousness coursing through his body.

"Oh, my mom wanted me to ask you to come to dinner tomorrow night," Mario said.

"Of course," Natalie said. After a little while, "Why's it so important that we go here?"

"I heard the seniors talking about it last year in orchestra. They said it was scary and that Tommy Doyle's cousin's neighbor saw a goblin there," Mario explained. "Tommy went and checked it out, and he was almost prom king, according to the voting committee."

"Is that right? You think if we drive all the way to Oakvale and see a gremlin or whatever, that you'll be prom king next year?" She almost cracked up at the thought.

Mario shrugged. "I don't know. Tommy's pretty cool, I just thought it'd be fun to do," he said.

"Oh, hey, listen to this," Natalie said, using her knees to steer the car. Mario, instinctively, reached over to take the wheel as she changed the music on her iPhone.

Trumpets and guitars. Ska music. Reel Big Fish.

The two bopped along, Natalie taking the wheel again. "Remember when we used to listen to this back in the day?"

He nodded and smiled. "I just moved here. You mentioned how much you liked my *Turn The Radio Off* button on my backpack."

"I thought I was the only one who knew who Reel Big Fish were. Man, thank god your parents are as old-school as mine," she said.

"You're still the only one I have anything in common with in this town," he said with a sigh. "I've been thinking of going to back to the city for school. Have you submitted your early-acceptance apps?"

"Absolutely not," Natalie said. "You?"

"Yeah, I sent out four. Probably wait until September to send the rest," Mario said. "Why haven't you?"

Natalie shrugged. "I dunno. Just don't care, I guess."

"It's only your *future*, Nat."

She scoffed. "You sound like my dad."

Mario laughed. He checked his iPhone. "Oakvale has a lot of creepy stuff, apparently. I read on this website that there was a Satanist Church here once."

"Is that so?" she laughed. "That's pretty badass. I only know the legend of the gremlin and that a couple college kids went missing like ten years back during East Islip's homecoming."

Mario stared at her. "Goblin."

"What?"

"It's a *goblin*, not a *gremlin*."

"What's the difference?" she asked.

"Gremlins attack planes and shit, goblins live in places like this: woods, near water, that kind of thing," Mario explained, gesturing to the thick trees lining the highway leading outside of town, stretching along the eastern shore of Pequot Lake.

"Why do you *know* all this stuff? Take the wheel a sec."

"I told you, that website," Mario said. He took the wheel as Natalie lit a fourth cigarette.

"Right," she said, cigarette dangling from her lips. She re-took the wheel.

"I didn't see anything about anybody disappearing in the area, though," Mario said. There was a hint of anxiety in his voice. Natalie knew he was nervous again.

"We don't have to go, Mario. Tommy Doyle thinks he's hot shit because he went to a scary place? *You're* hot shit because you're friends with *me*, so what does it matter? Let's just go to the diner, eat until we puke, fork someone's lawn and call it a night."

"No! I want to go! I want to be able to tell everybody we did this, Nat," he said.

Natalie nodded. "The college kids were drunk. They found their car in a pond at a roundabout in the center of Tiny Town."

"What about the kids themselves?"

Natalie shrugged. "I assume they found them in the car, too. I don't really remember. I was like, seven. They didn't have *that* on your spooky folklore website?"

Mario shook his head.

#

Tiny Town sat beyond the large brick and stone structure that was once home to the Vanderhugh family's servants. In its heyday, the development of homes was something to behold, but now, nearly a century after its completion, many had long-been abandoned for a variety of reasons, not the least of which was the softening of the land over the years.

Jack O'Lanterns sat on the dilapidated steps of the stone structure, glowing in the fading evening light. Their smiles greeted Mario and Natalie, and were one of the traditional "rites of passage" for the younger kids who had heard of the area and wanted to show how tough they were. Middle schoolers, mostly. They'd carve a quick and dirty pumpkin, stuff a candle or LED light inside and drop it on the nearest front stoop at the entrance to the town.

Typical kid stuff in a town filled with specters.

The Vanderhugh family was deeply-entrenched in the history of the region, investing early in the fishing and importing/exporting operations of Long Island. They turned a huge profit while creating an economy open enough to draw folks from New York City to the "boonies" further east.

Beyond the servants' quarters, there were rows of houses built on the grounds of what would have been Vanderhugh's stables. A large, open area, houses spaced in neat rows, trees lining their properties.

A hurricane did a number on many of the houses, most built under Long Island's natural water-table, due to the proximity to the ocean.

The two sat, staring at the massive brick and stone servants' quarters.

"Are we lost?" Mario asked. He checked his phone's weather app. "Looks like rain in a bit."

"It's just through there," Natalie said. "I think, anyway."

"We have to go in on foot. That's what Tommy said."

She rolled her eyes. "Fine."

The pair climbed out of the car and locked the doors. Natalie sparked another cigarette and the two walked through a large archway of brick into the darkness of Tiny Town. They both turned on their cell phones' flashlights and made their way through rows of homes, many of which nature reclaimed ages ago, or were sinking into the Earth, bit by bit, as the years crawled by.

"Weird that nobody's developed the land," Natalie said.

"They've tried. About six times. Everything sinks. No one knows why. They say the ground is sour."

Natalie rolled her eyes. She wiggled her fingers at Mario and whistled the theme to *The Twilight Zone*.

He laughed. Then something froze Mario in his tracks.

"The website said that nobody lived here," Mario said, pointing to a window in another section of the large stone structure, where a solitary candle cast an orb of orange-yellow light in the vicinity.

Natalie looked over the property. Mirrors were scattered everywhere, directed outward. She furrowed her brow, confused to see her distorted reflection in the darkness. For a moment, she thought she caught the glimpse of a shadow, small, fast, darting between rows of mirrors.

"What was that? Was someone behind us?" Mario asked, his voice rising in slight panic.

"Relax," she said, putting her hand on his shoulder. "You're all freaked out because some kids put some pumpkins and fake spiderwebs up. Jesus, you're such a wimp sometimes, dude."

"I thought I saw someone in red standing behind me," he said, softly.

"That's weird," she said, the tiniest hint of anxiety creeping into her voice. "Why are there so many mirrors?"

"What do they mean?" Mario asked, his voice shaky.

Natalie smiled. "It means you're *doomed*, Mario. Tiny Town has you in a death curse!"

She wrapped her arms around Mario and squeezed. He shouted and tried to wiggle free.

"You can't escape, Mario! This was my plan all along, to lure you here. *I'm* the goblin! Look at my reflection!" She laughed.

Finally, she let him go, laughing too hard to maintain her grasp.

"Nat, that wasn't funny!" he shouted. He was struggling to catch his breath and even in the dark, she knew he was upset. She stopped laughing at him.

"Mario, I'm just kidding, dude," she said, reaching out to him.

"No! Don't touch me, Nat, I'm serious, I'm already creeped out being here, I don't need you messing with me," he said.

"Mario, this was *your* idea, relax, I'm just playing around."

"You think everything's a joke. It's so obnoxious. Like you're too cool to have fun anymore."

Natalie stood, shocked by his words. "Mario, I—"

"It just sucks, you know? You're my best friend, and you quit on me in orchestra, we don't do video game nights anymore, we don't have sleepovers," he said quickly, as though he'd been waiting to unload.

"Mario, we're kinda' too old to be having sleepovers," she said with an awkward smile. "I don't know if my folks would be cool with that."

"Still, you *know* what I mean. You've changed so much, it just *sucks*. I only joined orchestra *because* of you. Most of the things I do, is *because* of you."

She had an inkling of what he was saying. She wasn't prepared for this kind of discussion. Not this night. Maybe not ever.

"Mario, you're second-chair clarinet, that's awesome," Natalie said, trying to calm him down and steer the subject away from the eventual declaration of love that was bubbling under his surface.

"Yeah? Is it? To the drummers and the guys in the locker room, it means I'm good at *blowing* things."

Natalie tried to stifle her giggle but failed.

Mario noticed and shook his head. An expression of hurt mixed with betrayal claimed his face. "Fuck this, I'm out of here."

He charged past her, towards the brick and stone archway they passed through moments earlier.

Guilt washed over her as she heard his footsteps grow distant. Sighing to herself, she turned after him. "Wait up, kid."

Natalie turned toward where she thought he would be but was met with empty space.

"Mario?"

She looked around. The area was vacant, with the exception of the houses, the mirrors, and the lone candle burning in the window of the servants' quarters.

#

Mario had been walking for a good ten minutes in the dark. Houses, half-submerged in the ground, sat around him. His anger was fueling him, and he hadn't noticed he passed the same houses two or three times.

Eventually, he stopped and looked around. Natalie was nowhere to be found. Neither was the car. He checked his phone. No service.

"Nat?" he shouted into the dark. Blackness stretched before and behind him, rows of houses, all of them abandoned and overgrown lined the street on both sides, and beyond them, impenetrable darkness.

His voice echoed in the night, as though bouncing off unseen walls in the dark.

He looked around. "This isn't possible."

He continued walking but tripped and landed on the cold asphalt. He brushed himself off and checked his phone. The screen was broken, but the flashlight still worked. He noticed a chalky-black substance on his hands and tried to brush it off, which took a good amount of effort. Kneeling down, he ran a digit along the ground and lifted it to the light of his phone.

Thick, black ichor dripped down his finger, to his wrist. When he rubbed the strange blackness off, it wasn't so much a fluid, but more like the chalky substance he had brushed away seconds ago.

"What the hell is this?"

Confused, he rose and walked toward one of the houses nearby and noticed the black chalk on the walkway and sidewalk, in various patterns and designs, most Mario had never seen before. Others were more familiar: stars, moons, squares, all thick with the same black substance.

Mario tried to cut through the backyard of the abandoned home. He climbed the fence and started toward the rear of the house, and smacked directly into a wall of blackness, falling backward.

"Jesus," he said, standing up. More of the substance, cast high, created a literal wall of crystalline blackness that stretched skyward behind the home, like a barrier, serving to separate the property from whatever lay on the other side.

#

Natalie snubbed out her cigarette on the heel of her black combat boot, and walked up to the brick house with the candle in the window. She checked her phone, but it wasn't working, the battery had apparently died.

"Hello? I'm sorry to bother you, but it's an emergency," she said as she knocked. She looked into the windows of the home and saw movement.

Eventually, the door opened and she stood in the doorway, peering into the dimly-lit home. Candles were strewn about. More mirrors, most covered with black or red satin. White candles dripping red wax onto their holders and the floor.

She stepped into the home, muttering under her breath that "this is how every horror movie starts."

Natalie was always one to take stupid risks. Even as kids, she'd jump headfirst into the ocean from the pier as summer vacation kicked off. She would jump off the roof her house when her parents weren't there, into the above-ground pool in her backyard. Mario would watch, in awe, as she held onto bottle rockets, waiting until the last second to let them go before they exploded in her hand.

She loved doing stupid stuff, but walking into a house like this gave her pause.

Paintings littered the walls. Folks from various ages. The eighteenth century, the modern one. Many of them wide-eyed with confused expressions on their faces, as though caught by an unseen surprise. As Natalie navigated the long hallways of the home, she studied the paintings curiously.

In more than a few, groups of people, stared directly at her. Their eyes seemed to follow her as she moved, but she knew it was just an effect of the artwork itself. There was a haunted quality to the images, definitely oil-based paint, if her time in art class was any indicator, thick globs in many sections.

Eventually, Natalie found one of a car, half-submerged in a small pond. Three figures stood beside it, staring blankly and wide-eyed, mouths agape at her. One of the figures wore a hoodie with Natalie and Mario's high school mascot on it. Pins and needles ran up her spine.

"That can't be..." she said quietly, staring at the photo.

The tiny hairs on the back of Natalie's neck radiated cold and she spun around, expecting a shadowy figure to pounce on her any second. She was relieved when she was met, instead, with a painting of a boy standing at the base of a massive black wall that seemed to emerge from the bushes of a home. She was curious why this figure wasn't facing her and instead felt a familiar connection to the image.

Leaning closer, she thought the figure in the photo could've been...

"Mario?" she whispered to herself.

She continued looking for a phone. The hallway of the home stretched farther back than she initially thought, and soon, she found various entryways to various other rooms before stepping carefully into a sitting area, the walls lined with ancient and modern tomes.

Books by people she never heard of: Anton Szandor LaVey, Jack Parsons, Poke Runyon, etc.

She ran her fingers along the spines of the books, while a soft breeze blew through her long hair. She caught a whiff of what she first believed to be roasted marshmallow, but altogether more vanilla than campfire.

"Can I help you?" a voice came from behind her.

Natalie spun again, and came face to face with a small-framed elderly woman. Her back was hunched, and her head hung low. Natalie noticed how difficultly the woman seemed to move as she shuffled toward her.

"I'm so sorry, ma'am, I saw the candle, and well, your door blew open and I desperately need to use a phone. Mine is dead and my friend, Mario ... he's missing."

"Goodness, that's terrible, come here, sweetheart, it's in the kitchen," the woman said, turning toward the hallway.

She waited until the elderly woman was a good five feet away. As she watched her lumber slowly out of the sitting room, Natalie swallowed hard, and nervously fingered the keys in her pocket.

She followed the woman out of the sitting room.

\#

Mario continued staring at the monument of obsidian before him. He ran his hands along its cool surface. The wall seemed to buzz at his touch, and he placed his ear to the smoothness, listening carefully.

He could hear what reminded him of whale calls, deep, guttural, distant. His parents used a sound app to get his little brother to sleep at night, and Mario could often hear the whale calls through the wall. They had the complete opposite effect on him, and all of sixth grade was sleepless nights.

The noises beyond the wall were pitched lower. The calls were stretched-out, sounding so far away. Whales weren't particularly common in the waters off the southern coast of Long Island, but they weren't exactly unheard of. Mario thought "Rare" was perhaps a better term.

A crash like thunder erupted beyond the wall, muffled but sharp, and caught his attention. The crystalline darkness seemed to glow faintly in-step with the sound on the other side, and Mario figured it had to be lightning. A storm in the distance. He listened more, and leaned back when the lightning flashed again, illuminating creatures of impossible size beyond the wall. As the lightning struck, flashes of what lie on the other side were lit up briefly. Figures that resembled something closer to a beast of imagination than any animal he could recognize.

Huge figures lumbering among an impossible, vast horizon of blackness, where the lake *should* be. Elephantine, with tremendous legs, heads, all seemed to lumber among the clouds, dark and tremulous, a purple-red haze lingering among them. There was no definition, just simple shape, rough, obscured by the glass-like wall between Mario and whatever was on the other side.

"This...this can't be..."

He placed his hand on the wall as one of the enormous figures made its way toward him. The flickering lightning didn't allow for detail, simply the shape of images beyond the blackness, which was more like a geode in structure than solid black. The whole thing reminded Mario of shadow puppets, the kind he and Natalie used to make during sleepovers as kids.

The figure seemed to glide over the expanse of distance rather quickly, covering an impossible distance in mere seconds. Paralyzed by fear, he kept his hand on the wall, hoping for more lightning to strike so he could satisfy his curiosity of what the creature on the other side looked like.

"You know you're stuck here, right?" a voice said to Mario's right.

The boy turned and spotted the source of the voice. A man, middle-aged, balding. Naked. In his right hand, he held a pipe.

"What?"

"The mirrors. You saw them. They keep us here. *She* keeps us here. Think of them like doors. She puts coverings over them to close them when she finishes the ritual. Keeps us stuck here."

Mario stared. "Why are you naked?"

The man laughed. "No need for clothes here in the dark. There's never any light."

"Where am I?"

"You're on my property, young man. All of this. Vanderhugh property. I'm Arthur Vanderhugh."

The man extended his hand to shake Mario's, when a sudden *thump* drew the boy's attention back to the cold, crystalline wall.

Mario got his wish. A blast of lightning illuminated the space beyond the darkness briefly, the figure's tentacled hand pressed to the structure, lined up with Mario's, a dozen slender fingers, squirming and wriggling as they squeezed against the opposite side of the wall.

Mario screamed and fell backward.

When he rose, he was beside a small pond. The backyard was gone. The wall was gone. It was as if he traveled somehow during the fall. He never lost consciousness, and he remembered taking his eyes off the wall for only a second.

"What...?"

The houses and road had seemingly melted away and he stood, alone, beside the pond, red lights of a car deep beneath the surface cast the only illumination in the area.

He looked around. The blackness had seemingly swelled around him, blocking the view of anything, even as he tried to use his flashlight to get a deeper look beyond the dark. Impenetrable darkness met his every turn, as though some unseen force was commanding his attention to the car beneath the water.

He stepped toward the pond and struggled to see anything beneath the murky overgrowth that had begun to reclaim the pond in the same way it had the nearby homes.

"Nat, where are you? I don't want to see this. I can't see this," he whispered to himself.

#

Natalie continued trailing the woman, shuffling slowly down the hallway.

"You have a beautiful home," Natalie said. "I love all the candles and that sitting room is amazing. I could spend hours in there if I enjoyed reading."

"Smart young lady like yourself doesn't enjoy reading? What a shame. The written word is our link to the past and the key to the future," the woman said, her voice dropping an octave from the last time she spoke.

"You sound like my dad," Natalie said, chuckling nervously to herself. "Your throat okay? I have lozenges, I think."

"No no, Natalie, I'm fine, you're a dear to ask," the woman said, turning a corner down another hallway.

How does she know my name? Natalie thought to herself. The girl bit her lower lip and furrowed her brow, turning the corner with the woman. More oil paintings. More candles. She wondered how the paintings didn't melt with the oppressive heat and humidity she was feeling deeper into the house.

Faces of people, some seemingly in agony, others, smiling, or looking confused, stood in various points of what Natalie imagined to by Tiny Town before it began its descent into the earth.

"Is that music?" she asked, hearing the distant sound of an old tune playing somewhere in the house.

The old woman laughed. When she did, her hunch tremored and its shifting sent chills up Natalie's spine. "The Merry Macs," the woman said. "My favorite group. Do you like music, Natalie?"

Natalie froze in place and looked around. She had started to sweat and feel nauseous, the air heavy, the smell of musky vanilla overwhelming. The scent of cedar and the ocean mingled with the vanilla and created a heady aroma that disoriented her.

"It smells like Christmas and a bonfire...what's happening?"

The woman turned to Natalie and smiled. "Do you like it?"

"Ma'am, where's the kitchen?"

"What kitchen?"

Natalie began to feel dizzy and braced herself against the wall, knocking one of the paintings down in the process. "I don't feel so good."

"Oh, sweetie, it's alright, just close your eyes a moment," the woman said, stepping closer. As she did, even through blurry vision, Natalie could make out the woman's void-like black eyes.

"How do you know my name?" she asked. "What *are* you?"

The old woman smiled. Natalie caught a glimpse of rows of jagged teeth, brittle like shards of thin glass. Her mouth resembled that of a shark's more than it did a human. Her maw seemed to stretch on forever as Natalie stared, almost drawn into the gaping void of nightmarish teeth.

"Get...away..." Natalie sighed, the world around her going dark.

#

Mario stared at the illuminated brake lights of the car under the water. They were the only source of illumination in the area, outside of his phone's flashlight.

He tried walking away from the area, but even as he was able to take the steps, he never physically moved from the scene. He knew he was forced to remain, waiting and watching the car in the water.

"Just do it already," he said, sitting beside the pond. "I don't care. I don't know what's happening. We can't get home. There's monsters in the darkness. There was a naked billionaire industrialist. There's a fucking car underwater here. I don't understand any of this. Can the goblins just come out and kill me already? Or do I drown myself in the pond? What are you waiting for?"

"That's some attitude, kid."

Mario turned, the voice causing him to jump. He thought he heard the voice in his head, as though it were one of his own thoughts, but behind him stood a young man, a little older than Mario, wearing a hoodie emblazoned with a Native American warrior on it.

"Who are you?" Mario asked. "Where'd you come from?

The young man shrugged and sat beside Mario. "I went to East Amity High School. I'm at Rocky Brook University now."

Mario looked at the young man's hoodie. "Hey man, like, that's not cool. You can't wear stuff like that."

"What do you mean? I love our mascot. Go Redmen."

"You went to East Amity? We're the Red *Storm* now, we don't use that logo, it's offensive."

The young man nodded. "Oh. Sorry."

That sat for a moment.

"You're stuck here too?"

The young man nodded. "Been here a while."

Mario sat in silence a moment. "Who'd you have for English?"

"Mahoney. She's the worst. Such a phony."

Mario laughed. "I had her this year, too. Agreed on the phony part."

The two shared a laugh.

Finally, the young man looked at Mario. "You know your friend is going to die, right?"

He looked at him. "What?"

The young man nodded absently. "She's with *her* now. She pulled you away from her. Put you in another place. Where she put me and my friends."

"Wait, are you...?" Mario asked, gesturing to the car under the water.

The young man nodded. "How long has it been? It was nineteen-ninety-two when my friends and I came here."

"I'm sorry, it's twenty-twenty-two now."

The young man nodded. "Wow. I can't believe Mahoney is still teaching all these years later."

"Some people hold on, I guess," Mario said. "Like you."

The young man smiled. "You're a smart kid. You have to help your friend."

He shrugged. "How? I tried leaving here, but I didn't get far."

The young man stood up and extended his hand to Mario, helping him to his feet. "I make no guarantees. Hell, you might be stuck here with me for all I know. But we can *try*, okay?"

Mario nodded. "It has to mean something that we're *here*, right?"

The young man nodded. "Everything *means* something to these creeps. They live for synchronicities, as they call them. It's part of their belief system."

"How do you know so much?"

"When I'm not *here*, reliving the moment she threw my car into the pond and reliving her tearing me and my friends apart, she calls upon me to witness her rituals. Something about my purity."

Mario's face turned red. "Am I dead too?"

The young man shook his head. "Nah. Not yet. Think of this place like a waiting room. Divide and conquer. She went for your friend because she's stronger than you. No offense. She makes us watch. We'll be drawn to her temple soon. That's where she feeds."

"Great," Mario sighed. "No offense taken, by the way, Nat always was the strongest," Mario admitted. "Wait, 'purity' as in..."

"Yeah, kid. Exactly that. My dad said I was a 'late bloomer,' alright? You're the first virgin to come here since me. I think we're the only ones she holds no control over. You want my help or not?"

Mario chuckled. "Guess I'm a late bloomer, too."

The two shared a laugh. "Here, take my hand. Maybe I can slip us into the real world. I've never tried this before with a live person, so, it might be...weird. I can't guaranty that you won't piss your pants."

Mario, anxiety racing through his body, extended his hand and the young man took it.

"Hold on tight, okay?"

Mario nodded, as the world around them began to illuminate. The great blanket of darkness began to swirl, an explosion of the red lights of the brakes under the water, the green of nature that encircled the pond and the colors of Mario and the young man's clothes all swirling together in intense brightness.

"I think I might throw up," Mario said softly in the swirl of color in the dark.

#

Natalie opened her eyes and looked around. She was in a large, cathedral-like space, walls lined with candles, black symbols and folds of dark-colored velvet undulating softly from the light breeze.

Attempting to move was an impossibility, as Natalie's arms and legs were bound with leather straps to an upright wooden table, angled slightly. At her feet was a large copper bowl.

The source of the scents that had wafted through the home was a great pyre in the center of the room littered with various sprigs of branches, Robed figures routinely tossed leaves and packets of colored spices into the fire, creating a colorful and disorienting explosion of scent and intensity.

Nude men and women stood around the room, holding snakes, black cats, ravens and other creatures. About a dozen or so of them stood beneath different symbols, some recognizable as simple stars and moons, others, completely foreign to the girl. They were pale. Ghostly in a way.

Mirrors, draped in various coverings, stood on the walls, each with a symbol on whatever covering lay over it, matching the ones above the men and women.

The old woman from the home stepped toward Natalie, a gray-haired Pomeranian in her hands. Her hunched body looked even worse with no clothes on. Her smile sent a cold shiver up Natalie's spine.

The others around the room stood in stark contrast to the old woman. They were younger. In their prime, even. Natalie recognized some of their faces from the paintings in the home.

"You should really do something about that back," Natalie said, feeling bold.

"Oh, we will, you'll see," the woman said, licking her lips.

She held the Pomeranian up to Natalie's face, and it nipped at the girl's cheek, gnawing at her flesh. Natalie screamed as the dog began taking smaller bites out of her face, slurping the blood in a frenzy, its tiny legs running in place with impossible excitement.

The old woman tremored, her body shaking more.

"More, my baby, take more," the old woman cooed, the Pomeranian tearing into Natalie's cheek.

Natalie kept her eyes shut tight, as the furry nightmare continued to assault her face. Finally, she felt the attacks lessen and she exhaled, opening them slowly.

The old woman's body began to shake with greater violence, her gray hair whipping around wildly. "Delicious...so delicious!" the woman cried, running her hands all over her body, releasing the Pomeranian onto the carpet.

Natalie watched the dog spin in circles, chasing its tiny nub-like tail. When she looked back at the woman, she was on her knees.

Her once-gray hair had begun turning red, similar to the fire blazing in the center of the room. When the woman lifted her face to Natalie, the old, terrifying visage was in a state of flux, and hints at the beauty within began to present themselves.

The woman stepped closer to Natalie and ran a finger along her damaged cheek. "I'm sorry, Natalie. My baby gets excited to eat. No hard feelings."

Without missing a beat, Natalie spit whatever saliva she had in her mouth directly into the woman's face.

Smiling, the once-old woman licked her lips, drawing Natalie's saliva into her own mouth. "Thank you," she said, patting the girl on her damaged cheek, sending a shock of pain through the teenager's body.

Once the pain subsided, Natalie looked up and watched as Mario and a young man in a Redmen hoodie entered the room. Her mind immediately connected to the painting she saw earlier.

The two moved amongst the figures, slow and low, avoiding the gaze of any onlookers.

"So this is it, huh?" Natalie asked between sharp breaths.

The woman turned to her. "What do you mean?"

"All the stuff about gremlins and ghosts and blah blah blah...it's just an old bitch bleeding the younger generation dry so she can keep on living?"

The woman laughed. "An oversimplification, but sure, if that's how you see me. My race has been here since the beginning of this place. We came from the woods and claimed the coast as ours, and then you came along. Your rich privilege. Driving us deep into the forest, further north, to the mountains. 'Tiny Town' as your generation call it. I got the Vanderhughs out. I keep the *undesirables* out. My presence poisons the land. The people here exist for my pleasure and my whim. I make them watch as I devour the children in the region. Pathetic little girls like *you*."

Natalie kept her talking long enough for Mario and the young man to begin gathering materials to help free her. Mario slipped one of the velvet coverings off a mirror in the back, far from the crowd. He slipped down and moved closer to the woman and Natalie's position at the back of the cathedral, moving unseen among the figures writhing in the candlelight.

"That's a great scheme..." Natalie sighed. "Be a shame if someone messed it up for you."

The woman smiled. "It's been centuries, darling. People mess it up all the time, but I *always* make a comeback."

"So what happens next won't be much of a surprise then," Natalie said, smiling at the woman.

Moving quickly, Mario rose from his position behind the woman and smashed the mirror over her head, dropping her instantly. The Pomeranian yelped, nipping at Mario's ankles, drawing blood, it's tiny teeth annoying and painful at the same time. Rapidly, he began untying the straps, setting Natalie free.

"She's a *goblin*, not a *gremlin*," Mario said.

The young man stood nearby, flanked by the other figures and holding a blazing candle holder, the fire burning red and black in impossible brightness.

"Tonight! We get our justice! She is the enemy, not these kids! Remember what she did to you! To *all of* us!" the young man shouted over the roar of the fire and the barking of the dog. "Get out of here. She's ours," the young man said to Mario and Natalie.

"Come with us," Mario said. "You can't stay here."

"She has to pay. For what she did to all of us. This time it'll be different."

"Thank you," Natalie said.

The young man smiled. "He totally likes you, by the way. Get out of here."

Mario and Natalie made for the exit, and before leaving, she kicked over two candle holders, spilling wax and fire to the floor.

The cathedral went up alarmingly fast, and the young man remained between Natalie and Mario as the figures in the room began to attack the woman.

Her red hair streaking with gray, the woman rose and looked at the two teenagers at the far end of the room. She smiled and slowly raised her hands, giving them a round of applause, fire beginning to engulf her, spectral hands clawing at her, dragging her into the pyre.

"Go!" the young man shouted to them. The two teenagers turned and broke through the doors of the cathedral and found themselves passing through the brick and stone archway at the entrance to Tiny Town.

They climbed into Natalie's car and drove off into the night.

Eventually, they emerged under the archway outside of Tiny Town.

"We have to destroy the mirrors. Vanderhugh told me it was how she moves around. That's why they were all covered up, because she keeps the doors closed during the ritual."

Natalie nodded. "A little teenaged destruction never hurt anybody, right?"

"What's seven years of bad luck times a few hundred?"

"Who gives a shit, turn up the radio and let's trash this place."

#

Mario awoke with a start the next morning. He had slept on the floor of Natalie's room, and she was already awake, laptop open, reading the news. Her bandaged cheek was swollen and red.

"We should get you to a doctor, Nat, your cheek might need stitches," Mario said, rubbing the sleep from his eyes.

"It all burned down. All of Tiny Town. The entire Vanderhugh property. The archway. The houses. All of it. Gone. The fire department couldn't put any of it out," she said, amazed at the news.

He stared at her. "I'm sorry. About everything."

She looked at him, closed the laptop and slipped onto the floor beside him.

"You sorta' saved my ass last night, kid," she said, smiling. "Thanks."

He nodded. "You'd do the same for me."

"Doubtful, I would've gotten the hell out of there and left you to get drained by that old broad."

They shared a laugh. She rested her head on his shoulder and he put his arm around her. Suddenly, the yelping of a dog outside made Natalie's eyes go wide. She rose slowly and stepped over to the window.

On the neighbor's lawn, a gray Pomeranian watched. Natalie sighed, shook her head and closed the blinds.

Fichtner Meets Feldstein

"Thanks, Rico. Here, for your troubles," Fichtner said, slipping a fifty into Rico's enormous mitt. The guard stood a solid foot taller than Fichtner, a man who usually found himself described, at best, as "squirrely."

"Cameras are down, shift change just started. Twenty minutes," Rico said. "I come back and unlock after twenty minutes. You go right back out the maintenance door, same as you came in, yeah?"

"More time than I need, Rico." He nodded to the money in Rico's hand. "Don't spend it all in one place."

"Yeah," Rico said, walking away, tucking the bill in his back pocket. He slid the cell door open with a metallic groan.

Fichtner stepped into the cell. He looked around. Maybe ten feet by ten feet. One window, overlooking the water, beyond that, New York City glittered in the night.

"So, you're him. The guy everyone's talking about," Fichtner said, turning, after sliding the cell door back into place with a *clang*.

"Who might you be?" Feldstein asked, looking up. He wore the standard-issue orange jumpsuit provided by the Department of Corrections.

"Call me Fichtner. Don't matter much that you know my name."

"It 'doesn't' matter much. That would be the correct way of saying that," Feldstein said.

"Sure, pal," Fichtner said. "Here, take a look. I like to give my clients a choice."

Fichtner opened what looked like an old leather doctor's bag, the kind you see in black and white movies. Inside, a myriad of devices, each more medieval than the last. Some rusty. Most, dull, but sharp enough to do their job.

"What's this all about?"

"Just look in the bag, pal."

"That's quite the collection," Feldstein sighed. "Guess my number's up. Enough folks got together and decided I needed to be out of the game?"

Fichtner nodded. A tiny smile curled in the corner of his mouth.

"You know all about that, right? All you did to those girls."

"I suppose," Feldstein shrugged. "You here to lecture me, too?"

"I usually don't talk much to those I visit. But with you, the man of the hour, I'm gonna make an exception. You're all over the news."

"I figured as much."

"Too bad you couldn't be famous for something important, you know? Curing cancer or sending a bunch of poor kids to college, that sorta' thing," Fichtner said, taking the tools out of his bag.

"I sent a lot of girls to college. Some are doctors now. Some are scientists."

"Sure, pal," Fichtner said. "Look, I don't take much pleasure in this, but in your case, and for what I'm being paid, I'm going to enjoy it a *lot*. What do you say?"

Feldstein turned away and looked at the sky through the tiny, barred window. The moon, barely glowing behind a thick bank of clouds, struggled to peer out.

"The news said it'd be a full moon tonight. I don't see it yet."

"Feldstein, pick a toy from the bag. There's so many. I was told to make it quick, but some of these are fast, made for smooth jobs. Some aren't, I can't guarantee a quick shuffle off this mortal coil, you know?"

"I would've enjoyed one more night. One more...dance in the moonlight."

"My last client picked the rope. There's nothing more boring than the rope, so I didn't bring it this time. How about an old favorite? Razor down the street, not across?"

"Fichtner, do me a kindness, won't you? When I close my eyes, do your worst. I just want to stare at the moon a moment. I don't want to see it coming."

"Whatever floats your boat, short eyes. I can go down the street, not across, and it'll be like falling asleep, okay?"

The clouds slowly drifted from the moon's rays, and they landed squarely in Feldstein's face.

"Funny thing about the moon, Fichtner...*funny thing about it...it's always had...*" Feldstein doubled over, grabbing his stomach. Fichtner stood, unsure what to do, and looked around, the blank concrete walls could provide no guidance.

Fichtner stepped closer and watched as Feldstein began to convulse on the floor. Black, syrupy fluid erupted from his mouth, and he squealed in agony.

"Pal, you alright? Jesus, Feldstein, what *are* you?"

Feldstein, bathed in the glow of the moon, tremored violently, his back swelling, his orange jumpsuit tearing away, revealing beneath an impossible blanket of thick, brown-gray fur.

"*It's always...had...an...*"

"Hey, Rico, hey! Somethin's goin' on. Get me out of here!"

"*Closer...Fichtner...*"

Feldstein, more animal than man, lunged for Fichtner, grabbing his greasy face between two enormous paws.

"Rico! Ricooooooooo!"

Slowly, Feldstein slipped a claw deep into Fichtner's arm and began dragging it down. The flesh carved easily, like a warm knife through ice cream cake, dark crimson rivulets emerging from within the assassin's arm.

"*Down the street...not across...*"

"Feldstei - - Please...off...gurgg...hellllll...Ricooo..."

"*Your nose first, to spite your face...your nose...then the rest...*"

Feldstein's enormous mouth opened wide, and he scraped his teeth across Fichtner's head, his tongue flicking the man's nose and eyes as he dragged his sharp fangs backward, tearing and pulling the flesh from Fichtner's face.

Rico re-appeared, standing in the doorway of the cell beside a shorter, younger-looking guard. Rico's hand rested on his sidearm, the other slid the door open.

"Jesus, what's happening in here?" Rico screamed. "Code six!"

"What is that in there?" the guard shouted over the raucous.

"*Come closer...Rico...come closer...*"

#

Feldstein stood, his chest heaving in the moonlight. The alarm of the prison roared, piercing the night. His ears twitched with animalistic instinct, as other inmates, safely locked in their cells screamed, unable to comprehend the enormous feral creature that emerged from Feldstein's cell.

It didn't take long to slip Fichtner into his prison uniform. With the shreds and tears, even with all the blood and viscous meat stinking up his former cell, the assassin's body made for a convincing Feldstein duplicate.

He looked around, sizing up the other inmates in his wing of the prison. They recoiled, pressing themselves against the far walls of their cells. What could be considered the closest approximation of a grin crawled across Feldstein's snarling face, even with his more canine features obscuring any semblance of humanity.

Turning slowly, Feldstein stalked toward the door of the prison, tearing it from its hinges, and disappearing into the dark, ominously silent New York City night.

#

The following morning, the local news had a field day with the report from the prison. At various points throughout the day some variation of the following could be heard on any number of radio and television stations: "... mysterious death of Teddy Feldstein at the Metropolitan Correctional Center in New York has left local law enforcement stunned. It appears Feldstein killed two guards in a failed escape attempt, then cut his own face off, bleeding to death in his cell...updates as they emerge...and now, our top story, a thirteen-year-old Staten Island girl disappeared from her bedroom last night, leaving the police baffled, we now go live to..."

Hookman's End

Tenma sat quietly on the gunwale of *The Clamdigger*, the commercial fishing boat he'd spent the past three seasons aboard. He was good at his job, and the captain was quick to rehire him, year to year, expecting him every April, late in the month. Tenma spent January through most of April traveling among the ports up and down the east coast of the United States, working aboard various smaller commercial fishing boats, making good money, and hunting good game.

In Tenma's hand was his primary hunting tool. The slender metallic glow of the hook, typically kept very clean, was caked with dried fish entrails, having hooked a large marlin earlier in the day. Tenma hadn't had a chance to clean it yet, but he would. He'd have to. Once they got back to port in Montauk, the hunt would be on.

For now, Tenma stared at the ocean. The smell of the day's catch wafted up from the cargo hold, and he smiled. He had been a migrant fisherman for twenty years now. Since he ran away from his adoptive parents at the age of twelve, Tenma found himself working on a variety of ships, small to large, learning more about the ocean than most sailors. He was a good study. Good with a rod. Good at the wheel. And damn good with the hook.

Tenma's nocturnal proclivities would be what pulled him out into the dark May night. Coming off Memorial Day Weekend, Long Island was about to enter full-swing tourist season, and there would be plenty of potential hunting partners running around East Hampton, Sag Harbor and even Montauk. Tenma was well-versed in the area. He loved working on *The Clamdigger* not only because it provided him the most work and the most money, but also the dumbest possible prey.

The partygoing Long Islanders who invaded the east end weren't the locals. In fact, the locals looked down on those renting beach houses, filling the hotels, and crowding their beaches. To the locals, they often referred to the tourists as "cityiots," a combination of "city" and "idiot" that always made Tenma smile when he thought of it. The locals weren't wrong, of course, as most of the time, the teenagers and twentysomethings who rented houses or filled hotels often drank to excess, wrecked the beaches and resulted in a massive spike in drug use.

Easy prey, Tenma thought. *The drunker, the better.*

"Plans tonight, Tenma?" the captain asked. He was heavyset guy, in his sixties, bearded. The stereotypical sea captain. The only thing missing would've been a peg leg, parrot or pirate-y way of speaking.

"Nothing too crazy, maybe grab a drink at The Dock," Tenma said. The Dock was his favorite hunting ground. No kids. No families. Dark. Old. It was a place most cityiots would find themselves in after too many rounds elsewhere. It was also a place where folks sometimes were last seen.

"Nice, maybe I'll drop down and join you, if the wife'll let me," the captain said with a smile. Tenma knew that wouldn't happen. The captain's wife often didn't let him out of her sight. Based on the stories the captain told, she sounded like a harpy.

"Cool, I'll keep a spot open for you," Tenma said, wiping his hook with a towel and slipping it into a sheath on his hip.

#

That night, true to his word, Tenma sat in the corner of The Dock, drinking a Coca-Cola, pretending it was a rum and Coke. He didn't like to actually drink while hunting, since he wanted to be in prime condition and savor the kill. While watching for prey, he thought about his first time. A young man who rebuffed his advances in Tampa, Florida. Tenma had been down south, as part of his usual migratory fishing ritual, working on a small swordfishing ship with an overbearing captain and his first mate of a son.

Tenma had spotted his first victim in a local dive bar, not unlike The Dock, but with more neon and less history. Tenma wasn't there to meet anyone, but he couldn't take his eyes off the man when he came in for a drink, Tenma assumed, after a day at work. They struck up a conversation, flirted a bit, but when Tenma made an advance, the man rejected him. After hours of flirtation, Tenma assumed this was a sure thing, and yet, the man shot him down.

Frustrated, Tenma waited for the man in the parking lot after the rejection, and when the young man walked toward his car, Tenma approached him, mostly to apologize, but also to try and change the man's mind. This didn't go well. They argued. The man insulted Tenma, and Tenma, frustrated, dug his hook into the man's crotch.

He didn't even scream. Tenma stared, surprised and confused at the man, as he doubled over, and went into a frenzy of tremors. Tenma removed the hook from the man's damaged organ and held it up, eyeing the blood and flesh still clinging to it in the neon light beaming from the bar's sign. The prey continued to twitch and shake, and Tenma, a sudden feeling of power and desire washing over him, slowly slipped the hook into the man's neck. He watched the blood pool and listened to the gurgling of his prey's final, pained breaths.

From that day forward, Tenma was hooked.

At every port, in every state, Tenma would find his prey. Male. Female. Young. Old. It didn't matter. As long as he was able to subdue his victim, and coat his hook with their blood, he didn't care what age, race or gender they were. He thought about one particularly difficult kill, a large, older man, Bucky, in South Carolina. He was a pawn shop owner that accused Tenma of trying to "Jap him" out of some money when Tenma offered him one hundred dollars for a guitar hanging on the wall that had a price marked at one-twenty.

Tenma nodded, then waited for him in the back alley. He stood by the man's truck, hook at the ready, and when closing time came, he sprung on Bucky, raining blows on him with the sharp instrument, plunging it into the man's back and sides, over and over. Bucky howled, but his size and strength were vastly superior to Tenma's small frame, and he ended up tossing Tenma away easily.

Bucky's undoing was trying to climb into his truck. He had barely gotten inside, when Tenma leaped on the hood and smashed the windshield to pieces with the hook. Tenma climbed in and finished Bucky off in a flurry of slashes and stabs.

Tenma smiled to himself, remembering leaving Bucky in the driver's seat, torn to shred. The old man had pissed himself when Tenma smashed through the windshield. Tenma finished his soda and ordered another.

He had seen the occasional article written about his murders. "Hook-Man Strikes Again!" read the Tampa Bay Tribune. "The Hook Returns!" read another, either some rag in Georgia or in Connecticut. Tenma couldn't remember. It was annoying that it took so long to give him a nickname. He preferred "The Hook" over "Hook-Man" because in his mind, "Hook-Man" sounded like a superhero, which he most certainly was not.

No superhero would sit in a bar on the east end of Long Island, waiting for a drunk twentysomething to stroll in. The Hook would, though. Tenma sipped his soda slowly and continued to wait.

#

It took a while, but eventually, a group of kids wandered in. By the looks of it, they were already plastered. Three girls, two guys. The girls, especially, were noticeably drunk, which didn't stop the bartenders one bit. The group ordered shots. Then more shots. Then more shots. Tenma smiled to himself, watching them, thinking how easily it'll be to separate one of them from the group and make an easy kill somewhere nearby.

The group continued to drink, while Tenma got up and paid his tab. He added a twenty as a tip, and left The Dock, heading to his rental, a gray Ford Taurus, parked across from The Dock. He watched as other patrons left the bar, then one of the bartenders. He knew the group would be leaving soon, and watched, hoping they'd come out and decide to head to whatever overpriced hotel or Airbnb they rented for the weekend.

When they finally emerged, they walked east, heading for a cluster of beach bungalows owned by a local hotel. Tenma followed them, pulling into the parking lot the bungalows shared with the hotel and watched as two of the girls and two of the guys coupled off and went into two separate rooms, leaving the one girl behind. She lit a cigarette and sat on a bench under the light of the bungalow's porch and Tenma was able to get a good look at her: brunette, attractive, late teens early twenties, glasses. Nothing to write home about.

Tenma got out of his car and went to the trunk. Inside, he slipped on his slicker from the boat, along with a ski mask. He started wearing a disguise after the incident with Bucky, as he was almost positive someone saw him fleeing the scene. Even though no one did, Tenma thought it better to be safe than sorry, and wore a disguise in some fashion ever since.

He pulled a small burlap bag out of the trunk and pulled the hook from it. At that moment, a car pulled into the parking lot, its lights on Tenma from behind, and he froze as it passed. He put the burlap bag back in the trunk of his rental car and walked around the back of the two bungalows. There were only five of the small rentals in the area, and Tenma wasn't sure which was the lone girl's.

Maybe she's bunking with one of the couples? he thought, watching her while moving. She hadn't lifted her gaze from her phone once since she started her cigarette.

This is almost too easy, he thought, eyes wide, drinking in the surroundings, trying to figure out the easiest and safest plan of attack.

He found himself on the side of the bungalow, watching her from the darkness. Inside, he could hear the muffled sounds of lovemaking going on from the girl's friends. Tenma hoped their noise would be enough to muffle the sounds his prey was about to make.

She stood and walked down the porch, toward where Tenma lurked in the shadows. Once close enough, Tenma felt every muscle in his body tense, ready to snap into action. She was still glued to her phone. Her cigarette was just about finished, and once she turned, Tenma would strike.

She threw the cigarette down and snuffed it out. She turned around and quickly, Tenma lunged at her. She kicked and screamed, but Tenma was experienced. He covered her mouth with a gloved hand and pulled her to the back of the bungalow. Though she was small, she was strong, and Tenma struggled to keep her in his clutches.

Once to the back of the bungalow, she threw her entire weight forward, catching Tenma off-guard, and pulling herself from his clutches. They both fell forward, tripping and collapsing in a heap. She screamed again, but Tenma acted quickly, punching her in the face.

"Shut up, Jesus, you'll wake the dead," Tenma hissed, punching her again for good measure.

Her head rolled, and she blinked rapidly, trying to fight losing consciousness. Tenma was surprised by the amount of fight in the girl, and he knew he'd probably have to act quickly, less she got a second burst of adrenaline. He raised the hook high and brought it down into her stomach. She lurched forward, eyes wide and mouth agape. Tenma stared into her eyes and watched as a look of confusion washed over her.

He removed the hook from her stomach and noted how she placed her hands on her injury, then held her hands up to her face, as if to check if she had, in fact, been stabbed. Tenma had seen this before. A few times. People were sometimes so confused by what was happening to them, they often needed confirmation of the horror that befell them.

Tenma raised the hook high and brought it down into her chest. She squealed and vomited, lurching forward again. *A lot of fight in this one*, he thought. He was trying to pull the hook out of her chest, when her slender hand wrapped around his fist, clutching the handle.

They locked eyes and she stared at him, pleading, in a way. For a moment, Tenma froze, and in that instant, she gouged at his eyes with her right hand, her left locked on his. He fell backward, and she struggled to her feet, a mixture of alcohol, adrenaline and anger fueling her.

"You motherfucker," she said, tearing the hook from her chest. It made a *shlorp* noise as she tugged it free and she stalked toward Tenma, who was still holding his face in agony.

As Tenma looked up at her, she slammed the hook into his skull. His body shook, and a variety of images passed through whatever was left of his brain. His first kill. His tenth. His thirtieth. There were so many, he lost count. They were blended with memories of his childhood, with the folks who adopted him, before that, in the orphanage in Japan, after that, his first time on a boat, his first time with a woman, his first time with a man.

Memory after memory, blood, death, love, sex, carnage, meat, bone. The images of all of these things continued to assault Tenma, over and over, so many nights, so many ports, so many cities and towns.

Tenma suddenly pissed himself. He fell over, the hook still in his head.

His last thought, as he watched his prey slink around the corner to the front of the bungalows, and felt the moistness of his own blood pooling around his head, was what name the papers in New York would end up using.

He hoped it would be The Hook.

Only That You Are Still Sane

Roger...

The name once held meaning to me. *Morris.* What was once my last name echoes through intangible walls of eternity, spoken by thousands of voices, from childhood to my last days in nineteen eighty-six.

The day the temporal radiation caught up to me.

In my previous existence, I remember that I was the chief engineer for VisionPark's World of Time attraction. Walcott had conjured the idea after a late-night drunken viewing of George Pal's *The Time Machine.* While Walcott's imagination wrestled with how to bring the experience of traveling through time to the Odessa, Texas masses, my mind was on what Yvette Mimieux was wearing under her pink dress.

"Surely, underwear would be phased out in a utopian future, no?" I remember asking.

I remember asking...

I remember asking how severe the radiation in my body was. *I had only stepped through the tear and into the future for a moment. It couldn't possibly be enough to kill me.* I remember the doctor's face, a blend of confusion and genuine worry. I remember his answer: "I don't know, Roger."

My name was Roger...

I remember...

"What are his options?" my wife asks. When the doctor fails to give her any, I submit all my saved sick leave, and spend the remaining months of my life wasting away at our vacation home in Corpus Christi.

Is there anything I can do for you?

I remember my wife asking that. Numerous times. Over the last months of life in this form. All she *could* do was provide meals, comfort, and tell me stories of our time together, as my memory began to fade, the radiation ravaging my body.

My beautiful wife. Aging yet ageless, as I hurtle through time. I see her young. I see her older. I see her as my angel and redeemer. I see her as my anchor.

At my bedside. Holding my hand. The feel of her warm, soft skin. The smell of her perfume. She wore my favorite every day. Towards the end.

Peale visits often. As does Walcott.

I remember asking...

"Is it because I went *through*?"

Peale nods. I knew my hands-on approach to creating a theme park ride worthy of H. G. Wells himself would backfire. We created a relative facsimile. A quantum of true time travel.

The tunnel itself allowed an experience that, to our workers handling the ride and to those enjoying it, appeared staged, through a mixture of animatronics and screen-projected imagery.

I remember...

"Can they tell the difference?" Walcott asks, watching the first few people through the ride. They had an adrenaline high and were exploding with excitement.

"They believe what they *want* to believe. There's no limit when it comes to the magic the human mind can conjure," I said, listening to the positive feedback of the park's first few visitors through The Time Tunnel.

I remember asking...

"Where is the tear?" as I stand inside The Time Tunnel, over a decade of wear and tear to the material of the structure itself. It had been abnormally hot in the tunnel, and I took it upon myself to investigate, after a few of our staff complained.

Walcott was with me, and once I traced the source of the split in the seam between the tunnel's outer structure, comprised of conductive metals, mostly alloys in an effort to harness and focus the tachyon emissions required to make the tunnel work. The fabric-nylon composite material we used was meant to be tear-resistant.

This was not the case.

As I investigate, I notice another tear. This one, through time and space itself.

Though the ride was shut down, and no electricity surged through it, a spectacular light and heat seemed to explode from the paneling beyond the one-foot tear in the protective seal between the ride itself and the actual time apparatus.

Intense, unfathomable heat beamed through. Human desire overwhelmed me. I *had* to look upon the world beyond with my own eyes. I had to *see* the future for myself.

I cracked the code. It seemed only fair.

I stepped inside...

One imagines something of a shock stepping from one reality to another. Some sort of friction that overwhelms the heart, the mind or both.

Gravitational forces stressing the body far beyond it's possible limit.

There were no gravitational forces.

There was a passing notion of friction. There was heat.

And blinding light.

Intense light, and impossible color, as though a box of crayons melted in the summer sun, swirling around me. The madness disoriented and confused, but it was momentary. I slipped through the gossamer threads of dimensional nebula and found myself on the shore of a great purple ocean.

This part of the ride was always the younger kids' favorite. There is always a direct correlation between the age of a child and their obsession with giant, terrifying monsters.

The future...

The vast violet sea raged. I could almost taste the salinity of the ocean, and looking around, I remember soaking in the sights of impossible creatures.

The sun, hanging low, singed my skin, and I felt an almost immediate sunburn begin to singe my flesh. Sweat began to form on my temples, and when I wiped my brow, my sweat seemed to be the same color as the raging waters before me.

I watched as a cluster of enormous mantis shrimp stalked and killed a crab roughly twice their size. We knew the future would be terrifying but seeing these creatures only a hundred yards away was something else entirely.

The shrimp glowed in almost-neon brightness on the shore, blue, red, some green and purple, not unlike the ocean roaring mere feet from me.

I trembled at the enormity of the creatures.

I feel fear for the last time...

I am sitting in a chaise lounge near the pool in Corpus Christi. My wife is beside me, holding my hand. My breaths are labored.

Speech is impossible. I have a vague recollection of pain, but my body has learned to ignore it.

She smells like heaven.

I pray for the last time...

The radiation is contained in my body. Of that, the doctors and scientists are certain. They are, however, less certain of what type of radiation this is. They've referred to it as "chronal" or "temporal," with the obvious implication that it has to do with passing through the threads of time and space.

I am thankful that the tests have indicated that my wife has shown no trace of the radiation that is coursing through me.

They do not understand why...

My wife, beautiful in a way that is beyond words, looks into my eyes. She wears sunglasses to hide how puffy and red her own eyes are. Tears are common for her these days.

My tear ducts have gone dry. The drops I am given to keep my eyes moist are oily and leave white streaks down my cheeks once it dries.

I am stricken with an insane thirst which never gets quenched.

In our church, where our son was baptized, the same one we stopped visiting not long after, I sit alone in a pew. My wife waits outside in the car. I walk with a cane and resemble a seventy-five-year-old man, though I am only forty-two.

"What a time to be struck with religious terror," I say aloud. The radiation has not yet claimed my ability to speak. I am not yet beside my wife by the pool, struggling to breathe.

I think of Wells. I think of Bradbury. I think of Irving. I think of Heinlein. Creative minds, like Walcott, who worked in the realm of time travel. All I did was step through a tear. I was only in the future for about twenty seconds.

I stare at Jesus on the cross.

That twenty seconds...

I am staring at the Time Tunnel. It is nine months before the opening of VisionPark. Walcott is worried it won't work. We had successfully sent our ride vehicles through eighty times, each time with a camera to record the sights and sounds. Each time, we reviewed the images. Each time, the machine worked.

I remember asking...

"And so what if it doesn't? We have the animatronics on standby, it'll be fine, Walcott, you'll see..."

We had cracked time and space. Standing on the shoulders of giants, we did it. Nuclear physics, combined with the astrophysics, mixed with a little theory and metallurgy and boom, time travel.

I am passing through time...

I am alone. Standing in the spot where I first entered the future. The tunnel is dark. The Realm of Time is closed. Time has ravaged the park. Nature has begun to reclaim the area. Cracks in the concrete and broken glass allow air into the ride where no openings existed previously.

Walking slowly, my footsteps echoing through The Realm of Time, I find discarded pamphlets, maps and gift shop items. Some have digital displays on them. They resemble alarm clocks, but not like anything in nineteen-eighty-six.

I see signs written in English, Spanish and other languages.

Advertisements for businesses I don't recognize.

I am not breathing...

In the chaise lounge, my heart begins to seize. A great pressure forms in my chest, and my eyes go wide, as though they, too, should be able to take in air to remedy the raging pain in my upper body.

My wife is inside, getting a glass of water.

Staring into space, I see the tear. I clutch my chest, squeezing hard, but the tear becomes wider, hovering a few feet away from me. I feel the intensity of the heat. I see the ocean of purple. I hear the sounds of impossible creatures roaring.

Silently, I thank whatever god is out there that my wife isn't here to watch me slip away.

I take one final deep breath and lean back in the chaise lounge. As I exhale, the pain evaporates from my body, and my eyes begin to lose focus, the outer edges of everything in my view becoming soft and dark.

The light of the tear washes over me.

I am gone...

I am outside The Realm of Time. The sky is dark. The desert stretches around me. The coldness of a Texas night feels good, even though I no longer have skin.

I am pure sensation.

I am a memory.

A memory of a man. An engineer. A man who worked hard to create a ride about time travel and through sheer luck, created time travel for real, even *if* in a limited capacity.

They'd never believe how real it all was...

Walcott would say that often. We'd share a beer after work and he'd marvel at how our team was able to truly create a way through time.

"Walcott, does it ever worry you? What we created here in VisionPark? What does that mean for us?"

I remember...

Walcott finishes his beer, wipes his face and smiles at me. "Roger Morris, my good man, it means only that you are still sane."

Roger Morris...

Morris...

A name that once held meaning but has since vanished. To time, to space.

My lifeless body sits in a chaise lounge by the pool in Corpus Christi.

I am approached to build a ride at VisionPark.

I create time travel.

The desert stretches before me.

The purple ocean stretches before me.

I watch my wife give birth to my son.

She sits at the bar, waiting for me. It is our first date.

I lift her veil on our wedding day.

I shake hands with Walcott for the first time.

A great expanse of white surrounds me. Color, unfathomable, bombards me. It is breathtaking in a way I have never experienced.

It is warm.

And I am whole.

Nibble

Eric hated flying. Nell never had a problem with it, but that was because the second any plane took off, she was out like a light while Eric had to white-knuckle it the entire way. His stomach dropped with every slight bump. No matter how much he dwelled on the statistics, it didn't matter that flying was the safest form of travel, Eric just knew that he hated it.

But he knew it'd be worth it. *Just relinquish control and focus on where you're going.* That's what his shrink had told him. Their destination was the goal. To make the delivery to the tribe deep in the heart of the Brazilian Rainforest, the Cumanagato. *To enrich the lives of the less fortunate*, their pastor had said.

Eric glanced over at his sleeping wife. His eyes lingered on her slender neck, then further down.

He thought of the pallet of goods that sat in the cargo hold of the plane. The goods he and his wife had spent a fair amount of money getting together to make the exchange with the tribe. He figured there wasn't anything wrong with quid pro quo when it came to missionary work. Not like their pastor would ever find out, anyway.

"It'll be worth it," Eric said softly as the plane entered a bit of turbulence. He adjusted in his seat, feeling the sting that still radiated down his neck.

He scratched at the wounds the insects left and smiled. He thought about how lucky he was to find the nest in the yard. Thought about the ritual of him and Nell slipping into their beekeeper suits. Carefully placing the wasp's nest into a leftover delivery box and taping it up.

The excitement that night of standing nude in the dark and pulling the tape off. Nell biting her lower lip in anticipation. Watching as the wasps took flight, swirling around the room, bumping into the ceiling fan, the windows, the mirrors. Tiny *thuds* against the walls and the glass that made Eric smile each time.

Taking his time exploring Nell's body. Taking his time and letting the wasps' stingers find homes in his and his wife's flesh. The pinprick of their perfect, deliciously sharp spears penetrating Eric and Nell's bodies over and over was almost enough to send Eric over the edge.

When they were finished, lying beside each other in their usual post-coital reverie, Nell began to count the stings on Eric's body. Ten running up his back, the flesh glowing red even in the dimly-lit bedroom. Twenty-seven in the sweaty, fleshy area of his thighs, running up to his testicles.

"Damn, babe," Nell said, breathlessly. She planted a kiss along each sting until she reached his neck.

"Let me look at yours," Eric said. He could still hear the wasps fluttering around the room. The air conditioning was keeping the room a brisk fifty degrees, and multiple oil diffusers were cranking to keep the bugs docile. Now that the couple had had their fun, they wanted nothing to do with their vespid partners. Their stings and the repeated penetration of their tender flesh were all Eric and Nell needed. Now, the creatures could freeze and spiral to the wood floor, drained of life and poisoned by the scented oils.

Nell sometimes joked that their bedroom partners weren't much different than the people she slept with in her twenties. Once she got what she wanted, the Earth could swallow them whole for all she cared.

Eric watched as Nell rolled over, wincing. She had it worse. Seventy-eight stings in all, up the back of her thighs, all over her rear and lower back. She had a few that were higher, above her neckline, and Eric rose to get the ointment he kept in the bathroom. Since they'd started their game, they had rules about bites and stings above Nell's neckline. Anything visible would surely draw questions, so the couple needed to keep their story straight. Can't let the ladies in the women's ministry know about their bedroom activities.

\#

When they landed, Eric felt jetlagged, so he wasn't too chatty as they rented the truck and watched as the airport personnel loaded it with the donated material from their church. Eric and Nell saw this missionary trip as an opportunity. Wasps, spiders, certain types of caterpillars were one thing, but the ultimate thrill lay in the rainforest. It was an opportunity to get their hands on something so exotic and unavailable back home, they couldn't pass up the chance. Not just their hands. Other parts, too. More *tender* parts.

Paraponera clavata. Commonly known as the bullet ant.

"The tribe's been using them in rituals for years. They even worship them," Eric said one day, standing beside Nell other parishioners as they handed out Styrofoam cups of electric-red fruit juice and small plates of sugar cookies after Sunday service. "Supposedly."

"Sounds crazy," Nell said, smiling warmly to some of the older ladies in their church. "How could we ever get there?"

"I have an idea," Eric said, taking a sip of the juice and recoiling at the sweetness of it.

As they bounced along the road in a rented pickup truck, the pallet of clothes, medical supplies and more securely fastened in back, Eric reminded Nell of that day in church.

"I can't believe it came together so easy," she said. "I still can't believe we're actually here."

"Here are the people we'll be meeting with. They set it all up for us." He showed Nell a picture on his phone. A group of people in various forms of traditional tribal dress sat in a circle around an intricately carved ant statue. Many of the men and some of the women were painted red and black, many of them wearing beautiful jewelry that looked carved from dark wood. "Their dresses are beautiful," Nell said.

"Maybe we can get one?" Eric asked.

"No, no, I think that might be too far. What they're doing for us already is more than enough," Nell said, squeezing the inside of Eric's thigh.

Thinking back, Eric knew that he and Nell's constant pursuit of an added thrill to their lovemaking was always there, even if it hadn't yet taken this "louse-y" turn. He chuckled to himself, thinking of the first time Nell used that very term to describe their predilection for being nibbled or stung on during their bedroom escapades. Voyeurism wasn't enough. Neither was exhibitionism. It was a sudden realization they both had, that their bodies demanded that flow of lymphocytes to the bit or stung area. The swelling and tenderness of the flesh. The reddening. Nell could no longer finish during sex if she wasn't swollen from some sort of bite, sting or scratch.

Eric, too. The carnal release had never felt better than when feeling the sting of dozens, even hundreds of tiny bedroom invaders all over his body, especially down south.

He felt a rush of adrenaline as he followed the GPS, turning off the paved highway and down a gravel road.

There were still a few hours of daylight left, and Eric's research into the jungles of South America told him that bullet ants were common in the lower rainforests. The couple were dressed sensibly, light clothes, shorts. Bottles of water and food in Eric's backpack, two EpiPens in Nell's clutch. He showed Nell a picture of the ants in question. They were larger than the average ant back home in New York, darkly-colored, almost a jet-black, with hairy legs and large, powerful-looking mandibles. Their stingers protruded from their abdomens and Eric caught Nell licking her lips as they cruised toward the jungle. *She's as turned on as I am*, he thought.

They'd have to cut through the town of Beso De Fuego to get deeper into the jungle, but they were assured that there was a trail the truck could handle. As the road turned from gravel to dirt, they approached the mouth of the jungle, with great tendrils of gnarled greenery, some with colorful flowers dangling from tree-trunk like vines.

Once to the edge of the rainforest, Nell slid a hand between her legs and smiled at Eric. "I'm so nervous."

He nodded. "Me too." The anticipation was killing him, and he began to feel the familiar stirrings of passion for his wife. He swallowed hard and continued their trek, letting his hand rest high on the inside of her thigh.

Slowly, they entered the jungle, vines grazing the top of the truck as they moved, scratching along the roof like the claw of some ancient tropical predator. As the jungle grew thicker, it grew darker. Whatever red and orange sky burned above was choked away by the deep shadow of greenery around them.

#

In the thickness of the jungle, Eric and Nell picked up the scent of smoke, mingling with some faint floral notes. They had been driving for about ninety minutes before it hit them, and they both realized they were close to...something. The dirt path they drove on had become overgrown in many sections, but the truck continued bumpily.

"That smell..." Nell said, trailing off.

"I know," Eric said. "Almost like patchouli, right?"

She nodded. After another ten minutes of driving, they found themselves on the outskirts of the tribe's village. For a moment, Eric thought he was lost, as the jungle was more of a maze, verdant and treacherous. "You can lose more than your way in here, man," he said quietly.

As Eric put the truck into park, Nell gestured to the Cumanagato tribeswoman who was walking slowly toward the truck, her hand up in a gesture of civility.

"Hello," Nell said, stepping out of the truck and returning the gesture.

The woman, older, possibly in her sixties, wore a beautifully-patterned dress and beaded necklace. Her long hair grew down to her backside.

Eric walked over. "We're from the church in New York. We have supplies for your people."

"How wonderful," the woman said. "I'm Kakury. I believe I'm the one you spoke to about your..." She looked Eric and Nell over. "Your *request*."

"I trust everything's in order?" Eric asked.

"Of course. We were just burning some guarana in anticipation of your arrival."

"Guarana? Like the drink?" Nell asked.

"It acts as a mild stimulant in ash form," Eric explained to his wife. Combing Wikipedia in preparation for the trip was starting to pay off. "Kakury's warriors place it on their hands when they perform the ritual."

Kakury smiled nervously at Nell. "We had to burn a lot in order to have enough to cover your entire, umm..." She trailed off, obviously embarrassed. "Either way, it is done."

"Excellent," Eric said. "If you send over a couple of your strongest, we can get the supplies unloaded and rest a bit before the ritual."

Kakury nodded. She turned and waved to two younger Cumanagato. Nell regarded them with a smile as Eric climbed into the back of the truck and began tearing away the plastic-wrapped containers.

#

"What has your husband told you about the ritual?" Kakury asked Nell as they stood together near the large metal urn of ashes that still smoldered.

Eric noted that Guarana wasn't the only thing that had been burned as part of the ritual, there were additional spices and flowers that contributed to the fragrant, alluring scent. He was sweaty from unloading the truck and was happy to see the Cumanagato enjoying the goods from his church's congregation.

"That it's part of your people's custom," Nell said, taking a sip of her water bottle. She handed the bottle to Eric. "That your warriors perform the ritual multiple times each spring."

Kakury nodded. "In a sense, yes." She handed Nell an intricately woven glove made of local leaves roughly the size of an oven mitt. "Our warriors place their hands into a pair of these. This one is empty, but when our people slip their hands inside, the gloves are filled with our ants."

Kakury gestured to the large wooden boxes scattered around the village at the base of large trees. Each was marked with a symbol that resembled a "U" but with an "O" beneath at the lowest part of the curve. As Eric stared at the containers more, he realized it was meant to be an ant's head with two mandibles extended. Two warriors, painted red and black, stood beside each box, blowing purple-tinged smoke into reeds that fed into the boxes.

"Inside each of those is a colony," Kakury said. "They cover the colonies during the ritual. Otherwise, we do our best to avoid them at night. It'll be dark soon. The smoke keeps them unconscious."

"Why do you avoid them at night?" Eric asked.

"Aggressive," Kakury said. "The moon sends them into a frenzy. Our rituals are done as day turns to night. *My* ritual happened as the sky turned black as sack cloth. It was the only one in a generation where the night came on too quickly. The elders knew that our people's leader would be in that group. That's how it's been done for generations."

"You performed the ritual?" Nell asked.

Kakury nodded. "I was bitten over two hundred times on my right hand alone. But I'm the leader now. No one questions my authority here."

Nell and Eric shared a look of pure excitement.

"I must express to you that we have never created a glove like this one," Kakury said. "To have so many inside...we just...it's never been done."

Eric turned and spotted a group of artisans carrying their prize out of a large hut. The men and women carried it carefully and placed it down on a long wooden table beside Eric and Nell. The "glove" was more akin to a sleeping bag in size, but thick, the leaves weaved together tightly, crisscrossed multiple times.

Nell ran her hands along the bag. "Oh my god," she whispered.

"I know, right?" Eric said, smiling. "It's perfect."

Nell nodded. She lifted the opening of the bag near the top and looked inside. "Big enough for both of us."

Eric's fingers interlocked with hers and he raised her hand and planted a soft kiss on her wrist.

"The colonies," Kakury said. "They tunnel deep underground. They're all connected. It is like your cities back home. Part of the same collective, but with different sections. The moonlight brings out their individuality."

"What do you mean?" Nell asked.

Kakury smiled. "Each colony's bite seems to do something different. When we do the ritual, we only use one anthill. To fulfill your request, though..." She trailed off.

"Go on," Eric said.

"We shall need all of the local colonies." Her voice sounded grim. "That's why our warriors are stoking the hills with the smoke."

Eric nodded. He looked at Nell. There was a slight look of concern on her face.

"We don't *have* to do this," Eric said. "If you're nervous, we can–"

"We do have to do this," she said. "You know I need this as much as you do. I can't wait to feel them crawling all over me." She inhaled and closed her eyes. Eric knew how turned on he was at the prospect of the ant sinking their mandibles and stingers into his flesh. He could only imagine how turned-on Nell was as she nibbled her lower lip.

He nodded, then turned to Kakury. "When can we begin?"

#

After what felt like an eternity, wooden platforms were erected, connecting the various colonies to one-another. A slat leading from the platform to the opening in the tops of the wooden boxes kept the ants from escaping. Eric lingered close by as he helped assemble the wooden platform where he and Nell would be performing their own version of the tribe's ritual.

"Are you worried about the visions?" one of the tribesmen asked Eric as they screwed the last section of wooden platform into place. From multiple areas, leading from the boxes to the village center, thin wooden paths would pave the way for the ants. It reminded Eric of the Hot Wheels track he had as a child, even as the tribesmen coated the "track" with the fragrant-smelling ash.

"Visions?" Eric asked.

"Their bites take you places," the young warrior said. "They are not always places you wish to go."

"What did you see?" Nell asked.

"I saw two bodies become one in the glow of the night," he said, fastening another section of the track in place. "Thought it was nonsense. Until I saw you two."

"The glow?" Nell asked.

He nodded. "Heat. Fire. Passion, maybe? I do not know."

Eric placed his hand on Nell's shoulder and smiled. "I think we'll be okay."

The tribesman nodded. "If you say so."

As they finished, Kakury assembled her people and addressed them in their language.

"They won't bother the ritual," Kakury said. "The children, especially, are to be kept in the village longhouse, where they will receive a special dinner and treats from our new American friends." Eric was thankful for this part of the "ceremony," as the last thing he wanted was for prying eyes to be watching as he and Nell made love. It was Nell's idea to bring a variety of toys to keep the kids occupied for the evening.

There were some strange looks given to Eric and Nell from the tribal elders. Eric chalked it up to them not understanding why any outsiders would wish to take part in their ancient tradition, let alone in the fashion they'd requested. Eric knew he'd never see the tribe again after tonight. He didn't care much what anyone thought.

This would be worth their stares.

Once the tribe's children and most of the villagers were in the longhouse or back in their own homes, Kakury nodded to her warriors, who took up their posts at the various colonies in the village.

Eric and Nell shared an excited look and kissed. Slowly, they ascended the assembled wooden platform, which had been placed over the large pot of ash from earlier in the center of town. The pot still smoked, and had some remnants of the guarana-burned concoction. When the couple finally stood above it, the scent was intoxicating.

In the dark, lit only by the torches that served to guide the villagers from structure to structure, Eric and Nell began to disrobe. The only eyes that remained close were Kakury's, and even then, it wasn't the couple's first time with exhibition. As they rubbed their bodies down with the fragrant ashes, Eric found himself becoming aroused at the thought of what was going to happen. He smiled, watching as Nell rubbed the ash all over her lithe, nude body.

Nell grinned when she saw how Eric was ready to go, and she climbed into the ritual bag first. Eric followed suit, lying beside her, feeling the dry grass and fibers scratching into his backside. The feeling made him anticipate what was to come.

The bag was big enough to fully cover the couple, while also allowing them room to move within. It was entirely possible for one of them to stand up and still be draped in the material. Even in the flickering light of the torches in the area, the intricate nature of the bag could be admired, as the strands formed a lovely pattern of stars and other celestial bodies, that, while crude, were still remarkable.

"Are you ready?" Kakury asked.

Eric and Nell shared one more look before Eric gave Kakury an anxious thumbs-up in response. He then slipped deeper into the bag, kissing his way down Nell's body until he found himself between her legs.

He could hear Kakury shout something in the tribe's native tongue, and he assumed it was her signaling for the ants to be released. As Eric worked on Nell, she began to writhe with pleasure, and his mind raced at how long it would take for the ants to make their way from their respective colonies all the way to the center of the village.

The thought only turned Eric on more. The idea of the creatures' tiny legs crawling all over him, their pincers sinking into the hard flesh between his legs, biting the backs of his thighs, his neck. The thought alone was working Eric into a frenzy. Nell bucking against his face wasn't helping, either.

"More, Eric, more," Nell whimpered as he continued working on her.

The two remained like this for a while, Nell running her fingers through Eric's hair as his mouth grew tired from working on her.

The ache in his jaw was nothing compared to the sudden feeling of being stabbed with a hot poker in the bottom of his foot. He moaned in pain, but Nell continued to grind herself into him.

They're here, Eric thought, a smile creeping onto his face.

"Oh, fuck," Nell whimpered. She patted Eric's head, the international symbol to "hang on a second," and he looked up.

"You okay?" Eric asked.

"These fuckers bite hard," Nell said. "Caught me off guard."

He kissed his way up her body and noticed the walls of the bag seemed to be rippling with his and Nell's movement. He slipped his hand between Nell's legs as he kissed her chest. She grabbed a handful of his hair and moaned in delight.

They stayed like this a moment, until Eric could feel what he thought at first were raindrops on his back. Turning from Nell's chest, one of the ants landed just above his left eye, where it promptly sank its mandibles into his eyelid. Almost immediately, a metallic heat-infused pain ripped through Eric's skull and he recoiled hard, almost headbutting Nell in the process.

The pain radiated and he cradled his head a moment, feeling the fire crawl around the inside of his skull for what seemed like eternity. The pain ebbed a second, and he suddenly became aware of another sensation. Warm wetness between his legs. He looked down and Nell winked as she worked on him. In the dimness of the bag, he could see the welts on her back beginning to take shape. The ants were crawling all over her, some in lines, some just moving mindlessly over the flesh of her body.

The bag seemed to swell in size and Eric began to feel as if he were in a room covered in the tiny biters. "Baby?" he whimpered as Nell continued pleasuring him.

He closed his eyes and felt her finger against his lip, *shh*-ing him. "They're *inside* me," Nell whispered softly. When Eric opened his eyes, he could see her hand was covered in ants, and they crawled onto his face, all taking bites in the process. Eric brushed them away and looked down at Nell.

In her place, an enormous bullet ant, mandibles wrapped around his erect flesh.

Eric watched as the gigantic ant pleasured him, its mandibles gliding up and down, saliva dripping from the creature's hairy mouth onto his lower abdomen and groin.

"Please...please..." Eric pleaded, as heat began to overwhelm him. He felt as though he were surrounded by steam, and the world within the bag began to ripple in confusion, the walls growing darker as the tiny creatures swarmed every surface of the bag around him.

Eric began to feel lightheaded as confusion washed over him. The ant was still fellating him, but Nell was gone, and he looked around for her, seeing only a vast wasteland of tropical hell around him, great tendrils of hairy vines suddenly cushioning him, welcoming him into his heat-induced abyss.

The ant suddenly rose, and straddled him with three legs on one side and three legs on the other. Eric watched as the stinger of the ant moved dangerously close to his still-erect member until finally tearing into him.

The pain was searing at best. An explosion of color, pure yellows, reds and greens erupted through Eric's mind. Shape and form were no longer visible, as though he were somehow regressing into some kind of just-born state. There was nothing to discern beyond the agony splitting his body apart, and he felt as though his appendages could tear themselves loose any moment. His muscles tensed, and it was as if his body had been seized from him, replaced instead with pure, unadulterated agony.

Except between his legs. He could feel the heavy weight of the creature atop him as it thrust its stinger deeper into his crotch. They had become one. Eric couldn't tell, because he had essentially gone blind, but he and the ant were pressed together so tightly, it was impossible to tell them apart.

"More," the ant hissed, saliva dripping from its serrated mandibles and onto Eric's chest.

Eric reached up and gripped the ant by the slender part above its abdomen and thrust into it. Lost in a kaleidoscope of color, Eric screamed Nell's name over and over, hoping to hear her voice return his call.

The ant lowered its head, its three-segment body curling forward unnaturally. Eric continued his manic thrusting, feeling fire at the tip of his manhood, wetness, sweat and tears drenching his body. He felt the mandibles open around his mouth and felt the tickling of tiny hairs as his partner attempted some sort of spastic kiss.

No, not yet, Eric thought, as he began to feel his orgasm mounting. It wasn't far off. But he didn't want to finish with this creature. He wanted Nell. He wanted this colorful nightmare to be over with.

As the ant pivoted on its back legs, repositioning and putting more pressure on Eric's stomach and chest, Eric's hands roamed the creature's thorax, gripping its legs tightly.

More pressure. The ant was leaning backward. Eric could feel it.

The tiny hairs on the back of the creature tickled his face, his neck and more. The ant's mandibles grazed the side of his own head as they continued their rhythmic collision of color, heat and sweat.

Feeling his way up the creature's body, Eric gripped the mandibles hard and began to pull. What began as a low grumble turned into a garbled squeal as he continued pulling with every ounce of strength he had, until an audible *crack* sent the creature into violent paroxysms.

"Nell! Nell, baby!" Eric screamed in his colorful cavern of confusion as he continued tearing the ant's face apart with his bare hands. He could feel the burn of the creature's venom radiating from the tips of his fingers, down his arms and through his chest. It was warm and wet in his blindness.

Eric could feel a heavy warm fluid dripping all over his face as more bites and stings from the world around him sent him over the edge.

As the fluid entered his mouth, Eric picked up the taste of something metallic. *Copper.*

The enormous ant continued grinding against him even as he felt the creature's head begin to fall apart in his hands. Eyes. Mandibles. Fleshy sacks that Eric couldn't place. Slick with fluid.

He screamed as the first pulse of his orgasm racked his entire body.

Then, darkness.

A Letter to the Ghost in my Basement

Dear Thing That Goes Bump in the Night,

    Hello from the other side. That is, to say, the side of the living.

    I understand that the realtor who sold me this house, a bubbly, all-too-excited gentleman in a blue suit that really was too bright for any normal human to wear, didn't exactly tell me the entire truth while going into his spiel about the beams, the foundation, the expert molding, etc., but still, what's your *deal*?

    Yes, he talked about how beautiful the house is-slash-was, how the recent renovations and vinyl siding would last for about twenty or thirty years, and that the kitchen cabinets were all new and the bathrooms recently redone, but when it came to the basement, he simply stated that it "wasn't finished," and that it was the perfect "workspace" for a "young guy like me," and that I could turn the space into a "craft beer laboratory."

    I didn't really know what that meant. I never *made* anything in my life, other than a bowl of cereal, toast, or a half-burned bowl of ramen. I guess he assumed by the flannel shirt I was wearing or the beard I had that I was some kind of woodworker, or perhaps a guy who only drinks obscure IPAs. I didn't correct him, and instead marveled that a house with four bedrooms and three bathrooms had an asking price of only $280,000 in this area of Long Island. That was an impossibility in itself, so I shrugged off the assumption of manliness made by my realtor and jumped at the chance to own the place, which was nestled among houses that would easily go for two to three times as much. My own slice of the overpriced American dream.

    I know, I know. If it's too good to be true, then it probably is. I expected the oil furnace to explode a week after moving in. Or maybe that there were drafts from the windows upstairs that would need replacement. Maybe the plumbing was about to go? These would be costly fixes, sure, but in the end, none of these things happened. The house was damn-near perfect.

Except for the basement.

Walking past the basement door in the hallway resulted in a feeling of chills up my spine. What a cliché you are. You can't even do something nice, like make the air smell like coconut or cookies or potpourri? You *have* to make the air around the door cold?

So lame.

Then you started banging around and there's that weird creaking coming from the "workspace" below me and soon that grew to louder, angry sounds that seemed inhuman.

You sound *inhuman*, dude. I don't know what you are, to be totally honest, since you scared away the psychic I hired to find out what your deal is, but my man, you've gotta' chill.

Maybe I'm offending you by assuming your gender, and for that, I'm truly sorry. You may be a vengeful *female* ghost. Maybe a crabby trans ghost. But I don't know, I think women are typically more creative than men, so, throwing things around a basement definitely has a more male quality, so, I'm going to keep calling you "dude." Do you even know what that word means? How *old* are you, anyway?

I don't even store anything down there with you, yet somehow you find ways to throw things around. Like that phonograph, one of those old-timey record-player things I've only ever seen in movies about old haunted houses. I didn't bring that here. Where the hell are you finding these things?

Do you have a secret space, maybe beneath the stairs, where you're hiding all this old stuff? I couldn't get that door open when I was down there last, so, maybe you live there? That's weird, dude. You can have the whole space down there, I don't really mind.

What's with all the old medical equipment, too? Stuff that's ancient and rusted that looks like it's from the eighteen hundreds? This place was built in nineteen-seventy-five, how do you have access to old pictures of creepy little kids in white dresses and ill-fitting suits sitting in the laps of people who have never heard of smiling when their picture is taken?

It was easy enough to find the previous owners who built this place. They're perfectly normal. In their sixties. Retired. They never had any issues. In fact, they only sold this place because they started having issues with *you.* They didn't wanna deal with it, so they moved to the next town over and that's why the place was so cheap.

You cost them around three hundred thousand dollars. What kind of a *jerk* does that?

A jerk like *you*, dear ghost in my basement.

The noises are one thing. I can shrug that off. But the *slime*? On the steps? The walls? The floor? Do you really need to leave this goo *everywhere*?

Ectoplasm, it's called, apparently. I just call it gross.

That time your weird, glowing red eyes appeared in the laundry chute? Yeah, that was scary, but really, I just thought you were a raccoon, so, I'm not sure what the endgame was there.

At the end of the day, you're only throwing around your own stuff. I don't care about the creepy pictures. I don't care about weird, old medical equipment. The slime doesn't even smell bad or anything, it's just a nuisance. I can't even hear you when I'm upstairs trying to sleep, so I appreciate that.

It's just that I'd like to be able to watch my shows from the hours of seven to eleven at night without hearing wind howling and footsteps running up and down the stairs to the basement, you know? Make all the noise you want when I'm at work or not here. I don't really care. Do your thing. I'm not here to infringe on your rights as a dead person.

You only seem to like the wide open, dusty space at the bottom of the stairs. The basement proper. Not even the extra space near the boiler and tiny room where the sump-pump are, so I appreciate that.

Live your truth, annoying ghost in my basement.

But live it any *other* time and not when I'm trying to watch YouTube videos or *Hell's Kitchen* or *Beforeigners* or while I'm playing *Overwatch*. I just want to unwind a bit after work and dinner, you know what I mean?

Thanks in advance.
Sincerely,

Grover Blake

Grover Blake, new homeowner.

The Aluxes

Maria had been driving through upstate New York mountain roads for entirely too long when she noticed the tank was almost on "empty."

"We better stop soon, we're low," Maria said, softly, careful not to wake the toddler, Alejandro, in the back seat.

Craig lifted his head from the window and rubbed his temple. He had been asleep since the Cross-Bronx, having gotten home from his night shift shortly before they hit the road. He looked over and nodded. "Okay, sweetness."

He turned around and looked into the backseat. Alejandro sat, looking out the window at the evening sky, burning orange-purple, the sun setting behind the mountains.

"Hey, look who's up," Craig said, smiling.

"Up! Up!" Alejandro said, extending his chubby arms toward Craig, expecting to be picked up.

"Soon, baby, we're almost there," Maria said, smiling.

Craig turned the volume up, "Alice's Restaurant" by Arlo Guthrie played on the radio. "This is like, the *only* Thanksgiving song, right?"

Maria shrugged. "Dunno, babe, this is white people shit. This further cements you as the whitest boy I know."

They shared a laugh. "That's true. They didn't have anything like this in Mexico?"

"Thanksgiving's not a thing in Mexico, babe," she said, chuckling.

He shrugged. "Guess not. At least baby boy gets to eat turkey with his cousins and run around in the backyard a bit."

"I just wish it wasn't so far from home," Maria said, wistfully. "Such a long drive."

Craig reached over and rubbed Maria's neck. "I'm sorry baby, want me to take over?"

"When we stop, sure."

"Up there," Craig pointed. About fifty yards up the road sat a small gas station and convenience store. Craig took Maria's hand and squeezed it. "I promise a massage when we get to my brother's house, okay?"

"I'll take you up on that, Mr. Calloway," she said, smiling.

He squeezed her hand tighter.

#

As they rolled into the parking lot, Maria noted one other car, a standard pickup truck that seemed to be a prerequisite of upstate New Yorkers. The times she and Craig talked about moving to the area, Maria knew she'd have to ditch her Civic for something else, as the roads, especially in winter, were particularly treacherous, especially some of the tighter turns.

"I'll meet you in the store, I'm gonna use the bathroom," Craig said, handing Maria his credit card.

They kissed quickly, and he slapped her rear end as she scooped Alejandro out of the back seat. Maria checked her phone and noted the lack of service.

"What happened here?" Maria asked the toddler, who had, at some point, kicked one of his sneakers off. Craig was halfway to the restroom, while Maria dug around the floor of the Civic searching for the lost shoe.

The sound of an engine roaring caught Maria's attention and as she unbuckled Alejandro's seatbelt and pulled him from the car seat, she craned her neck to see what the noise was about.

A classic black mustang with an obnoxiously-loud engine rolled into the lot, pulling up at the pump opposite Maria's. The driver, heavyset, dressed like a mechanic, his coveralls stained with grease and oil, hands filthy, eyed her carefully.

A Confederate Flag decal obscured the back window of the Mustang. A bumper sticker with the word *Burzum* in gothic-looking font, silver on black. As the door to the mustang opened, loud, oppressive metal could be heard, mingled with flutes and more folk-sounding instrumentation.

Alejandro looked at the sky, giggling at nothing. Maria bent over and resumed her search for the missing sneaker. As she did so, she heard the Mechanic whistle.

Fucking really? she thought, rolling her eyes.

She rose and slipped Alejandro's sneaker back on. She looked toward the store and saw Craig standing in the freezer section, studying the various energy drinks and iced coffees within.

Maria walked, carrying Alejandro across the parking lot, feeling the eyes of the Mechanic on her. This wasn't a new thing, but it wasn't something she ever got used to. When she was a little girl, her mother would warn her that "such a pretty girl would be the envy of boys her entire life," and Maria wondered what, if anything, she could do about it.

Her mother's friend, Francisca, their small town's medicine woman, spoke of old-world treatments and traditions. Things that would take men's gaze off Maria. Simple poultices applied in the mornings and at night that Maria could use if she truly wished to avoid a man's lecherous gaze.

Wish I had it now she thought, glancing at the Mustang driver from the corner of her eye.

#

Inside the store, Maria joined Craig at the fridge. "Anything look good?"

Startled, he turned. He gave her a kiss, and gave Alejandro a kiss, too, the toddler squealing. "I was thinking a couple coffee-drinks?"

"Whatever you want, let's just be quick, okay?" Maria said, gesturing to the Mechanic, who had entered the store. "Dude was blasting some *Lord of the Rings*-sounding metal shit in the parking lot. Bad vibes for *days.*"

Craig nodded. "Everything okay? He say something to you?"

Maria shook her head. Best not to mention the catcalling. Just get what they needed, fill up the car, and get back on the road.

The Mechanic stood at the counter with the clerk, a small red book in his hands. They were talking. Whispering about something. More than once Maria saw The Mechanic look toward her.

"No, no, just a bad vibe is all," she said, re-balancing Alejandro on her other hip.

They walked up to the counter, and Craig placed two cans of Starbucks Double Shot coffee on the counter. The Mechanic stood nearby, watching the couple closely. The clerk, behind the counter, pimply-faced and young, name tag reading "Rusty" rang them up.

"Also, can we get twenty on pump one?"

Rusty nodded. He produced a small paper cup and spit some tobacco into it.

"You two ain't from 'round here, huh?"

Maria didn't even look at The Mechanic. Craig did, smiling and nodding.

"Where y'all from?"

"Not around here, that's for sure," Craig said, chuckling.

The Mechanic nodded. "I can tell. Don't really get mixed folks up here."

Craig cocked his head.

Maria could tell he was annoyed. *Just let it go, baby, it's not worth it.* "Just about ready to go? Maybe keep the change, Rusty?"

"What does 'mixed folks' mean, *Jethro*?"

Maria closed her eyes. *Dammit, Craig...*

The Mechanic smiled. "No harm meant, friend, just sayin', you and your little mamacita here ain't usually the kinda' folks in these parts."

Craig nodded and stared into The Mechanic's eyes.

"Right. Have a good day," Maria said, grabbing the change from Rusty, and placing a penny in the "Leave a penny, take a penny" jar, before walking out of the store, practically dragging Craig and carrying Alejandro.

#

Maria sat in the passenger seat, shaking her head as Craig drove, a little too fast, down the road.

"Babe, why'd you ever say anything?"

"Because fuck that guy, that's why. I may be from Long Island, but my family can buy and sell that piece of shit hick motherfucker ten times over, I'm not gonna have him—-"

"Enough!" Maria cut him off. She knew Craig was out of control when he was mad. He never got angry at her, but when something bothered him, slighted him in some way, she knew her husband could fly off the handle far too easily. "Let's just get to your brother's, have a drink, relax and enjoy Thanksgiving, okay?"

Craig took a deep breath. "Yeah, no, you're right."

He looked into the rearview mirror at Alejandro, the baby's eyes glued to the passing scenery, the ocean of trees, dark against the fading light and the purple-navy sky burning beyond the mountains.

"Little guy likes it up here," Craig said, smiling.

"Little guy likes it *anywhere*," she said. "But it *is* nice to ditch the Bronx once in a while."

Craig reached over and squeezed her hand. He ran his pinky along her wedding ring and smiled.

This always comforted Maria. She thought back, again, to when she was a child growing up, listening as her mother told her stories of ancient beliefs and the traditions of her people. Maria was always fond of the stories of La Llorona, the weeping woman. Even though it was meant to scare her, the excitement at seeing a spirit was altogether too much for the little girl to handle.

Her mother would hold her hand, and trace her finger along the girl's slender digits, back and forth, telling her stories. The aluxes. The roadside seductress. Stories that stayed with Maria into adulthood. Stories she found herself telling Alejandro, late at night, when he couldn't sleep. She wondered if he understood what she was talking about but figured he probably couldn't.

There was a truth in folklore. The seductress preyed upon travelers along the Baja. The aluxes, goblin-like creatures, their bodies slick with mud, would demand satisfaction, and play tricks upon those who scorned them.

Maria smiled, thinking of her mother and her tales.

"Shit," Craig said, turning on the wiper blades.

"Oh no," Maria said. "Forecast didn't call for rain tonight, did it?"

Craig shook his head. The sky had begun to turn a deep navy-black, the sun finally vanishing behind the mountains. The Civic's daytime running lights immediately turned brighter, and without warning, a pair of brights lit up behind their car.

Maria turned and spotted the Mustang, right on their tail, honking and swerving on the slick road.

The same nightmarish cacophony of metal and wind instruments filled the air.

"What the hell?" Craig said, checking the rearview mirror.

Maria's heart leapt into her throat. "That's the guy from the gas station."

"What?"

"*Jethro*. The big guy. That's him."

Craig stuck his arm out the window and waved for the Mustang to pass him. When it didn't, and continued honking, Craig accelerated, pushing the Civic faster down the road.

"Babe, just pull off the road somewhere," Maria said, calmly.

"What does he want?" Craig said, nerves getting the better of him.

Suddenly, the Mustang slammed into the bumper of the Civic. "Holy shit!" Craig shouted.

Alejandro, confused in the back seat, began to cry.

"It's okay, sweetie," Maria said, reaching into the back to comfort the toddler. "It's okay, it'll be okay."

They were rammed again, harder. Craig felt himself lose control of the car for a moment, and they fishtailed, the tires screeching maniacally along the slick road.

Maria climbed into the back seat and held Alejandro. She buckled herself in next to him, and whispered softly. Told him stories from when she was a little girl. Some in English, some in Spanish. Her brain raced. Craig struggled to keep ahead of the Mustang, and the ramming continued. *Jesus, is this it?* Maria thought. She checked her phone. Still no service.

All of a sudden, the Mustang rammed the Civic still-harder, and for a moment, Maria felt what it was like to lose all sense of gravity. The Civic spun in the air, completely tossed on its side, and rolled hard along the road, eventually coming to a stop in an embankment on the side of the road. The rain had continued down, harder, and the Civic sank into the mud.

#

Maria sat with her mother, watching the crowd assemble in their tiny town square. She watched as a man was dragged to the edge of town, near the forest. The man, sweaty in the midday sun, his clothes ripped in places, screamed and cried out, declaring his innocence.

"What did he do, mama?" Maria asked.

Suddenly, Francisca was there, too.

"Tell her," Francisca said, nodding in the sun-drenched afternoon.

"He...*attacked* a young woman from the next town over," Maria's mother said, choosing her words carefully.

"Why?" Maria asked.

"Some men can be beasts. They can't always...*control* themselves around a beautiful young girl."

Maria watched as the man was dragged into the forest.

"What will happen to him?"

"The stuff of bedtime stories, Maria," her mother said, placing her hand on her daughter's.

"Justice, little one. Simple justice. The aluxes will judge him." Francisca stood, a small smile crawling across her face as she watched the man dragged deeper into the forest.

#

Maria struggled to hang onto consciousness, realizing her head had slammed into the rear window the Civic, cracking it in a spiderweb design. Craig's head rested on the airbag, white dust and powder hanging in the air of the car.

Maria reeled as she realized that they were upside down.

She felt a warm fluid run down the middle of her face, mingling with her hair. Being upside down, she was disoriented. Alejandro screamed, his crying sharp. Shaken to consciousness, she looked over at the toddler and started whispering to him, saying "It's okay, sweetie...shhh...go to sleep, it's okay..."

Craig unbuckled his seat belt and braced himself against the driver's seat. He turned and looked at Maria and Alejandro, struggling to right himself in the flipped car. "Maria? Baby? Jesus, you're bleeding..."

Maria, slowly losing consciousness, watched as Craig checked the toddler, unbuckling him from his car seat, and carefully slipping him out, turning him rightside up. The baby's face was red from crying and screaming, and Craig rubbed his back.

Craig slipped out of the car and checked Alejandro over again. "You're okay, my sweet boy, you're okay..."

He rested Alejandro against the car and turned back to Maria. He started undoing her seatbelt, when suddenly, the roar of the Mustang's engine caught his attention.

Alejandro, shivering in the downpour, watched as the muscle car rolled up slowly.

Maria, from inside the Civic, watched as The Mechanic stepped out of the car, and walked over to Craig. It was impossible for Maria to hear, but the two men exchanged words. Craig stepped closer to The Mechanic, and without warning, Craig fell to the mud.

Alejandro started crying.

Maria's vision began to blur as The Mechanic fired a shot into the back of Craig's head, killing him instantly.

She began to shake, rage and terror overwhelming her, then watched as another person joined The Mechanic. *Rusty.*

"Jesus, holy shit, you shot him," Rusty said, nervousness in his voice.

"Don't be a pussy. When the master comes, there won't be room for race-betrayers like this city faggot."

Maria reached toward Craig's face, far beyond her reach outside the car. He was frozen in a state of confusion, half-buried in the mud.

"We need the boy to be scared, the blood needs to be fueled with fear for the ritual to work," The Mechanic said. "The Master *needs* the fear."

"What do we do with the body? We can't take him up the road with us!"

"Just grab the kid and throw him in the car, I'll roll daddy into the embankment."

"Be quick," Rusty said, grabbing Alejandro.

"Tell me my business one more time," The Mechanic said, annoyed.

Maria listened to Alejandro scream, then heard a car door slam. She could barely make him out any longer.

The Mechanic rolled Craig's body over the edge of the side of the road, down into the muddy ditch. He then rose and walked back to the Civic.

The world began to grow dark, as The Mechanic knelt down, looking into the car. "What a waste. Definitely good enough for a poke," The Mechanic said, squeezing himself through his coveralls.

#

Maria walked with Francisca, playing among the Mayan ruins her hometown was famous for.

"Do you see them, child?" Francisca asked, gesturing to a deep, verdant region of the woods.

Maria stared. She saw a shift of leaves, though there was no wind. Her eight-year-old mind couldn't comprehend what it might be. Tiny creatures moved, their flesh slick, glistening in places, beyond the dark green protection of the woods.

"Yes. I see them..."

Francisca handed Maria an apple that had been cut into four pieces of equal sizes. Together, they slowly stepped closer to the forest. The rustling in the leaves stopped and Maria, curious, extended her hands, offering pieces of apple to whatever was in the woods.

She waited. Francisca beside her, a gentle hand at the girl's back.

Slender gray-black hands stretched out from the woods, plucking the apple quarters from her tiny brown palm.

#

Maria's eyes bolted open, and she looked around the inside of the car, panicking. Her head throbbed, her hands shook, and her neck was killing her. She looked at Alejandro's car seat. He was nowhere to be found.

She unbuckled herself from her seat and fell to the muddy floor, slamming her head into the oily muck as well as the roof of the car.

She braced herself against the ceiling of the car and crawled through the smashed window beside Alejandro's seat.

As she did so, she found herself caked with mud. Once out of the car, she looked around for Craig. Walking to the embankment, she saw his body, drenched in blood, mud and rain. Climbing down, she slipped at first and landed beside him, crying hard. She leaned down and planted a kiss on his cheek.

Seething, she looked around. Her head was bleeding, and the warmth of her own fluid was dripping down her face. She imagined her nose might be broken, but there was no pain beyond that of taking a hard bump to the head.

She walked back to the car and looked down the road. In the distance, she could see a clearing. Lights on in the parking lot. At the very least, she could call the police.

At her feet, Maria spotted one of Alejandro's sneakers. She reached down, picked it up and stared at it. *They have Alejandro.*

She tucked it into her back pocket and started limping down the road.

#

After limping for what seemed like an hour, but was probably only about twenty minutes, Maria stood, obscured in the woods surrounding a small concrete building with a gravel lot. Only one car sat in the lot.

A black Mustang. One with a Confederate flag in the back window.

Maria looked around and thought, for the faintest of moments that she caught movement beside her in the woods. She felt like she was outside of her body, as though she was watching the scene from a quiet movie theatre. The sounds of the rain were muffled. Lightning crashed, but it, too, was muffled. Maria could hear her own heart beating.

Slowly, the rain pouring around her, she crept from the woods and made her way to the building. She tried the front door, which wouldn't budge, then found her way to the back door. It, too, was locked.

The building was only one floor. She watched as a light came on in one of the windows along the rear of the building. A wave of panic washed over her, and she hugged the wall, hoping not to be seen.

She crept, ever so slowly, closer to the window, and listened as a toilet flushed. Peeking through the window from the lower portion of the frame, she saw it was The Mechanic. She watched him tuck his meager offerings back in his coveralls, and zip himself back up.

She could hear intense, loud music from within. Now, though, The Mechanic sang along. Lyrics about "brother mountain," "sister moon," "Master Dreamer" and other concepts Maria couldn't understand were all she could make out.

For an instant, she caught her own reflection in the window. Gray-brown, caked with mud and filth. Behind her, in the woods, she saw similar figures. More slender. More slight.

Absently, she raised a hand to the window and tapped lightly with her fingers, mimicking the sound of the rain pouring around her. Not getting a reaction, she tapped harder. *That did it*, she thought.

She ducked back, waiting to see if The Mechanic would investigate. She heard the window open and watched as he poked his head out. In the darkness, he hadn't seen her.

He looked to the left of where she was hiding. Almost in slow motion, he turned toward her, and she prepared to grab him. Maybe try to pull him through the window. *But he's enormous.* Whatever she did, it would have to be quick.

The Mechanic turned and stared directly at her in the darkness. Confusion crawled across his face, and he opened his mouth, uttering what might have been "What the fuck?" Maria never knew, the sound of rain and distant thunder too loud to make it out.

In a flash, three tiny, gray, wet creatures launched themselves from the woods, all pulling at The Mechanic's head. Maria watched, confused. Aluxes. Petite, slender gray-black hands pulled The Mechanic's eyes out, and he roared, screaming obscenities, some of which Maria could make out, others she couldn't.

The aluxes backed off, and The Mechanic hung half-outside the window, his legs still in the building, gurgling and groaning in the roar of the rain.

Maria grabbed him by the lapels and pulled him through the window completely.

"*Where is Alejandro?*" she heard herself growl, her voice inhuman, distant.

The Mechanic simply continued his parade of obscenity. Maria wondered if he knew any other words. She knelt down and pulled the gun from his belt, tucking it in behind her in the waistband of her jeans.

She saw the red book poking from his coveralls. Grabbing it, she leaned in the building and flipped through it quickly. Latin words.

Illustrations. None of it rational. All of it disturbing. "Blood sacrifice." "Child." "Impure." "Infused with fear."

One drawing depicted a child on an altar, and a robed figure above him, brandishing a knife. Behind the figure, a creature of darkness, eyes piercing red, loomed, a hungry smile on its face.

She looked down at the eyeless Mechanic at her feet. "Take him."

"You fuckin' bitch...what the fuck are you..." he grunted, followed by a rainbow of more cursing. The aluxes grabbed The Mechanic and slowly pulled him into the woods.

Maria watched as one of her nocturnal companions tore out the man's tongue.

#

Maria slipped through the window into the building. *Let them have their fun*, she thought. She hoped it would be slow. She knew, in her heart, that it would be.

She rounded a corner out of the bathroom and entered the building proper. Wood paneling greeted her, the kind one might find in a 1970's rec room. Hung on the walls were pictures of old men, all of them white. Some in robes. All of them wearing some form of Klan uniform.

A chill ran up Maria's spine as she moved through the citadel of hate she had found herself in. In the dark, she could hear Alejandro's distant cries. *Still alive!*

Nazi flags mingled with Confederate flags mingled with flags dedicated to a failed Presidential fascist.

She found the source of the music. An old cassette deck littered with tapes all with bands Maria never heard of. Peste Noire. Hate Forest. Bands with absurd names. One of them was even called Absurd. She rolled her eyes and turned to the window she just slipped through, watching as one of the aluxes crept in, crawling almost on all fours through the bloody space The Mechanic once occupied.

Eventually, Maria came to a door leading to a basement. She could hear Alejandro's cries louder, further down in the darkness.

Mommy's coming...

She descended the stairs slowly. She listened to Rusty trying to soothe her child. She could hear him singing "Twinkle, Twinkle Little Star," which filled her with rage.

At the bottom of the stairs, she saw Alejandro tied to a makeshift altar in the center of the room, his screams echoing off the cement walls.

Candles hung from sconces on the sheer, empty space. They littered the floor in a pentagram pattern. Heat hung in the room, and Maria dripped a mix of mud, blood and sweat as she moved. The aroma was altogether intoxicating.

Walls adorned with swastikas, pentagrams, and other dark madness. Robes hung along the walls were the traditional Klan white, others were red, black and purple. Maria didn't care what the colors meant, all she knew was that she had to get Alejandro off that slab of rock.

Rusty stood, hunting knife in one hand, cell phone in the other, frantically typing.

"The fuck you go, man, I been textin'..." he said, turning, and seeing Maria at the bottom of the stairs, her eyes stark white in the flickering candlelight of the basement.

He stared at her. Slowly, he tucked his phone in his pocket. Maria could see a look of terror wash over his face.

"You?"

Me.

Maria pounced, tackling Rusty to the ground. While he was certainly the easier of the two men to engage physically, Rusty swiped and slashed with the hunting knife, finding his mark on more than one occasion.

She wrestled with him, knocking over candles, sending some rolling to the corners of the basement.

Rusty drove the knife deep into Maria's shoulder. She recoiled, rolling off him, and then scrambled quickly to her feet. She placed a bloody finger to Alejandro's lips, shushing him. He immediately quieted down.

Maria tore the knife from her shoulder and charged Rusty, stabbing him in the throat. She then tossed the knife aside, and began tearing at the wound with her bare hands, pulling the flesh apart, practically bathing in Rusty's blood.

She rubbed it all over herself, lost in a frenzy of crimson mania.

Rusty's body twitched in the candlelight. Maria regained her composure and looked around. On the steps, the aluxes stood, watching her. She stared, breathing heavy, her chest heaving, blood pouring from the wound on her shoulder.

In the darkness, they looked frightened.

In the darkness, Maria wept. Her body shook with adrenaline and anger, tinged with heartache. She collapsed to the ground and for a moment, found her mind flooded with images of Craig, their wedding, the last time they made love, him holding her hand, squeezing her thigh.

The smell of smoke shook the cobwebs loose and Maria rose, the room beginning to darken and haze over.

She walked over to Alejandro, untying him from the table. She kicked more of the candles around the basement, the robes catching quickly. She took the red book out of her pocket, used one of the candles to light it, and tossed it beside the altar.

She then took the gun from her belt and threw it into the darkness of the basement.

#

Outside, Maria stood in the rain, holding the sleeping Alejandro in her arms. The meeting hall burned behind her. Sudden movement in the forest around the parking lot caught her attention.

Slowly, she slipped the sneaker back onto Alejandro's foot. It was slick with Rusty's blood. She smiled, caressed Alejandro's sleeping head, turned, and disappeared with the baby, vanishing into the slick, verdant gloom of the woods.

For the Gods

DeAndre stood in his new bedroom, staring in the full-length mirror his sister Amara gifted him before heading off to college. Twelve years old, DeAndre already felt something of a crisis about his scrawny frame. His arms were thin. His legs, too. He had hoped running track would somehow turn him into a muscle-bound speed demon.

"You're just a late-bloomer," his father told him, time and time again, when he questioned himself for joining the team. Not the fastest or the slowest, he considered middle of the pack an apt descriptor. "You'll see, bud, you'll grow into yourself soon enough."

The added stress of moving to a smaller house in a new town worsened matters. His room was fine, and they had a pool, but in the end, he was without what few friends he had back in the Bronx, and couldn't imagine how he'd go about making new ones during the summer. The town itself, Resting Hollow, was nice and all, *quaint* was the word that seemed to flicker through DeAndre's mind more than any other, probably because of his last vocabulary test featured it and he misspelled it, but it wasn't the bustling metropolitan atmosphere DeAndre was used to. He'd have to get used to "quiet nights in the country," something his dad was all-too-excited to enjoy.

Wearing his Teenage Mutant Ninja Turtles bathing suit, DeAndre hoped a summer of swimming and working with his dad would help bulk him up. With school over, DeAndre was praying he'd be sent to summer camp with his friends from the old block, holding onto a distant hope that a summer together would help bridge the gap between his leaving the city and heading to the country. Maybe it would give him a chance to tell his friends how great his new house and pool were so they'd make the forty-five minute drive out to see him?

"Hey bud, dinner first, then pool time, okay?" he heard his dad say. "Look at you, you're getting ripped!"

DeAndre rolled his eyes. "Dad, come *on...*"

"Sorry, just bustin' chops. Five minutes, butt in seat outside," Dad said, smiling. "You excited to see Amara?"

DeAndre shrugged. "I guess." He looked around his room at the other items he inherited from his sister. Her record player. Her New Kids on the Block, Madonna, MC Hammer and other albums. Amara's Patrick Swayze and Brad Pitt posters secretly hung in DeAndre's closet, their intense looks greeting the boy each morning as he picked out what to wear.

Various items remained scattered around, most still waiting to be set up.

"You're too early for this 'moody teenager' shit, buddy-boy," dad said, furrowing his brow.

"Dad, you cursed! Swear jar!"

"You're right, I did. Sometimes it's worth it, though," dad said, pulling a quarter out of his pocket and turning towards the hallway.

As dad turned, the closet door in DeAndre's room unlatched and opened ever so slightly with a creak. Dad walked over to it, looked at the latch, examined the hinges and closed the closet.

"Another project for us, eh, bud?" With that, dad turned and walked down the hallway, toward the kitchen.

DeAndre heard the satisfying clink of the quarter slipping into the former spaghetti sauce jar sitting on the counter of their new kitchen, one of the last of the renovation projects dad had planned.

He hoped by the end of summer, the jar would be filled with enough quarters to buy the weight set he had his eyes on at Terry's Gym Supply in town.

#

DeAndre and his dad ate cheeseburgers fresh off the grill in their backyard. Lightning bugs danced in the sky, sparking, then fading in their usual summer choreography. The sky burned an intense orange-purple.

The pool sat nearby, stealing most of DeAndre's attention. The house needed updates and repairs, but the pool was perfect. It even had a heater. DeAndre, used to the square and rectangular pools in the city's various YMCAs and Boys' Clubs, found a kidney-shaped pool weird. But he realized that a pool was a pool, and at the end of the day, he'd be spending as much of the summer as possible swimming, floating and enjoying his own private slice of watery heaven.

"I saw that *Batman Returns* is coming out in a couple weeks," Dad said. "You wanna go?"

DeAndre thought about when he saw the first *Batman* movie. His mom, still around then, hid her eyes during the fight scenes, which made DeAndre laugh. This was before she decided to head out for a pack of cigarettes and never return. DeAndre wondered, late at night, whether she *really* did head out for cigarettes and something awful just happened to her, or if it was just an excuse to slip away.

"Sure," DeAndre said. "That baseball movie's coming out, too, I thought that looked pretty funny."

"Baseball movie? *Major League*? Didn't that come out already?"

"No, I think this one's different," DeAndre said. "It's like, about women playing baseball."

Dad laughed. "That *is* funny. I'll look into it, kiddo."

Without warning, a backpack sailed over the fence to the side of the house, and with it, DeAndre's sister, Amara, bounding after it. Athletic, tall, hair that curled in perfect impossibility, the girl was a blend of their mom's beauty and dad's natural athleticism. DeAndre's self-worth always took a hit when she was around, even though she never intended it.

"Something smells good!" Amara shouted, running over and hugging her little brother, giving him a big kiss on the cheek. He winced and tried to wipe his face. "You better leave that kiss on there, buddy-boy, otherwise I'll give you ten more."

DeAndre knew this wasn't an empty threat. He took another bite of his burger.

"How's my little girl?" Dad asked, hugging her and lifting her off the ground.

"Didn't you get my grades?" She asked, smiling.

"We got a letter, but we've been busy, and it's not addressed to me, so I didn't open it," dad said.

"Dad, if it's from school, dive in, I don't give a shit," Amara said, grabbing a cheeseburger, and pulling the bun off it. "No carbs for me, this summer, dad, I need to cut weight for the fall."

"Swear jar!" DeAndre shouted.

"Swear jar?" Amara mumbled, her mouth full of burger.

Dad nodded. "Swear jar," and pointed toward the kitchen. He handed her a quarter and she slipped into the house.

#

That night, Amara and DeAndre sat by the pool, draped in towels, both of them drying off. The night air radiated warmth, and they kept their feet submerged.

"How was the end of the school year, kiddo?"

DeAndre shrugged. "Good, I guess. I got a C in Woodshop."

"Woodshop? Making birdhouses and stuff?"

The boy nodded. "I forgot to drill the hole for the birds in mine when I submitted it."

Amara laughed. "Yeah, that'll do it."

"What's college like?"

She smiled. "Amazing. There's so many people. Everyone's different, and interesting, and there's so much creativity."

DeAndre smiled. "That sounds cool," he paused and looked at the water. Soft light lit the entire pool from within casting an almost-radioactive glow to the area and bathing DeAndre and Amara in white-blue light. "Do you miss the city?"

"Nah," she said. "There are so many people at school, even though we're in a small town, there's so much to do. The city is a different animal, but like, at school, literally, every night is something new. It's so much fun." She looked at him. "Do *you* miss the city?"

He nodded. "Yeah."

She put her arm around him. "I'm sorry, Dee. I promise you'll get used to life here. You'll make new friends. You'll miss your old ones, sure, but you're young."

"You made new friends, right?"

She nodded. "A lot."

"Any...*boy*friends?" he asked, teasing, stretching "boy" out to obnoxious lengths.

She laughed. "You're such a dork."

"That's not an answer," DeAndre said, laughing.

"If you *must* know, yes, a few boys have taken me out," she said. She looked at him out of the corner of her eye. "Some girls, too."

"What?" he asked, looking at her. "Girls? What do you mean?"

"You know, like, I've gone out with guys, and some girls, too. Like, on dates and stuff."

DeAndre stared at his big sister. He was confused. DeAndre didn't know how to react. "Huh."

"That's it? Just 'huh'? Don't tell dad, okay?"

"Sure, yeah, okay. So...you like girls, then? Does that mean you're gay?"

"First of all, how do you know what that means? Second of all, I don't know, that's kinda' what college is all about. Figuring your shit out."

"Swear jar," DeAndre said.

"Damn it."

"Dad was watching *Roseanne*, and it was the one where Dan, the dad on the show, was upset because his son wanted to dress up as a witch for Halloween," DeAndre explained. "I asked why it was a big deal, and dad told me that some people aren't accepting of people who are different."

"How did dad sound when he told you that?" Amara asked.

A sudden splash in the water caught their attention. They looked into the pool, and seeing nothing, looked at each other.

"Maybe it was a rock?"

"It's late, who's out throwing rocks into random people's yards and pools?" Amara asked.

DeAndre slipped his goggles on, dipped into the water and slowly treaded over to where the splash erupted. He slipped under the surface and looked around. The section of the pool where the splash happened, the eight-foot area, had been separated from the three-foot area by a plastic safety rope connected to white and red flotation devices.

Empty. DeAndre re-emerged, took his goggles off, and looked at Amara, standing nearby wrapped in her towel. The wind picked up and she shivered. "Let's go inside, okay?"

She helped DeAndre out of the pool, and he placed his goggles down on the side, near the ladder out of the water and wrapped him in his towel. They walked through the sliding doors and into the living room, where Dad was watching the news.

#

That night, DeAndre lay asleep in bed. His Ninja Turtle night light cast yellow-green illumination around the base of the floor between the door to his room and the door to his closet.

With a ferocity, the closet door swung open, slamming into the wall. DeAndre awoke with a start and looked around. His half-awake mind re-focused and he glanced toward the closet. He thought he caught a wisp of breeze float through the room, pulled toward the closet. The boy shivered in the dark and tucked himself further into his blankets.

He watched as the closet door started closing slowly. Again, it slapped open. DeAndre rose, and walked over to the closet, one hand on the door. He reached in slowly and grasped the chain hanging from the ceiling lamp. Clicking it on, he sighed at the piles of boxes still waiting to be unpacked, shelves stacked with various GI Joe figures, Amara's old Barbie and Ken dolls, a half-deflated basketball, pairs of sneakers, baseball caps, a glove, etc. His clothes hung on the left and right sides of the large space, which, if there weren't any boxes on the ground, would truly by the walk-in closet his dad promised him.

Looking around inside, he couldn't find any vents or openings. He still felt the wisp of cool air pulling him in, but he couldn't figure out where it could possibly be coming from.

He leaned into the closet more, trying to feel the air flowing around him. He moved his clothes around on the left rod. Just an empty wall. No space for a draft.

Why would the air be flowing into *the closet?* he wondered. A thick musk suddenly filled the space, and DeAndre breathed deep. It was heavy, but not unpleasant, almost minty in fragrance.

Turning to the clothes on the right, he heard a low *hiss* from within. Slowly, he began to part the clothes, expecting to find a snake, a Komodo dragon, or some other nocturnal hissing nightmare, and instead met a pair of glowing purple eyes.

Almond-shaped, piercing and beautiful. DeAndre froze in place, his body betraying him, as every muscle tensed to burst from the closet. The light above flickered, and slowly, a hand emerged from the darkness behind the clothes. Thin. Bone-white. Fingernails sharpened to a point on each finger, more claws than anything else.

DeAndre shivered, and felt a loss of bladder control. The hand caressed his cheek and wiped away a tear that suddenly fell. As quickly as it emerged, the hand slipped back into the darkness, the eyes closed, and the aroma and wind vanished from the room.

After his mind stopped firing in eight thousand different directions, his legs fired only one. Directly out of the room, and into Amara's, where she helped him get cleaned up, and slept, uncomfortably, through the night, his mind racing at what was lurking in his closet.

#

The next morning, DeAndre sat at the kitchen table, eating Pop Tarts with his dad, who read the newspaper. He didn't know if he should tell his dad about what happened the night before, since he couldn't be sure if it *actually* happened or not. He knew that he peed himself, and it had been easy enough to change his clothes and wash himself before sleeping in Amara's room, but the entire ordeal felt more like a dream than reality.

Before breakfast, DeAndre checked his closet again, and found nothing. No wind. No smell. No purple eyes hiding behind his Starter jackets. *Had to be a dream*, he thought, taking a hearty bite out of his second strawberry Pop Tart.

"Buddy-boy, today, we tackle the basement steps, then we work on that loose railing," dad said. "If we get done early enough, maybe we grab some pizza in town?"

"Sounds good," he said.

Amara entered the room, scruffed DeAndre's hair, and grabbed the rest of the Pop Tart in his hands, scarfing it down quickly.

"What was going on in your room last night, bud? Why were you slamming the door?" Dad asked.

DeAndre looked up at Amara, trying to think of something. Dad heard the door slamming. At the very least, the part about his closet door opening on its own happened. "The wind, I guess. The door doesn't latch very well."

"Right, right, we can grab some stuff at the hardware store to fix that, bud," Dad said, placing the newspaper down. "Sweet girl, you wanna join us for lunch later? We're gonna hit that pizza place in town."

"Barf, dad, no carbs, remember?"

"They have salads, I'm sure," dad said, rolling his eyes. "You about ready, Dee?"

DeAndre nodded. He and dad rose from the table and started for the closet in the hallway. They grabbed the tools, and headed for the basement door, which sat in the hallway, connected to the stairs leading to the second floor.

#

DeAndre hadn't spent much time in the basement of the new house, so he didn't know exactly what to expect once able to explore the space. He imagined the Rat King or possibly Baxter Stockman doing experiments to finally figure out a way to defeat the turtles and Splinter.

Instead, he found some broken steps, a busted railing, and some broken light bulbs. The rest of the space, empty, other than the crawlspace between the first floor and basement that started about five steps down.

The air near the crawlspace felt cold, and DeAndre noticed the faintest hint of mint coming from within. "Do you smell that?"

Dad sniffed the air. He shook his head. "Smells like a basement. Why?"

DeAndre shrugged. "Nothing, I guess."

"You know, buddy-boy, once we get all the repairs in the house totally done, we could maybe turn this basement into a cool den or something for me and you. Maybe hang some Yankee posters? Put up one of those huge televisions? Sound system? Hell, even a mini-movie theater!"

DeAndre couldn't take his eyes from the crawlspace. Inside, he heard the same hissing as in his closet. Then, softly, a sensual voice quietly said *"DeAndre..."*

DeAndre bit his lower lip, a shiver crawling up the back of his legs, the feeling becoming more of a tingle as it rose, the voice lingering in his mind, his body reacting as though tiny, sharp icicles were gliding their way up his spine.

DeAndre exhaled slowly, and thought, for a moment, he saw his breath in the dim light of the basement.

Dad stared at the boy. "Dee? You okay, pal?"

DeAndre looked around. As quickly as it came, the sensation vanished just as fast. "Yeah, sorry, spaced out, I guess."

"I know, I even cursed and you didn't yell at me to put a quarter in the jar. Hand me that screwdriver, will ya'?"

#

That afternoon, DeAndre, Amara and dad headed into town. DeAndre was exhausted from a day of working on the house. After the basement, they tackled the railing, then did a quick assessment of the needed items for the closet door. Dad also wanted to get an idea of what he'd need to finish the basement, once they were done with everything else, so, he was in a deep conversation with the two clerks at the hardware store while DeAndre's mind remained focused on the feeling that had been coursing through his body in the basement.

At the store, even at the pizza place, DeAndre couldn't shake the feeling from the basement. He couldn't get the voice out of his head. He couldn't escape those intense, purple, beautiful eyes. He remembered the cold feeling of the hand on his cheek.

When got up to refill his soda, DeAndre kicked his sister under the table.

"Ow, you ding-dong!"

"Shh. I think our house is *haunted*."

She smiled. "What makes you say that? Because of last night?"

"A feeling I had in the basement," he said, his voice low.

"Why are you whispering?"

"I'm freaked out about it," DeAndre said, with a sigh.

Amara made a pouty face. "Little dude, there's no such thing as ghosts, I promise. It's a new house, in a new place. I swear, nothing can hurt you. It's just your excellent imagination running wild, okay?"

DeAndre nodded. Amara usually made him feel better about things right away, but this time, he still felt nervous about whatever happened in his bedroom and in the basement.

He felt almost as though he kept some kind of dirty secret from his father, but instead of feeling guilt, DeAndre wanted *more*. He replayed the voice over and over in his mind, and each time, he felt the slightest hint of that familiar tingle in his legs, back and arms. He recognized the element of teenage hormonal reaction, sure, he learned about that in health class, but it felt more like the excitement when one tries something new and *loves* it, or the feeling you get while overcome with joy and happiness while dancing. Sprinkles of that level of love and joy, all through DeAndre's body, accompanied by an impossible heat in his chest, that at first the boy chalked up to being summer, but now, realized it had to be something *more*.

Pure, unfiltered *happiness*. And in that happiness, DeAndre felt remarkable *truth*. Whatever had been in his closet. Whatever hid in the crawlspace. Whatever lurked in the *house*. DeAndre wanted *more*. More of that feeling. More of the excitement. Just thinking about it sparked tingling in his chest. He hadn't felt this way before.

And he *needed* more.

#

When they got home, DeAndre made a beeline for his bedroom. The closet door creaked open slowly. Dad followed him, and the two started repairing the latch on the door. It seemed like it took forever for DeAndre's dad to make the repair, and the anticipation of having his dad out of the room felt palpable.

"How much longer?"

"Almost done, kiddo," Dad said, tightening the screws. He stood up and closed the closet, listening for the catch of the new latch. He nodded and smiled once it clicked into place. He tugged hard on the knob, trying to get the door to open without turning the knob and found it wouldn't budge. "There we go, bud. Let's go watch the ballgame, huh? I'd say you've earned a bit of relaxing."

"Be there in a sec," DeAndre said, his eyes locked on the closet doorknob.

"Hey, did you want me to get rid of Amara's old posters? The guy from *Dirty Dancing*? That's more for girls, isn't it?"

"I like *Roadhouse*," DeAndre said, eyes darting to the floor nervously.

The old man smiled and shook his head, then left, and DeAndre's gaze remained fixed on the door. Slowly, the knob turned and the closet opened with a soft creak. The musky smell of mint wafted into the room, and DeAndre stepped closer to the closet, slipping inside, clicking on the light above him.

He felt the soft breeze through the light hairs on his arms and legs. He closed his eyes and let the air swirl around him. *Through* him. A tightness in his throat caused him to swallow hard, and the familiar intensity of heat swelled in his chest, then his stomach.

"*DeAndre...*"

He opened his eyes and saw two violet orbs staring back at him. More animal than human, the eyes had flecks of gold in them, with inky dark pupils that seemed dilated.

The eyes belonged to a figure, slender, almost emaciated, skin a gray-white chalky color. DeAndre's eyes roamed the figure's form, and he noted that its face looked human, but after staring at it for a while, realized something was *off*. Almost a perfect facsimile of a person's face, smooth in the right places, angular at others, symmetrical in a way that doesn't often occur in nature. It wasn't beautiful. It just *was*.

"Who are you?" DeAndre asked, his voice shaking.

"I am whatever you want me to be," the figure said softly. DeAndre felt the icy pinpricks run up his spine whenever the figure spoke.

"You know my name already...I should know yours."

The creature's eyes darted around the closet, glowing an intense amethyst, the way a cat moves while tracing a fly in the air. The figure pointed a slender finger to one of the posters on the inside of the closet door: A chiseled, long-haired man in torn overalls stared into the sunlit distance.

"Patrick Swayze?"

"*Sway-zee...*"

"That's what you want me to call you?"

The figure nodded slowly, eyes locked on DeAndre's. "*Swayyyyyyzzzz...*"

"I like that. 'Swayz.'"

Swayz nodded, smiling, his thin lips stretching in an unnatural way, almost too-wide. At first, DeAndre recoiled, but after a moment, he found it funny.

"What *are* you, Swayz?"

Swayz shook its head. It rose from its crouched position and stood about as tall as DeAndre, if slightly smaller. The creature appeared to have no gender, as it had nothing on its body to indicate male or female. DeAndre covered his eyes, embarrassed to see the "nude" creature before him.

"*Why cover?*"

"Not s'posed to see other people naked," DeAndre said quietly, hand still over his eyes.

Swayz reached over and placed an icy hand on the boy's wrist. With little force, he lowered DeAndre's hand, and the two stared into each other's eyes.

"*A face fit for the gods,*" Swayz whispered in the dim light.

#

When DeAndre exited the closet, something he would do thousands of times over the next three years, he always buzzed with happiness and excitement to face the rest of his day.

First thing in the morning, DeAndre would find himself slipping into the closet, to greet Swayz, who, over the years, grew and matured as well, its lithe body changing, ignoring gender, while also showing signs of both sexes. Swayz seemed unaffected by it. The being cared more about spending time with the boy than the gender-swapping that its body was soaring through every day. DeAndre found his eyes roaming over the creature's body more and more as they both grew older.

Over time, the house took shape, too, with DeAndre and his dad making renovations as they went slowly along. The basement turned into a man cave of sorts, decorated with Yankee memorabilia, neon beer signs, a bar, and other items. DeAndre's videogames were down there, so when DeAndre would slip downstairs after dinner, Dad just assumed he was playing videogames before bed.

Instead, DeAndre and Swayz were relaxing, listening to music while DeAndre did his homework. Sometimes he'd talk on the phone with Amara, who was going to law school, working hard, and partying even harder. She loved divulging the details of her nights out with her teenaged brother, and sometimes, during DeAndre and Swayz's basement dance parties, the boy would imagine himself in a Brooklyn nightclub, bathed in neon light, sweat glistening, music pulsing.

At bedtime, the two enjoyed each other's company, talking late into the night, Swayz on the floor between DeAndre's bed and the window, the creature's lavender-colored eyes beaming in the moonlight.

In those three years, DeAndre learned that Swayz didn't know his own history. Not a ghost. Not a mythical creature from another dimension. Not *anything*. Swayz explained, the best that he could over time, and with DeAndre's help, that he came into being that summer when DeAndre moved into the house. The world didn't exist for Swayz before then. He was tethered to the boy, and the boy, to him.

Borne from somewhere impermanent.

At track practice, DeAndre would sometimes spot Swayz hiding beneath the bleachers, watching him. He would wave to the huddled, nude figure hiding under the steel, and sometimes the creature would wave back, but mostly Swayz watched and waited for the boy to make his way home after school.

Dad had noticed how quickly DeAndre rushed through dinner, to head down into the man cave. It was a nightly occurrence.

"Did you have a friend over last night?"

DeAndre looked up, nearly finished with his meat loaf. "No, why?"

"Because, I thought I heard two voices. One of 'em was kinda' weird-sounding."

DeAndre thought quickly. "Oh, I'm sorry pop, I've been practicing for the school play. I'm trying to get a part, and thought it'd be cool to try a different voice."

Dad nodded. Part of him believed the boy. The other part of him knew better.

#

Eventually, DeAndre set up his record player in the basement, and he and Swayz would listen to Amara's old tunes. One evening, on the last day of school, while dancing around the space to Madonna, DeAndre heard his dad making his way down the steps. Swayz immediately rushed for the darkened space behind the bar and waited. It had become his usual hiding spot whenever DeAndre's father made his way down the steps.

"Hey bud, I was in the garage and finally opened that random box of your mom's stuff, and found a bunch of records I thought you'd maybe wanna add to the collection?"

"Oh, awesome," DeAndre said, lowering the volume on the stereo. He took the box from his dad and started flipping through the albums. He didn't recognize many of the artists, since they were from way before his time. Mr. Flagio, Fancy, Boney M. He did, however, recognize Abba, The Bee-Gees, A-Ha, The Pet Shop Boys and a few others.

"Your mom loved her dance music," dad mused, a hint of sadness in his voice. "We met at a disco, actually."

"You still have the leisure suit in your closet," DeAndre said, smiling.

"I do indeed," dad said. "One day, that'll be yours, too."

"Oh goody," DeAndre said, laughing. "Thanks for these, dad, I love them."

Dad hugged DeAndre. "You wearing cologne? You smell minty."

DeAndre looked toward the bar nervously and shrugged. "I'm trying a new deodorant?"

"That must be it," dad said. "Can't believe how old you've gotten. Amara, too, seems like yesterday we left the city. Time really flies, you know? Another summer in the boonies lays ahead of us."

DeAndre smiled and nodded. "I love it here, dad. I don't miss the city much."

Swayz's eyes locked with DeAndre. They shared a secret smile.

\#

After dinner, Swayz and DeAndre rode over to the park. DeAndre's dad thought his son had been joining friends for a night game of basketball, but instead, Swayz scaled the side of the house, hands gripping the siding like Spider-Man, effortlessly climbing down to the ground.

DeAndre handed Swayz an old wool coat, red with white trim, and the creature wrapped itself, smiling at the comfort. "*This is beautiful...*" the creature whispered in the darkness.

"It was my mother's. Climb on," DeAndre said, gesturing to the seat of the bike.

Nervously, Swayz climbed onto the bike, and after settling in, the two rode off into the night, down the street, under cover of night, toward the park around the corner from the house.

Once there, they found a bench under a large dog tree, white blossoms spreading above them, nestled in a canopy of green. Swayz sat, looking tiny in the large, comfy coat, looking around the park. The creature could easily pass for human with the right clothing, even though this jacket wasn't doing any favors to Swayz. If anybody passed by, they might've thought DeAndre was sitting with his grandmother or something.

DeAndre placed his backpack gently on the table between them and smiled.

Slowly, the boy reached into his book bag and pulled out a small white pastry box, tied with purple string. He held it out to Swayz.

"Happy birthday, Swayz," DeAndre said, nervously.

Swayz stared at the box, confused. "*What is a 'happy birthday'?*"

"You have to find out, silly, open the box" the boy said, smiling.

"*I have never had a birthday before,*" Swayz whispered. "*I do not know what it means.*"

"It's to celebrate the day you were born. Like when we have other holidays, presents, gifts, that kind of thing."

"*My...birth-day?*"

"We met three years ago today. Technically, it was a few days later, but, when we moved into the house, that's when you came to life, so, *that's* your birthday. The string even matches your eyes."

Swayz smiled. With bony fingers and sharp nails, the creature carefully untied the string, noting the color. "*Thank you, DeAndre...*"

Opening the box, inside, was a large cupcake. Chocolate, with purple frosting. Three candles sat in the center, and DeAndre reached over with a Bic lighter and lit them. Swayz recoiled from the flames.

"It's okay, I won't let the fire hurt you," DeAndre said softly. "You have to think really hard, make a wish, and blow out the candles. Don't tell me the wish, because then it won't come true."

"*There are many rules to birthdays...*" Swayz said, staring at the lit candles. The creature thought for a moment, and a soft breeze blew through the area, blowing the candles out while its deep violet eyes remained closed, and its thin lips remained tightly shut.

#

That night, in DeAndre's bedroom, the two sat in complete silence. Friday, late, and DeAndre couldn't sleep.

"*Did you mean what you said? About the city? With your father in the basement?*"

"Of course," DeAndre said in the dark, his voice soft. "If I didn't come here, I never would've met you. You're my best friend."

"*And you are mine...*"

DeAndre felt a swelling of tension in his chest. Whenever Swayz was around, he felt what he began to realize could only be described as "butterflies" in his stomach. An intense desire that seemed to flutter, with flaming, acid-tinged wings, inside his belly and chest.

"Swayz?"

"*Yes, DeAndre?*"

DeAndre bit his lip and felt a swell of nerves lump in his throat. "Would you want to sleep in the bed with me tonight?"

Swayz sat up, cast in the silver glow of the moon outside the window. DeAndre sat up and looked at his friend. Slowly, DeAndre scooted over, the bed sheets rustling a bit.

Swayz, more animal than person, climbed into the bed. He felt the springy reflex of the mattress, and sat, cross-legged at the edge, confused, eyes looking around the room. The heavy, musky mint aroma was almost overwhelming.

DeAndre stared at Swayz. He gestured to the spot next to him. Slowly, the creature crawled up the bed toward the boy, and rested its head on the pillow beside DeAndre.

"Isn't that better than the floor? More comfy?"

Swayz's eyes glowed in the darkness. "*My chest feels strange,*" it whispered.

"Mine, too," DeAndre replied.

DeAndre and Swayz inched closer to each other, awkwardness growing between them. The tension they felt seemed to draw them nearer, until finally, they were nearly face to face. Cautiously, slowly, they kissed, and both felt an explosive rush of pure desire between the two of them.

Their lips touched merely for a second, but the imprint left on both of them felt impossible to shake.

DeAndre's first kiss. And if Swayz had never existed until the boy entered the home, it certainly had been the creature's as well.

Swayz's slender fingers reached up to DeAndre's face and caressed his cheek in the dark.

DeAndre, his head still spinning from the sensation of Swayz's thin lips on his own, was racked with intense pangs of guilt and confusion. He had never felt anything for anyone at school before. At least, not in the way he was feeling for Swayz.

But what does this mean? What is Swayz? DeAndre slipped away from the pale, slender fingers and rested his head down. "Good night."

Confused, Swayz closed its eyes. "*Good night, DeAndre.*"

#

DeAndre floated lazily on his back in the pool, dad and Amara nearby, setting the table for dinner. The boy's eyes were on his bedroom window, where Swayz watched him, unable to join the family. DeAndre often wondered how his dad and sister would react to the weird creature that emerged from nowhere and had become such an integral part of his life. He wondered how they'd react if they knew that the night before, he had shared his first kiss with this being.

"Dee, almost time to dry off, bud," Dad said.

DeAndre didn't answer. He kept replaying the kiss over and over in his mind. He didn't know what his feelings were, the mixture of guilt and confusion and desire perpetually running through his mind the entire day, while helping to clean the house, taking a bike ride into town, and getting coffee with his sister.

It didn't help that Swayz had no clear gender. This added to DeAndre's confusion. Some days, Swayz resembled some of the girls DeAndre knew at school, others, he looked like the guys on the track team. No matter how Swayz appeared to DeAndre, the one thing the boy knew was that he loved and desired the creature that came from his closet more than any human in his life.

Being gay, or being bisexual, those concepts scared confused teenagers all over the world, but being *in love* with a creature from some impossible time and space?

That scared and confused DeAndre the most.

#

As DeAndre prepared for bed, Swayz rifled through things in the closet. He shifted some clothes around and took others off the racks.

"What're you doing?"

"I thought you might prefer if I stayed in here tonight..."

DeAndre sat down on his bed. He looked out the window, the moon hanging high and bright. His Ninja Turtles night light cast a glow on the floor, a remnant from his childhood.

The boy shook his head and scooted into bed. "No, come here."

Cautiously, Swayz stepped closed to the bed, nervously looking around the room. All these years with DeAndre, and the animal fight-or-flight instinct in the creature remained ever-present. A light minty musk filled the room, and DeAndre realized Swayz must have been scared.

Swayz climbed into the bed and sat on its knees, the being looking as though they were in prayer. DeAndre looked over the creature, noting how distinctly feminine Swayz appeared in this moment, shoulders low, the smooth flesh of the creature's chest budding a bit where breasts might be on a female's body.

"Come here," DeAndre whispered in the dark. He took Swayz's wrist and pulled the creature closer, their lips locking together. Passion overwhelmed the two of them, until their mouths were no longer two distinct concepts, instead, they simply became one.

There was no telling where DeAndre's ended and Swayz's began.

Swayz straddled the boy, its legs on either side of his body. They pressed hard, together, the heat between them sending them over the edge, their minds focused solely on the intensity of the moment, a first for both of them.

"I've been thinking about this all day," DeAndre whispered into Swayz's mouth.

"As have I..."

DeAndre's hands roamed all over Swayz's chest and back, as the two continued kissing. Suddenly, the boy felt something hard begin pressing into his stomach. Confused, he broke the kiss and looked down, seeing a bulge beginning to form between Swayz's legs.

The two locked eyes. DeAndre's lust shifted to confusion, and he pushed Swayz off him, nearly throwing the creature to the floor. Though Swayz had the advantage of height over the boy, DeAndre remained the more powerful of the two.

Swayz scrambled off the bed, bracing itself like a cat on all fours on the ground near the closet door, hissing and confused, glowing violet eyes flashing all over the room, searching for an unseen threat.

"I'm sorry, I just—" DeAndre began.

Quickly, Swayz opened the closet door and slipped inside.

DeAndre never saw such hurt or pain in another creature's eyes before.

#

DeAndre awoke the next morning, after getting barely any sleep, and felt awful about how he treated Swayz. The creature was his best friend, his first kiss, and deep down, the first person the boy ever *loved* outside of his family.

Slowly, he walked over to the closet, and opened it, expecting to find Swayz huddled in a mass of clothing on the floor.

Inside, he found nothing.

He sniffed the air, hoping for the hint of mint that accompanied Swayz whenever he was around, but instead, just the musty, woody smell of a closet in an old house.

Confused, DeAndre closed the door and went downstairs.

And so it went. For the next two years. Each morning, DeAndre would awaken, no matter the season, and check his closet for Swayz, but the creature vanished. As time went on, DeAndre fell out of the habit of checking for the creature. They were simply gone.

Over time, the closet changed. DeAndre returned home from school to find Amara's posters missing, but when he saw them in the garbage behind the house, he knew his Dad had gotten rid of them.

DeAndre, to fill the void left by Swayz's disappearance, settled into a friend group of kids from the school's theater department, and teammates from track. Straddling both worlds.

The boy felt at-home both on the stage, and on the track. Knowing that eyes were on him as he performed, DeAndre felt incredible explosions of energy, nerves and more, feelings he first felt with Swayz. The acid-winged butterflies in his chest and stomach only returned when he was under the lights of the stage or pushing himself further on the field.

In those moments, for DeAndre, it felt as if Swayz had never left.

When DeAndre had the house to himself, he would listen to his mom's records and dance. He imagined himself performing for crowds of people. From disco to 80's synth to modern pop, the boy worked out a variety of routines that he carefully executed when his dad wasn't around.

These songs remained in his mind as he dashed across the finish line. Over time, he found himself gravitating more toward theatre and dancing and further away from track. Once senior year started, he had all-but-abandoned athletic pursuits in favor of artistic ones, much to his father's disappointment.

DeAndre had grown more muscular, and his body had finally begun to take shape the way he hoped. Dad was right, he was a late bloomer. The boy had gone from middle of the pack to being the second-fastest on the team, and while state records were attainable, none of it felt right to DeAndre. He simply didn't care.

From time to time, DeAndre thought he saw a pair of indigo-colored eyes watching from beneath the stands during his track meets, but when he'd investigate, there was nothing there, just a faint, familiar scent in the air.

"Kiddo, are you *sure* this is what you want to do? They give more scholarships for track than they do acting," dad said one night at dinner.

"It just doesn't feel right anymore, pop," DeAndre said.

Dad nodded. "I don't get it. But, if you want to throw away your talent and hard work, then so be it. You'll regret it later."

Little comments like that remained with DeAndre. *What didn't he get?* DeAndre would think, confused not to receive the support from his own father that he was getting from his former coach.

"Is it the theater-stuff? Is that what's making you do this?" Dad asked.

"What do you mean?"

"Dee, look at how you're dressing, I mean, you don't look—" Dad stopped. He sighed and lowered his head. "Dee, sometimes to *get along*, you've got to *go along*. It's rarely a good thing to stand out."

DeAndre fidgeted in his seat. He was wearing a neon-green hoodie, Madonna's face in black and white emblazoned on it. Black bike shorts hugged his thickening, muscular legs. "What's wrong with how I look?"

Dad just shook his head, got up slowly from the table, and walked into the living room. "Never mind, bud."

To Dad, these were signs.

To DeAndre, they were just who he *was*.

#

Prom rolled around. DeAndre asked a girl from the theater department, who had become his closest friend since Swayz vanished. Dad took pictures and chatted with the other parents, happy to see his son with an actual *girl*.

At the dance, DeAndre and his date swirled and put on a show. DeAndre could really move, and so could his date. They hardly left the dancefloor that night, and they certainly didn't mind, the night too perfect, too fun to settle down and relax.

Afterwards, DeAndre found himself in the backseat of the girl's car. They kissed, touched, and squeezed each other, but DeAndre barely felt anything for the girl beyond a friend. This had been especially noticeable when she looked him in the eyes and asked if he'd ever gotten a blowjob before, to which he nervously replied he had not.

When she started, he didn't find himself reacting in any way. He just laid back and remained nervous.

"What's wrong?" she asked in the dark.

"I'm sorry, I—umm—"

She sat up and sighed. "Why can't you get hard?"

"I don't know, I'm just, I guess I'm nervous..."

"Don't you *like* me?"

"Of course I do," DeAndre said, unable to look her in the eye.

She ran her hands all over his body, and DeAndre began to feel a level of discomfort he had never experience before in his entire life.

"Stop, I don't—"

"Don't be a fag, let me do it," she said, her voice harsh, hanging in the air.

DeAndre started pushing her off him, but her entire weight on top of him pinned him down. "Please..."

Her hands squeezed moved lower and squeezed harder. The boy's groin tensed, and he buckled at the assault.

"I know you want this, even if you *are* a queer..."

Tears began welling in DeAndre's eyes as she continued her assault on his genitals. She removed her underwear and mounted him, and through gritted teeth, continued an array of insults, his body never giving her the reaction she desired.

Fag.

Queer.

Gay.

#

DeAndre sat motionless in the hospital bed, waiting for his Dad to pick him up. He wondered if it was the cocktail of pain medications he was on, but either way, he felt destroyed, internally and externally.

The doctors examined his lower regions and noticed swelling and bruises, but nothing that would remain permanent. The entire examination left DeAndre feeling raw, embarrassed and heartbroken.

Distinct tension hung in the air as DeAndre gathered his torn tuxedo and his father watched him.

"Not getting the deposit back on this," Dad said.

"I'm sorry, dad," DeAndre said.

"Your sister's at the house, I don't wanna talk right now," Dad said, exiting the room, carrying his son's belongings.

#

At the house, DeAndre sat on the couch while Amara looked him over. She started working in the city, had her own apartment and lived with her boyfriend. She wept when she saw her brother's injuries, and held him almost too-tightly, almost trying to heal him through her arms and chest, radiating love.

"What happened?" Amara whispered.

"You *know* what happened, Amara, don't get him started," Dad said, waving the question away as though it were a fly in the air.

"I want to hear it from *him*, dad!"

"We were in the car, and I don't know what happened next, but she—"

"Bullshit!"

"*Dad*, stop!" Amara shouted.

"You know why this happened, Amara, just *stop*. I don't want to hear this. I *can't* hear this! How does a boy get *raped*? The *police* won't even hear it, they say he's lying!"

"This happened to *your* son, dad," Amara said. "How could you not want to hear what happened?"

"Because he's not my son, okay? I've been living with him the past couple'a years and he's not my little boy anymore," dad said, bubbling over with emotion. "The god-damn posters he was hiding in his room? The music? His *clothes*?"

Amara and DeAndre stared at him.

"You think I didn't notice? DeAndre, I clean your room at least once a week. You think I didn't notice Amara's old lipstick in your sock drawer? Christ, what I wouldn't give to find nudie mags, instead, I find out my son is a cross-dresser!"

"Dad!" Amara said, standing up. "That's enough!"

"Growing his hair longer, quitting track, the clothes he wears," dad rambled. "I can't take it anymore. I can't take what's happening to him."

"Nothing's happening to me," DeAndre said, softly. "I'm still your son, I'm still me."

Dad stared at him. "I don't want him here in the morning. I don't care where you go, but I don't want you here, Dee. I can't take you like this. Boys don't get raped. *Faggots* do."

DeAndre's eyes began welling up with tears. With what little energy he had, he stormed up to his bedroom.

He began packing a bag the best he could, hearing the muffled fighting of his sister and father downstairs.

He heard a creak of the closet door opening. Slowly, DeAndre turned, eyes tearing, his body wracked with pain. He desperately needed Swayz. Memories of their time together flooded his mind. He breathed deep, hoping to pick up the musky, pleasant smell of mint in the air.

He walked to the closet and looked inside.

Nothing.

#

"Don't try to lift anything, Dee, I got it," Amara said, taking DeAndre's luggage from him and helping him up the stairs at her and her boyfriend's apartment.

They had driven from Resting Hollow back to the city that very night, Amara agreeing immediately to take her brother in. Their dad gave her some money, and the two left quickly, emotions and adrenaline fueling the drive. They didn't speak.

Amara's boyfriend, Todd, came down to meet them on the street. DeAndre had met him only twice before, and he had always been sweet, a lawyer, and working his way up the ladder at the firm he and Amara met at.

"Hey Dee," Todd said, hugging the boy. "I'm sorry about everything. I set up the guest room for you, fresh sheets on the bed. It's not as big as your room back home, barely any closet space, but we can maybe get you one of those portable rack things, if you like?"

"Thanks, Todd," DeAndre said, feigning a smile.

Once settled into the guest room, DeAndre found himself crying again. Todd brought him some hot chocolate and Amara sat with him, holding the boy close. He was holding a letter from his high school. He opened it and inside was his diploma.

"I won't even get to graduate with my friends," DeAndre sobbed. "They took that from me. I hate them for that."

"I do, too, buddy-boy," Amara said, tears forming in her eyes, too. "Graduation is overrated anyway. They say your name, you walk across a stage, it's dumb. Who needs it?"

DeAndre smiled. Amara was doing her best to cheer him up.

Deep down, DeAndre cried for Swayz. Yes, he'd miss his friends at graduation, if they even *were* his friends any longer, after what happened to him got around town, he wasn't sure what to think, but he missed the love of his life, the one who accepted him no matter what. The mythical being sprung from the boy's own desires and heart.

#

DeAndre enrolled in Queens Community College, and quickly joined the theater department. He hadn't seen or heard from his father once during that time and he didn't care to. Amara would exchange emails with her dad a bit, something that was foreign to the old man, but DeAndre couldn't be less interested in learning what his dad had going on back in Resting Hollow.

In class, DeAndre's skills were apparent, and he felt immediately accepted by his peers. Nights out with new friends, his sister, her boyfriend, who saw DeAndre as his own brother, and days studying, working part-time at a record store around the corner from their apartment, so he could help pay the bills and eventually get his own place.

One night, DeAndre was tying his hair up. It had grown long, curling in the same way Amara's tended to. She watched him working with the curls and smiled.

In the mirror, DeAndre thought he caught a glimpse of a familiar face, smooth skin, thin lips, larger than he remembered, eyes glaring with amethyst intensity, but when the boy spun around, it was gone.

The room had evolved over time from the empty space and bed of their guest room to a beautiful, warm space littered with costumes for shows DeAndre performed in, a large vanity mirror purchased and refurbished by Todd as a birthday present a year after DeAndre moved in. Makeup, wigs and more littered the vanity, colorful and explosive, catching the eye immediately upon walking in.

Photos of DeAndre in various costumes from school performances hung on the walls with thumb tacks, others in frames. In some photos, in full drag attire, something he had become exceptionally good at. A few school recitals required him to explore this side of performance, and he relished it. So much so, he started attending drag shows at Queen Mab's, a Chinatown club that featured weekly performances by local drag queens.

"What's funny?" he asked, noticing Amara smiling in the mirror.

"You look like mom," Amara said. "You're beautiful like her. I wish I had your face."

"Stop it," he said, smiling.

"Hang on," Amara said, ducking from DeAndre's doorway. She returned a moment later with a shoebox and sat next to her brother. She opened it and inside, there were dozens of photos of their mom. She had dark skin, like DeAndre, and a bone structure that indicated way more of a resemblance than DeAndre ever imagined.

He held up one of the photos and looked in the mirror. "Amara, my god," he said softly.

"I *know*. I see it more every day."

"I always thought *you* looked like her," DeAndre said.

"When we were younger, sure. The hair. But I'm lighter than her. I'm more dad's complexion. You're her in body and soul, I think." Amara played with some stray strands of DeAndre's curls.

"I miss her," he said, softly.

"I do, too," Amara said, hugging him. "I got an email from dad. He wants us to come home for Thanksgiving. I told him I'd think about it."

"I don't wanna go," DeAndre said. "You can go, obviously I don't want you to be swayed by me."

"I figured," Amara said. "You're my baby bro, we're ride or die. You should keep this one, she looks amazing here."

DeAndre looked at the photo. Their mother was wearing the red and white wool coat from Swayz's birthday. A flutter ran through the boy's chest as he looked at it. Amara rose and left the room.

He hung the picture on the vanity, tucked into the mirror and frame.

#

In the darkness of the stage, the opening string-plucks of a haunting Madonna track floated through the empty theater. DeAndre stood in the center of the stage and performed his routine, pushing his body and mind further than he ever had on the track in high school. Shirtless, beads of sweat forming on his muscular, toned body. Gym shorts allowed fluid movement.

Being the month of April, DeAndre had been preparing for his final exam. This routine took a while to prep, but he had nearly gotten it down. He knew every action, every fluid gesture, and executed it to the best his design and body could allow.

He allowed a few moments for improvisational movement to accompany the song. As Madonna's perfect whisper echoed, DeAndre imagined his impossible love in the audience watching him. He wondered what Swayz looked like now.

As he finished his dance, DeAndre caught his breath, his mind still on the lust and love he felt for his long-lost friend.

A sudden clapping in the back of the theater startled DeAndre and he covered his eyes to block the little bit of light preventing him from seeing who it was.

"Bravo, Dee," the figure said, stepping into the light.

Dad.

"What're you doing here?"

"I wanted to see you, buddy-boy," dad said, stepping closer to the stage.

"I don't want to see you," DeAndre replied, starting to walk off the stage.

"Dee, please," dad called. "I'm sorry, I didn't know what to think, it all just happened and I know—"

"You *don't* know, dad. You pushed me away when I needed you the most," DeAndre said, his heart racing. He imagined this confrontation a hundred times in his head, and felt well-prepared for whatever nastiness his father had in store for him.

Dad nodded. "You're right."

DeAndre stared. "What?"

"I've been talking to a therapist. And getting updates about you from Amara. You're absolutely right. About all of it."

"Okay...?"

"Not seeing you this past year. Learning how amazing you are, how hard you've been working, how you're becoming exactly who you were meant to be, on your own, you're amazing."

DeAndre held steady, even though hearing the emotion in his father's voice broke the boy's heart for the third time in his young life.

"Thank you," he said, softly.

"Dee, I love you, and I'm so, so sorry for how I treated you," Dad said, openly weeping. "I just want my family back. Losing you and Amara, talking to my doctor, I just can't bear to lose you two."

DeAndre stepped off the stage and walked toward his dad. "You broke my heart, dad."

Dad nodded. "I know I did. I'll spend the rest of *my* life making it up to you, if you'll have me back in *your* life."

#

The stage at Queen Mab's wasn't the biggest DeAndre had been on, but it would do for his debut as DeeAgio. He chose his on-stage persona based on the song he chose for his debut at the club: "Take a Chance" by Mr. Flagio, one of the records in his mom's collection that had quickly become his favorite.

The Emcee stood on the stage, wearing a glittery top hat, monocle and little else. The performances were about halfway done for the night, and in the back of the club, Todd and Amara leaned against their high-top, drinking cocktails that seemed to glow with electric fury in red and green.

The entire club seemed bathed in neon-blue light, with pinks and gold accenting throughout. Many of the queens who had performed earlier littered the crowd, enjoying time with friends and family who came to see them perform.

Dad entered the club, waved to Amara and walked over. They hugged. Dad shook Todd's hand. After a moment, dad hugged Todd and thanked him for being so good to his daughter and son.

"Ladies and gentlemen, we have a virgin to Queen Mab's tonight!" the Emcee cooed into the microphone.

The crowd erupted into cat calls and hollering. Amara smiled, and dad looked around, more nervous for DeAndre than anything else. Todd catcalled, which cracked Dad up.

"Ladies and gentlemen, for the first time, may I present to you, a face for the gods...DeeAgio!"

Darkness engulfed the stage. A hush came over the crowd. Sharp, heavy footsteps plunked across the stage in the darkness, and everyone awaited the visage of the latest to take Queen Mab's stage

As 1983's Italo-Disco classic "Take a Chance" thumped with progressive abandon over the sound system in the club, purple light slowly lit up the stage. DeAndre, looking impeccable, stood, in platform chunk Chuck Taylors, red and white wool coat draped across his form, presenting an air of modesty.

His face, upturned to the lights, was that of an ancient goddess, painted and decorated perfectly, eyes glittering, lashes long, lips wet and supple. He looked otherworldly, a gift truly from whatever heavens saw fit to grace the assemblage in Queen Mab's that night.

As the infectious synth beat thumped forward, building to a pulse-pounding explosion of electro-tinged lyrics, DeAndre removed the coat, the light shifting, allowing his outfit to be revealed. A play on classic disco-chic, the entire outfit composed of purple pleather, encrusted with sequins that seemed to radiate the reflective light on the stage.

No need for a wig, DeAndre's hair was long enough and curly enough to stand on its own, the only addition that of sparkle-dust (a gift from Todd, who believed it would "tie the look together"). DeAndre's strong chest stuck out from the outfit, covered in body glitter.

He stood, beginning his performance, glowing like a moving disco ball on stage. In the crowd, the veteran performers and regular attendees stared in brilliance at the young man's moves and his impeccable look.

As DeAndre performed, he spotted his family in the crowd.

Suddenly, the smell of mint wafted into the room. DeAndre didn't react in motion, but he scanned the crowd more. In the corner, under the glowing red "EXIT" sign stood a figure, wearing a trench coat and baseball cap.

Purple eyes glowed from beneath the cap.

Butterflies on acid wings formed in the pit of his stomach and in his chest. Ever the professional, DeAndre continued dancing, intoxicated by the musky mint aroma of his love in the room.

DeAndre smiled and felt tears begin to well in his eyes.

A Year of Bloody Gums

"Dentistry is practically a pseudo-science," Carolyn said. She finished her Manhattan, and chewed on the blackened, soaked cherry at the bottom of the glass. She chomped on a piece of ice and Kiara shuddered, watching her teeth crunch into the stiff chill.

"I mean, I'm pretty sure it's like an *actual* science, Car ..." Kiara said, furrowing her brow. A dull ache, firmly rooted at the base of her lower front teeth, her *central incisors*, throbbed. She was on a steady diet of six Tylenol a day, which was about the only thing that seemed to help.

They sat outside a trendy Italian-fusion joint right on Main Street. The entire town was framed by the Dunderberg Mountains of upstate New York, tucked away, secluded, without feeling disconnected from the more metro region of the state.

Carolyn waved over the waitress, a young brunette, attractive. "Two more doubles, yeah?"

"Absolutely," the waitress said, turning and heading toward the bar. Kiara watched the girl bounce away.

"Dentistry is like, one step above being a chiropractor," Carolyn said. "You see the ass on our server? And that *Mad Max*-type buzzcut on the side of her head? My *god...*"

"Easy, tiger, flirt with her when I leave, I can't handle another awkward encounter between you and a waitress, bartender, postal worker or—"

"*Excuse* you. That weekend romance with the UPS worker was delicious, and that uniform..." Carolyn groaned, eyes rolling and tongue hanging out, like a cartoon character.

Kiara laughed. "You're a creep."

"I've been sorta' seeing someone anyway, but a gal must keep her options open, right?"

"Do tell," Kiara said, absently rubbing her chin, favoring a particularly soft region of gum the dentist highlighted on her last visit.

"Well, I shouldn't say anything, but...the hell with it, it's too delicious not to share," Carolyn said, pulling her phone out. "Just don't scroll through the pictures too far, otherwise, you may see something you don't want to see."

Kiara rolled her eyes and took Carolyn's phone. She began flipping through the pictures, a woman, clearly young, her body firm, in a variety of poses, her dark, curly hair obscuring her face. Caramel skin. Kiara felt a pang of sadness remembering when she was once as youthful and sexy as the mystery girl on the phone. "What's her name?"

"Oh no, no, I don't kiss and tell, it's bad luck," Carolyn said with a grin.

Kiara continued to scroll, until eventually, she recoiled, realizing she had, in fact, gone too far. The photo depicted Carolyn between the young girl's legs.

"I told you not to go too far," Carolyn said, snatching the phone back as the waitress returned with their drinks and placed them down. Carolyn smiled, eyes shooting hearts the young girl's way.

"You're new, right? You're doing fantastic," Carolyn said, nodding.

"Thank you, let me know if you need anything else," the waitress said, grinning, turning and walking off.

"I don't know what to do," Kiara said.

"I could definitely show you," Carolyn said, staring at the waitress.

"I mean about my teeth, Car," Kiara said, running her tongue along the gumline where her bottom teeth sank deeper into her jaw, her gums pulpy, red and, according to her dentist, "inflamed."

"The X-rays didn't show anything?"

Kiara shook her head.

"Then maybe it's stress. Maybe you're doing too much at the office?"

"Maybe," Kiara said, glancing down Main Street. She watched as people bustled around town, dipping in and out of shops, restaurants, bars, the usual spots on a busy main strip in a quaint locale like Resting Hollow. It was rare to get out of the office for lunch on a Friday. Carolyn had texted at just the right time, and Kiara was taking the afternoon off to head home and get a head start on sulking in pain in the darkness of her living room, where episodes of *Kitchen Nightmares* waited for her on Hulu. Watching Gordon Ramsey scream at people was just about the only thing that took her mind off the fact that for the past year, her gums would cake over with blood, crusting and forming along the lower sections of her teeth.

"The last X-rays showed something in the gumline, sorta below the front bottom teeth, a black space," Kiara said absently, remember staring at the X-ray on the glowing computer screen. A cavernous black void greeted her, and the dentist couldn't make heads or tails of it.

Two different dentists expressed concern over the gum line receding, which was certainly the case, but nothing Kiara did helped. Fancy mouthwash? Nothing. Flushing her mouth with coconut oil / eucalyptus oil / sesame oil / peppermint essential oil / whatever the fuck else oil? Nada. Quarterly deep cleanings? Zip. Flossing ten times a day? Zilch. Brushing after every meal? Zero.

The blood returned. She worried that the constant attention she was paying her gums was doing far more damage, but she persisted.

"I think we're just getting old," Kiara said, a hint of wistfulness in her voice.

"Oh most definitely," Carolyn said, finishing her cocktail and waving the waitress over. "We're absolutely getting old, but at the same time, you're only as young as you *feel*."

Carolyn, in her mid-fifties, was just as beautiful as when she and Kiara were roommates in college. Getting older only added an air of authority to the intensity of her sharp, gray eyes. Her hair, a vivid blond, was not store-bought, or at least, Kiara didn't *think* it was.

Kiara, however, felt older every day. The gum issue was the latest in a series of nagging problems, starting with her "tweaking" her knee while jogging one morning five years back. She knew menopause was kicking in, and had been feeling her sex drive backing off for a while. Once the aches and pains really set in, Kiara hoped that would be the worst she'd be dealing with, but then, the blood. The aching gums.

When the waitress arrived, Carolyn produced her business card and handed it to the girl, introducing herself.

"If you're ever interested in learning about investing. Options. Positions. I could even teach you about the *spread* of certain things. My personal number is on the back. I suggest you use it."

The waitress looked at Carolyn and smiled, her cheeks red.

"I know what you're thinking. Just tuck it in your front pocket there. Use it later. I have a house account here, look me up in the system and charge it, would you? Tack on an extra thirty percent for yourself.

"Jesus," Kiara said, stifling a laugh.

"Umm...I will. Thank you so much," the waitress said, turning and heading to the nearest server station.

Carolyn smiled. "Eh? How could I *not* make that happen, Kiara like, *look* at her."

"She could be your daughter, Car," Kiara said, laughing.

"Oh, Kiara, they *all* could," Carolyn cackled.

#

"Carolyn was in rare form this afternoon," Kiara said, looking herself over in the bathroom mirror. She paid extra attention to her midsection, which she had noticed grown thicker over the past year. She felt bloated. Run down. Her body, it seemed, had begun to betray her.

Harlan sat on his side of the bed near the window, reading a horror novel. Something with a ridiculous cover, two hairless baby birds screaming in a nest, bulbous purple-blue eyes looking like shimmering galaxies. "Is that right?"

"That woman's sex drive is insane," Kiara said, pulling her lower lip down to examine her ailing gums. "She was practically raping our waitress."

Kiara could see Harlan lower the book. "Oh? Do tell."

Of course that gets his attention, Kiara rolled her eyes. "You're a creep just like her," Kiara said. "I don't know how you two keep your sex drives up."

"Well, I've got *you*, that's more than enough for me, that's how I do it," Harlan said, smiling.

Kiara sloshed some coconut oil around in her mouth, counting slowly in her head. *One, two, three...*

As she counted, she hung her head low, the ache consuming her. She checked her phone, noting that she only had another half hour before she could take her next round of Tylenol. The pills were making her a little constipated, so on top of the normal bloating she had throughout the day, the only minor pain relief she could get made it somewhat worse. It seemed for every bit of relief, there was another problem to be had.

She spit the coconut oil into the sink and noted how it, too, had an annoying reaction, making her teeth slippery. The oil was tinged pink, and as Kiara ran the faucet, she watched it circle, then slip down the drain.

On the bathroom counter was the microplane grater she picked up at Williams-Sonoma last Christmas. She held it up and examined it, noting flecks of pulpy, dark matter wedged in the grates. She rinsed it, and carried it into the bedroom.

"Do my gums look any better?" she asked, lifting her chin and pulling her lips up and down, examining her gums.

"Your gums, much like the rest of you, looks fantastic, baby," Harlan said, slipping the bookmark their daughter, Maggie, made for him in elementary school. Two glued-on googly eyes sat on a puppy's smiling face, his floppy ears made of felt, and his paws making it look like he was resting above whatever horrifying thing Harlan had been reading.

Kiara flipped the light off in the bathroom. She ran her tongue along her gums absently, standing beside the bed in her underwear and one of Harlan's old Sleater-Kinney t-shirts.

"Let me get a closer look," he said, shifting over to her side of the bed and leaning closer to her neck. Without warning, he began an assault of kisses and nibbles up and down Kiara's neck, pulling her onto the bed in the process.

"You dork! Stop!"

"Absolutely negatory," he said, kissing around to her lips, then down her neck, lifting her shirt and kissing his way up her stomach.

"Harlan, I'm just ... "

He stopped. Kiara could practically feel the energy drain from his body as he sat back up on the bed, looking down at her. "Sorry, babe, but...you look so good. It's been, you know, a little while."

"I know, I'm sorry," she said.

"It's okay, I just miss our...naked time."

She laughed. "Well, when you call it that, how could I resist?"

He rested his head on her chest and she held him, scratching the side of his head. She imagined if he were a dog, his leg would be twitching and kicking, he loved being scratched in that one spot more than anything else.

After a while, Harlan was asleep, and not long after, Kiara was too.

#

Saturday arrived, and Harlan sat on the back porch, talking on the phone. Kiara assumed it was to Maggie, their daughter, away at school. Kiara usually eavesdropped, her husband typically asking about Maggie's classes. If she'd been eating healthy. If there were any "special someones" (Harlan's term, not Kiara's) that Maggie was spending time with.

But not today. Kiara couldn't make out much of anything. Harlan wasn't his normal loud self, instead, it seemed as though whatever conversation he was having involved every ounce of focus he could muster. From the upstairs bedroom window, Kiara could hear the warm breeze rustling the leaves of the trees that lined their property better than her husband's conversation.

Maggie being away was supposed to re-open doors to Kiara and Harlan's shared youth, and instead, with her gone, Kiara had little to no desire to do much of anything. Jogging had become agony. The stand-up paddleboard she bought the summer her daughter prepared to head off to school had remained unused.

Rising, she walked to the bathroom and examined her gums again. Obsessively, she leaned close to her reflection, straining to see any sign that her hard work was helping. Instead, it looked as if her gums had receded further, shifting along their downward descent.

A light lump had begun to form just under her front lower teeth. The area where the black hole on her X-rays was.

Her hands gripping the bathroom counter, Kiara began to shake.

#

Once in her favorite hoodie and sweatpants combo, Kiara headed downstairs for much-needed coffee. She wore a pair of enormous sunglasses, a Christmas gift from Carolyn, and poured a hefty amount of the miraculous dark liquid into the company mug Harlan had made up to celebrate his business' twenty-year anniversary. In twenty years, Kiara still didn't fully understand what his company did, something about eCommerce for financial institutions and banking systems.

"There she is," Harlan said, stepping into the kitchen from the porch. He moved to the refrigerator and grabbed the hazelnut creamer.

Kiara turned, smiled, and took it from him. "Thanks," she said, pouring what some might call an absurd amount into the mug.

"You look like a sexy Unabomber," Harlan said, tugging on Kiara's hoodie strings.

"Oh, why thank you," Kiara said. She sipped the coffee. "How's Maggie doing?"

"Good, good, she's happy to be coming home soon," Harlan said. "She's taking a Film Noir class, how cool is that?"

Kiara nodded. "Neat."

"What's wrong, babe? What can I do?"

Kiara rolled her eyes. "Nothing, Harlan, just, do you still want me?"

"What?"

"Like, I know I rejected you last night, it's not like it's the first time or anything. At some point, you're going to go elsewhere," she said, softly.

"Baby, that's just silly," Harlan said, placing his hand on hers, as she leaned against the counter. "I wish we could figure out what's up with your teeth. Your knee. All of it. So what if your sex drive isn't like when we were younger? Who cares? I still love you so much and would never dream of being with anyone else."

"A year of headaches and toothaches, Harlan. I'm so sick of this," Kiara said, taking an exasperated sip of coffee.

Harlan sighed. "Why don't we take a drive? Maybe head up to the mountains for a hike? Nothing too crazy, just a little meander through the foothills north?"

A little meander...Kiara thought, rolling her eyes

"I'll pack us a picnic or something, it'll be fun," Harlan added.

#

About an hour or so later, Kiara stood along the trail leading through the northernmost section of Resting Hollow, hands on her hips, hiking boots on, soaking up the warm sun. Harlan trailed behind, which wasn't unusual, as he liked to take in every sight possible. What was once a cute trait of her silly husband had become an annoyance, as he seemed to examine almost anything that came within his view.

As she waited, she felt the dull throb in her gums. She thought back to the mirror. The sliver of tooth visible as the gums tore themselves away from her teeth. She ran her pinky along her gums and winced at the new ache of whatever it was slowly growing beneath her teeth.

"Come on, slowpoke," Kiara called.

Harlan walked slowly, tapping away on his phone. *He texts like an old man*, Kiara thought, watching as he hovered over the keyboard, tapping like a bird. He finished and tucked the phone in his pocket.

"Mr. Popular today with that phone. Even for a *meander* through the foothills, you are moving at a snail's pace, Harlan," she said, smiling.

"Sorry, got a text, work stuff," he said, shrugging. "How does it feel being here in the sun? Fresh air and all that. Little better?"

"Not too shabby," Kiara said, smiling. Even the simple action of a smile made her mouth hurt.

#

That evening, Kiara stirred a pan of taco meat, spicy scents accompanying the sizzling sounds, all of it intoxicating to her. She had been able to avoid taking any Tylenol that afternoon, letting the headache swell and die on its own. She was still riding the high of the walk in the foothills, with only minor knee pain.

Outside, on the porch, looking out over their large yard, Harlan stood, smoking a cigar. "You need me to do anything, babe?"

Kiara smiled and shook her head. "No, no, it's all good, just relax."

She watched as he took his phone out. He turned and Kiara noticed he had a slight smile on his face.

"Be ready in a few," Kiara said. "Who's that?"

Harlan continued to text. He finished and tucked the phone in his shirt pocket. "Who's what?"

"Texting you," she said, her cheeks heating up, from the spiced meat before her or something else, she didn't know.

"Work stuff still," Harlan said, tapping the cigar, ashing it off the porch, onto the cement.

"Tell them to kick rocks, it's Saturday," she said, smiling. She pulled a wedge of cheddar from the fridge and began grating it quickly.

"We just landed a new client, so lots of moving parts," he said, puffing away.

Kiara nodded. Harlan's phone rang. She listened as he answered, stepping off the porch, onto the lush, verdant grass. Slightly annoyed, Kiara pushed harder on the block of cheese in her hands, shredding it more. The heat in her cheeks had expanded, radiating out into the rest of her body. It felt as if her head was the focal point, radiating outward in waves.

She grated hard, pressing the firm cheese into the metallic slits in the handheld grater. She pressed harder, the cheese shredding, reducing in size with relative ease.

The taste of copper filled her mouth. Absently, she ran her tongue along her lower incisors and felt the familiar slick sensation of blood pooling between her gums and lower lip.

Pain flooded her mouth. It seemed to rocket up the front of her face, directly to her brain, where an explosion of agony tore through her.

She could feel the fluid in her mouth building up, and without warning, a few drips spilled from her lips, most landing on the stovetop, but a few splattering onto the meat, sizzling, adding a slight hint of coppery scent to the air. Flicking the stovetop off, she ducked down the hallway toward the downstairs bathroom.

Inside, she pulled her lower lip down and could see the root of her tooth jutting from her gums. She had never seen the gums so stretched down, and she began to tremor with anxiety as she examined herself. She could see the whites of her incisors stretching downward, only the barest bit of its tip resting in what was seemingly left of her gums.

Her gums had been shrinking for a while but nothing so dramatic over the course of a day. Panic began to overtake her.

As she examined her gums in the mirror, it looked as though the tiniest tip of bone had begun to protrude from within.

A tusk?

She leaned closer to the mirror, so close it began to fog, and stared. Blood oozed from the protrusion, and she ached. The pain caused her to hear a high-pitch buzzing, her brain unable to process the agony she felt.

Absently, she touched the tusk emerging from her gums, and picked at the flesh around it. She felt the tiniest hint of relief at the feeling of the flesh pulling back a bit from the wound.

She noticed shreds of flesh jutting from what little remained of her gums, ragged, rough-looking patches, some smooth, others, torn apart.

Kiara looked down at the counter. The microplane.

Slowly, she raised the grater to her mouth and, with one hand holding the wooden oak handle, and the other holding her lips as far apart as possible, Kiara dug in. There was no pain. As she ground the flesh away, the tusk began to emerge more, at the expense of the rest of her gumline.

Over and over, Kiara ran the tiny teeth of the grater against her gum, tearing herself apart. Exquisite agony tinged with impossible relief flooded every sense in her body, and her mouth oozed thick red fluid, her saliva mixed with blood.

Harder. More pressure. She could feel the brick of cheese in her hand giving her some resistance, when suddenly, with a hitch followed by a *clunk*, the hindrance vanished.

Finally, Kiara stopped.

Kiara looked down. In the sink sat the tusk. A deep red viscous fluid spewed from it, and fibrous black nerves clung to where it had been broken off by the grater.

She looked closer, noticing a sliver of white root protruding from the deep red meaty flesh of her mouth, and that its tip looked severed, blood streaming from where it had been sawed off. Somehow, it had dislodged from her jaw and skull.

"Harlan!" she screamed.

"Babe? Did you cut yourself? The grater—" Her husband appeared in the doorway of the bathroom, staring at her reflection in the mirror.

Kiara turned to him, hands shaking, covered in blood. Her mouth was open in an approximation of a grimace, teeth bared, mouth caked in dark, thick fluid. It dripped endlessly, splattering all over the ceramic countertop of the half-bathroom.

#

Later, at the hospital, Kiara lay in bed, heavily medicated. She could, however; hear Harlan talking to the doctor. Fragments of discussion.

Stress...

So much blood...

Annoyed easily...

Tried everything...

A cheese grater, of all things ...

Groggy, Kiara watched as Harlan was joined by Carolyn.

"Car..." Kiara attempted, her throat dry. She reached for her friend.

"I'm here, kid," Carolyn said, brushing Kiara's hair from her face. "Don't try to talk."

Kiara raised a hand to her face. It was heavily bandaged. She felt sore. Beat-up. A radiating, dull ache coursed through the lower part of her face, below her nose.

"She's heavily sedated," the doctor said. "She really did a number to her gums."

Carolyn caressed Kiara's forehead. Sleepily, Kiara traced her finger along the bandages. She felt the tinge of panic rising in her chest, but was far too weak to do much beyond sighing under the fog of sedation.

"If you need to have her see someone," the doctor handed Harlan a business card. Harlan nodded, and the doctor ducked out of the room. Once he was gone, Harlan stood beside Carolyn and stared down at Kiara.

Maggie entered the room. "Mom?"

Kiara whimpered, her eyes tearing up, as Harlan held their daughter. She watched as Maggie began to cry, too.

"Your mother's exhausted," he said, softly.

"Harlan, why don't I get the nurse to get her some more pillows?" Carolyn asked.

"No, no, you stay, I'll grab them," Harlan said, ducking from the room.

Maggie stepped closer to Kiara and held her hand. "I love you, mom, I'm so sorry I didn't get here sooner."

"No, no, it's okay, your mom's gonna be fine, sweetie," Carolyn said, putting her arm around Maggie and leading her to the door. They were framed by the light of the hospital hallway, casting their long shadows into the room.

Through blurry vision, Kiara watched as Carolyn leaned down and began kissing Maggie's neck. Her hand slipped down the front of her jeans, and Kiara, unable to move, felt panic replaced with anger deep within her, but far down, impossible to touch and impossible to dedicate true attention to. The rage was an abstraction, confusing, the semblance of a feeling more than a real, tangible emotion.

"I can't imagine why she'd do this..." Maggie said, throwing her head back, allowing Carolyn to kiss further down her neck.

Kiara watched as Carolyn's hand emerged from Maggie's jeans. Slowly, she cupped the young girl's face and kissed her softly.

Maggie returned the kiss and the room went dark.

\#

When Kiara was allowed to return home, she barely spoke to Harlan. She didn't know what to say, even if she could tell him about Carolyn and Maggie. She'd sit, on the back porch, watching as Harlan mowed the lawn, her face bandaged. He'd serve her meals on metal trays. Tiny cups of liquid medication. The wire that kept her jaw locked in place made the hinges of her mouth unbearably painful.

She tried to focus on the yard itself, with large topiaries shaped into a variety of animals, stretching to the sky, their hooves, tusks and trunks arching in an almost worship to the sun and moon. Kiara never noticed the bushes before. She wondered if Harlan had them installed to make her more comfortable.

There were no mirrors in the house. In fact, the house was different in every respect. Their two-story seemed to grow, somehow, in the time she spent recovering in her hospital bed. Long corridors. A constant light in the hallway beside the special bedroom Harlan had set up for her.

She'd lie in bed, each night, imagining the vile things Maggie and Carolyn did to one-another. Perhaps even in Maggie's childhood bedroom.

#

Kiara sat on the back porch, tucked tightly in a white robe, scratchy at the hips and elbows. She didn't love the material, but it was all she had.

She sat, watching Harlan mow the lawn. Her face, still wrapped in bandages, ached. Reconstructive surgery was still a few months down the line. She had to heal first. Then, surgeons could open her gums up and make the necessary incisions to fix her mouth.

Each night, Harlan left the house. Each morning, Kiara awoke to photos on her phone of Maggie and Carolyn in a variety of compromising situations. Sometimes with various third parties. The pictures were all sent from different phone numbers, none of them stored in Kiara's phone.

When Carolyn came to visit, Kiara wanted to confront her about what was going on, and almost did, but with her jaw wired shut, everything Kiara said came out as a stiff murmur.

Kiara rose and stepped into the home, making her way up the elevator, her robe dragging behind her, the bandages on her face coming loose.

Kiara tried begging Harlan to stay home, writing on pink and neon green Post-It notes her thoughts, her feelings and more. Her bedroom had become littered with these neon missives, which, Kiara realized, since Harlan would ignore, she had to display, not only in the hopes of him realizing that she knew what her best friend was doing with their daughter, but also because it helped her rage. A rage, like a tiny flame, burning deep within, consuming her every thought.

The door to the bedroom opened, and in stepped Harlan, carrying a tray with a yellow protein shake on it. Yellow, not unlike the walls of the bedroom, painted while Kiara was in the hospital after taking the cheese grater to her own face. Kiara remembered that now. Remembered the rage. The sadness. The stress. That dull, seething ache in her jaw.

Harlan, wearing white pants and a white t-shirt, placed the tray down beside Kiara. Nodding, he smiled nervously.

This was not Harlan's smile. His broad, sweet face, replaced instead with the pudgy, doughy expression of a man half Harlan's age.

"Your favorite, miss, banana smoothie," not-Harlan said, glancing around the room, soft, yellow walls obscured by thousands of neon notes, some with pictures drawn on them, others with phrases like "betrayal," "love," "touch me," "need" scrawled on them in red or green crayon.

"Thank you," Kiara said softly. The cell phone in her hand dropped to the floor and not-Harlan leaned down to pick it up. He placed it back on the table beside Kiara. No longer a phone, it was, instead, a photo of her, Carolyn and Harlan, with Maggie, taken the last time Maggie was home to visit.

The light above her flickered. Wincing from the abrasive fluorescent strobe, Kiara's eyes blinked, as not-Harlan exited the room.

She touched her face and realized, for the first time, that there were no bandages.

The fluorescent bulb in the ceiling flickered again, manic and intense.

As Kiara stared, she felt as though she began to float. The ache in her jaw, the closer she got to the light, began to melt away. In the light, she would finally heal.

The Girl in the Floor

Bev couldn't stop dancing.

At nine years of age, even after dancing for hours at the ballet school that cost her parents thousands of dollars a year in tuition, Bev often returned home after each three-hour session and continued practicing her moves in her bedroom.

Her parents didn't mind, in fact, they often encouraged her to continue practicing. Dad saw it as a blessing that he had such a focused, hard-working young lady for a daughter, and mom, who had danced all through college until an injury forced her to give it up, relished the fact that Bev was, in many ways, following in her footsteps. There were times, however; that mom worried that Bev might be overtraining, working herself entirely too hard. Overtraining was often worse than not training at all, and certainly had its dangers.

When they returned home from the ballet studio Tuesday evening, Bev went right to her room to continue training herself to stand en pointe. The girl could feel the tension in her ankles begin to constrict again, even after taking time during her recovery session to muscle scrape and ice, but she remained steadfast.

From this position, she twirled, spinning quickly. As she spun, flourished and assumed the starting position over and over, she barely noticed the hardwood floor starting to dissolve as she moved, a flurry of pink and white, her dark hair pinned tightly against her head.

Until she noticed that she had been sinking into the floor.

When she finally realized what was happening, panic set in, and she believed for a moment she might be dreaming. The impossibility of the situation stung her young mind, prickling at what she knew was reality.

Her eyes flickered multiple times, unable to comprehend what had been happening, and yet, here it was: she was slipping *into* the floor, as though the firm surface beneath her had become liquid, like a warm, welcoming oatmeal-substance beginning to devour her.

Her father's scream shook the notions of logic from her mind. When her parents burst into the room, she was bisected at the waist, her legs kicking in place in the air above the living room.

Her mother thought perhaps the floor had collapsed, but that wasn't possible because surely Bev would've tumbled through completely. No. The floor remained perfectly in place. The ceiling, too. Instead, it was as if the mass of the floor and ceiling was displaced by Bev's legs and lower half. While Bev's mom was shocked by how this could've happened, she knew her focus had to be on her panic-stricken daughter.

Her dad took her by the hands and tugged lightly, attempting to pull his daughter free. He wondered if perhaps the floor had become like quicksand, some kind of manufacturing default at the warehouse or something, either way, getting Bev out of the floor was top priority.

When she failed to budge, Dad released her hands and stood, unsure how to proceed, glancing around the room for some miracle that never materialized.

His mind raced. He wasn't a logical man by any stretch, that was his wife's territory. Instead of thinking, he acted, and grabbed his daughter's hands harder, pulling with greater fervor, but still she couldn't budge. Bev began to shake, the panic overtaking her, and her dad held her, tears in his own eyes.

Mom joined them on the floor and held them both. She didn't cry. When her husband and daughter fell to pieces, she held strong, and instead focused on the problem at hand: her daughter was somehow stuck between her upstairs bedroom and the downstairs living room, and there was seemingly no explanation as to how this may have occurred.

#

Mom remained with Bev, while Dad went downstairs to study the space in the living room where his daughter's tiny legs pierced through moments earlier. Instead of her legs, he found the ceiling was smooth, undamaged, and with nothing more than the recently-installed high-hat lights to greet him.

He walked into the kitchen, and that's when he saw them. Two slender legs, in her ballet school uniform of pink tights, black shoes and a black leotard, poking through the ceiling.

Above the kitchen was a bathroom. Staring, he simply couldn't rationalize what he was seeing.

"What the...?"

Dad took out his phone and dialed 9-1-1.

#

The police arrived, with members of the fire department in tow. An ambulance sat outside, parked on the street. The two firefighters made their way up to the girl's bedroom while an officer from the Nassau County Police Department waited at the bottom of the stairs for the emergency personnel to come into the large home.

Beverly's legs, meanwhile, had shifted from the ceiling of the kitchen, to sticking straight up out of the floor in the garage, then above the dining room table, and back to the living room, where they remained. For the moment.

A sharp "Holy shit," from upstairs caught the officer's attention, as two EMTs carried their emergency kits and stretcher into the home. Leaving the door open, the officer walked into the living room and saw Bev's legs dangling from the ceiling. Unable to process the reality of the situation, he removed his standard-issue cap and sighed, eyes locked on the perverse impossibility dangling above him.

The two EMTs walked upstairs and entered Bev's room. They saw her parents, huddled in the corner, dad crying, mom sipping from a coffee mug, a dazed look in her eyes. They saw one of the firefighters, on one knee, examining the area of the floor around Bev, who just looked at the officers, and her parents, tears in her eyes.

"How did this happen?" asked a second firefighter, heavyset, thick mustache on his upper lip, standing nearby.

"That's why we called you guys, we have no idea," Mom said. "She was practicing, dancing, like always, next thing we know, her legs were through the floor."

The firefighter, a confused look on his face, knelt down and looked around the girl. Her tiny waist met the floor, as though she had always been part of it. "Sweetie, are you in pain?"

Bev shook her head. "No, no pain. Just can't move. Your mustache sure is silly."

The firefighter smiled. "My wife tells me that all the time, sweetheart."

"Frank, look at this," the other firefighter said.

The firefighter rose and moved quickly to where his compatriot was kneeling down. "Beverly, I'm going to move your shirt a little, okay? Right under your arm. It might tickle, so, I'm sorry," he said, his voice calm in an effort to keep Bev relaxed.

The firefighter furrowed his brow and slipped on a pair of blue rubber gloves. He shared a nervous glanced with Bev's parents, who watched, anxiously, from the far side of the room. Bev strained to look but couldn't twist her body far enough in the direction of where they were looking to get a good view.

Pinching with gloved fingers, the firefighter tugged the thin fabric of Bev's ballet leotard just under her arm. The little girl snickered a bit, and he paused, frightened he may have hurt her.

"Sorry, kiddo."

"S'okay," Bev said, fighting another giggle at the light tickle beneath her right arm as the firefighter continued tugging on the fabric. "Are you gonna save me?

The firefighter smiled. "Yes, we will. Don't you worry."

As he did so, the emergency personnel and Bev's parents saw what caught the two firefighters' eyes. Along Bev's skin was a faint line. Deep red, almost black, running up her side. Both men pointed at it with gloved fingers, but everyone knew where to look.

"What is it?" Bev asked, her sweet voice shaking.

"Nothing, baby, we'll be right back," Bev's dad said, rising quickly and charging out of the room. "Everyone out!"

The emergency personnel followed Bev's dad out of the room, and Bev was left with her mother. She flinched when her dad slammed the door and watched as one of her stuffed animals fell the shelf the shelf nearest to it. She heard everyone charge down the stairs, her dad's voice muffled as they moved.

Bev placed her hands on the floor around where her hips would be. Though she was touching the floor, she felt as though her hands were resting on her sides, as though she was setting up to go into first position in ballet class. She spread her fingers and tickled herself but didn't laugh this time. She began pushing but felt as though she was shoving herself in place. There was no movement, just struggle, and it exhausted her small frame quickly.

Downstairs, in the kitchen, the emergency personnel stood, coffee mugs in hand. One of the police officers was on his radio, calling in updates to his superiors, noting how the legs shifted from the living room to the downstairs bathroom at the end of a hallway.

A crowd of neighbors began gathering outside, watching to see what was going on. Police officers and firefighters in their neighborhood was uncommon, so everyone was curious what the excitement was.

The cop eventually called for additional officers to set up a barricade around the house, preventing onlookers from getting close. He didn't answer any questions from curious neighbors, because, he figured, what could he possibly tell them that didn't sound completely insane?

#

As time passed, Bev's dad became anxious. Ideas were thrown around. *Should we cut her out? What was that line? Is she in pain? What do we do? What's causing this? Does she have a history of illness? Is that line a scar?*

Dad went upstairs and sat on the floor next to Bev and his wife.

"Go get some fresh air, babe," Dad said to his wife, and she kissed his cheek, then Bev's, and slipped from the room.

He asked Bev if she needed anything, and she said a glass of water would be nice, so he brought her one. He sat while she drank, and she stared up at him, her eyes watery from crying. "Daddy, am I going to get out of here? Why is this happening to me?"

He just stared at her. He couldn't lie to her, so he cleared his throat and said, simply "I don't know, Bevvy. I wish I could tell you that I knew why this was happening, and that I know how to get you out of here, but I don't. I'm sorry, lovebug."

She sighed and looked down. The two were silent for a moment as she finished her glass of water. "Could you move a little bit? My leg's starting to go numb," she finally said.

Dad looked at how he was sitting. Even though he was a good two feet from the girl, and believed he was sitting on the hardwood floor, he shifted further away, and she smiled up at him. "Bev, you could feel that? Where I was sitting?"

Bev nodded. "I still can."

He took a cautious step backward as he stood up. *Three feet around the girl*, he thought. *How in the world?*

"Sweet girl, I'm going to head downstairs, okay? Do you need anything else?"

She shook her head. "Can you have mama come up in a little bit? I don't want to be alone. And maybe if you could—" She trailed off.

"What, sweetie?"

"Maybe, if when people come in, they could take their boots off. It hurts when they walk in here. It feels like when the doctor was pushing on my stomach that time when I was sick."

"Sure thing, Bevvy," Dad smiled at her. "We're going to figure this out, okay?"

She nodded. Dad didn't feel good lying to her like that. *Was it a lie? Wouldn't they figure it out? Science and miracles happen every day, don't they?* Before he left the room, Dad noticed the red-black lines spreading across the girl's back like an absurdist roadmap.

#

Downstairs, the additional emergency personnel, along with some new faces. People wearing suits, some with white doctor's coats on, stethoscopes around their necks, all trying to come up with a plan to get Bev out. Dad walked over to Bev's mom and whispered the little girl's request to her.

"Everybody, Bev has requested that you remove your shoes when entering the room, apparently she can feel beyond three feet around her, and it hurts," Mom said.

"The lines on her back, how bad were they before?" one of the new faces, a doctor with University credentials, asked.

"What lines on her back?" the mustached firefighter asked, putting his coffee down. "We saw *one* line under her right arm. There are lines on her back, now?"

Mom nodded. "A bunch. Blood poisoning, maybe?"

"Blood poisoning can cause reddish lines on one's body, that's true," said one of the EMTs. "I'm no doctor, but..."

"I am. We should do a full battery of tests on her to determine if the girl has blood poisoning or not," said one of the guys with a white coat. He had a North Shore University Hospital badge on his lapel.

"Where'd all these doctors and stuff come from?" Dad asked no one in particular.

"The firemen made some calls. The EMTs, too. Nobody knows what to do," Mom said, sounding tired. She sipped coffee from a Styrofoam cup.

"How long will the test for blood poisoning take?" Dad asked.

"It's fairly quick, but if it's positive, we'll need to get her to the hospital right away," the doctor said.

"How do you propose we do that?" Mom said, her voice angry.

"Hey folks," a voice called from the living room.

"I don't know how we do that; we may have to consult an architect or construction crew to get her out of the floor," the doctor said.

"You guys can cut her out if we need to rush her to the hospital," Dad said, then, realizing his own words and how insane they sounded, recoiled at the idea.

"Hey! In here!" the voiced called again from the living room. It was one of the police officers. When everybody rushed into the living room, they look up at the spot in the ceiling where the legs were supposed to be. They were still there. *Sort of.* Somehow, they had blended into one solid mass. It almost looked like a stalactite one might find in a cave system, a deep, blurry gray, as though the color of Bev's black leggings had bled into the off-white ceiling.

The formation twitched a little bit, looking almost like the tail of a lizard, wriggling around the ceiling. A hush fell over the room and they listened, hearing Bev grunting softly above them.

Nearly tripping over each other, everyone rushed up the stairs and entered Bev's room. The girl screamed in agony as the boots and shoes trampled all over her. Mom quickly began shoving everyone out of the room, as everyone struggled to get a look at the girl. The reddish-black lines had begun to swarm up her neck, onto her sweet, youthful face. Her eyes were black marbles. She was struggling hard, pushing at the floor, at herself, trying to tear free.

An ungodly gurgle escaped her throat, her voice somehow five octaves lower. Intensely guttural noises emerged where once a soft, high voice once lived. A trail of black goo oozed from her mouth.

"Help her! Somebody!" mom screamed.

Dad looked around, again begging the walls decorated with pop stars, pictures of Bev and her friends dancing, family vacation photos, a pile of dirty laundry, for any help at all. Just a hint of guidance. Something, anything, to tell him what to do. When he looked out the window into the back yard, he caught, for an instant, the rustling of wind in the tall pine tree, swaying back and forth lightly.

"That's it," Dad said, barely a whisper, before bolting from the room.

Dad sprinted down the stairs and ran to the garage. Inside, he found the chainsaw he bought the year they moved into the house, when they decided to clear some trees in the backyard. Shoving the EMTs and emergency personnel out of the way as he made his way back up the stairs, he stood, ready to cut the girl free from the floor.

"I'll go get the ambulance ready," one of the EMTs said, running down the stairs. His partner followed him, and the ambulance's engine roared to life.

"Dispatch, this is Officer Chambers at the Ellis house. We're going to need to provide escort for the ambulance here, over," and with that, the cop, along with the other police officers in the house, ran down the stairs, to their squad cars, engines and sirens roaring to life.

The firefighters remained, as Bev's mom stared at the chainsaw, her eyes wide. "Daniel, that's my little girl in there."

Dad stared at her. She only used his name when she was deadly serious. It was rare. He sighed. "I know. We can wait and find another way. It's your call."

Mom looked around. Bev's dad stared at her, waiting for her to make the decision. She looked at the chainsaw, then into his eyes. "Do it."

#

Dad kicked off his boots and entered the room. Before exiting the garage, he grabbed the pairs of safety goggles that were hanging on the corkboard he installed when Bev was born. A little side project for himself that was pretty much gone untouched.

He also grabbed two disposable face masks and placed one over Bev's face. In her delirium and pain, her head lolled around, and she had begun to drool the black viscous fluid even more all over her once-pristine ballet outfit. Her cries were soft whispers, and Dad tried to make out any intelligible words, but failed.

Behind him, Bev's mom entered the room and closed the door. She removed her shoes and walked to her daughter's side, holding the little girl's hand.

"I don't have another mask or another pair of goggles," Dad said.

"I don't have another daughter. Just do it," Mom said.

He noticed that Bev's leotard had begun to blend into the floor, as well, making it remarkably difficult to tell where her flesh ended, and the wood floor began. He removed parts of the leotard to get a better visual as to what to expect, but found that it, too, in the same way that Bev was beginning to meld into the floor, had fused to the girl's flesh, and every time he tugged on the fabric, Bev elicited a sharp inhale, which he interpreted as pain.

"Jesus, this is a fucking nightmare," he said softly, shaking his head.

Mom held Bev's left hand, as the right one had all but melted into the floor. She gripped her child's slender fingers tightly, in the hopes that this nightmare would be over soon, that Bev would be in a hospital and would be back to dancing in no time. Therapy would be required, of course, but all that mattered was that Bev would be alright.

He revved the chainsaw to life, and mom jumped at the sharp, high-pitched sound. Dad stepped softly around her, doing his best to guess where the little girl ended and the floor began. If there was an ending or difference, he simply couldn't tell. He looked up at Bev's mom and she shouted "Do it!"

Dad looked at the floor and noticed it appeared to be mostly wood. There were the beginnings of soft, pink flesh about two inches above where he was aiming the chainsaw, but he dropped to one knee and lowered the chainsaw slowly to the floor. The teeth of the blade spun quickly, and as they connected with the floor, the high-pitched revving of the engine mixed with something else almost-equally highly-pitched.

It was at that moment a blackish-red fluid began spewing from the area where the chainsaw met the floor. The goo splattered his face, and as he recoiled, losing his balance, the saw dropping further into what he hoped was wood flooring.

More screaming. More viscous fluid. Mom dropped Bev's hand and grabbed the saw, pulling it from the floor, and switching it off. The parents turned to the girl, who was rocking back and forth, bellowing in agony. She pulled her fused arm from the surface, and it, too, erupted with the same blackish fluid from the wound in the floor.

"Bevvy!" mom screamed.

Bev's face, even with the mask and goggles on, was a blur of movement, screaming and rage. Her black eyes seemed to shimmer and her arm, torn free from the floor, slumped, as though it was being pulled back into place.

Her voice gurgled, unintelligible words. "Ma...da...mom..."

Dad ran to her side and pulled the mask and goggles from her face. They were splattered with the fluid. Whether it was from the chainsaw or her tearing her arm free, he had no idea. He held the girl. "I'm so sorry, Bevvy, I'm so sorry, sweet girl, I'm sorry," he cried. Her face was slick with what appeared to be a combination of tears and the ichor that was now spreading across the floor.

Beverly froze in place. She stared at her father, the black globes of her eyes becoming larger, almost as if they were stretching out, the sockets becoming hollow. She tried to reach up with her once-free left hand, but couldn't, as it had become fused to the left side of her body.

"I'm sorry, Bevvy, I'm so sorry..."

#

Downstairs, the emergency personnel who didn't prepare for the race to North Shore University Hospital, watched as the girl's legs continued to droop from the ceiling. Eventually, her toes (or toe, since the two legs had formed one amorphous blob) connected to the floor, and the entire shape began to fill out. One of the police officers placed his hand on the formation, and though it felt fleshy, soon, it began to harden. He noticed the black and red lines in the pillar of flesh before him resembled the ones on the girl's body, but over the period of a few minutes, they began to settle and fade in color.

Bev's dad walked down the stairs and looked at the new column in the middle of the living room. He walked over and touched it and felt a sting of cold emanating from the surface. Looking up, he noticed the ceiling had tiny cracks in it, resembling the pattern on his daughter's flesh. He stood, in shocked silence, as the pattern spread across the ceiling.

Back in Bev's room, mom watched as the little girl's body hardened and began to stiffen the veins in her back forming a stucco pattern, which had begun to invade her body. Her flesh, what was left of it, paled, and her face became a misshapen glob of spackle-like façade. Soon, what once resembled the tiny girl's upper body on the floor was nothing more than a pile of cracked flesh.

"M-m-m..." a gurgle came from Bev's widened maw. Her mother reached out and clutched what was left of her daughter's hand, but, as it melted and changed int one fleshy-hard substance, drew her hand back, unnerved by what was happening to the child before her.

Mom touched what was left of the girl, but recoiled when she realized that Beverly was, essentially, gone. In her place, this impossible statue. A hideous, Francis Bacon-like facsimile of what was once a little girl. Mom did note, however; that if one stared at what was once Bev's face long enough, the dark orbs of her eyes were grayish stains, melted next to each other into what looked like a pained expression.

#

As the years went on, Beverly's parents lived with the new column in the middle of their living room. It stood, a hardened flesh-like structure, rippled and muscular at points, at others, soft, and warm, as though life still coursed through its façade. Late at night, when Bev's mom and dad sat in the living room, they thought, for the tiniest of moments, they could hear Bev's voice, echoing down a hallway, or sometimes, sounding muffled beside the column, deep within, encased in flesh-like stucco.

Mom would often spend time sitting in her daughter's room, talking to the grotesque sculpture that now rested in the center of the floor. Dad would find himself in there, too, late at night, crying, begging for his daughter's forgiveness.

The thought of moving was an impossibility. Friends had recommended they demolish the home, as whatever that new structure *was* in the center of their living room, surely it wasn't truly their daughter. It was something *else*. A terrible stucco-ceramic tribute to their daughter, maybe. Not the bright, funny, sweet child that once was.

Bev's parents wouldn't listen. To them, their baby girl was still alive.

She *was* the home.

Always would be.

Wrapped in Plastic

David didn't know what to make of it at first.

"Thirty years on the job, never seen nuttin' like this," David said, wiping the sweat from his brow. It had been an uncharacteristically warm fall. "Not in all my life."

The others had walked over to stare. He didn't know why they would. Human nature, David guessed.

"These things don't happen here," Brody said, fingering the silver crucifix around his neck.

"Saved that cat that time," Kelly said, adjusting her glasses, bending over to get a better look. "Remember? Some piece of shit put a kitten in a paper bag and threw her away?"

"How *is* Waffles?" Brody asked, turning away, clearly no longer interested in being a lookie-loo. David knew that naming the rescue kitten "Waffles" was a risky endeavor but he didn't care. Certainly not when it came to Brody, whose opinion he valued even less than the three-year old tabby that greeted David at the door each night when he got home from the dump.

"Doin' just fine," David said, eyes on the foggy cellophane bag at their feet.

When the trucks dumped their refuse that morning, David was doing his usual inspection, when he noticed the cellophane bag sitting a good ten feet from the nearest landfill. Confused, he walked over and prepared to toss it onto the mountain of trash before him, but froze when he got a closer look.

Someone in the cellophane bag stared back.

Ants crawled around inside the bag, skittering across what was the apparently-untouched face of a beautiful young woman. Her lips were painted a light shade of green, and a large smear ran across her cheek. She wore light makeup around her eyes and had the faintest hint of freckling across the bridge of her nose.

Other than her head, the rest of her body was missing.

Crinkle-crack. The bag shifted in the breeze. He knelt down for a closer study.

The bits of meat that peeked from within the stiff cellophane bag made David's stomach lurch, but that wasn't what pushed him over the edge.

She was smiling.

#

"We're going to need a record of everyone who was in and out of the depot since yesterday evening," the detective told David. As foreman, it was his responsibility to provide these things to law enforcement. David didn't mind one bit. Part of the job.

"These things aren't supposed to happen here," Brody repeated. It was as if he'd rehearsed his outrage, playing a part, saying what he was supposed to say. They were now in the can, the portable office that had been set up years back and never dismantled. The simple crucifix dangled from his neck, occasionally catching the light, casting off-hand flashes on the walls. David used it as his home base of operations once he became foreman and was able to keep the space long after the renovations on the main building had wrapped construction.

"Best if you all go home and get some rest," the detective said. David was surprised at how young he was. Couldn't have been more than twenty-five, with long hair and a scraggly beard that couldn't possibly be regulation. The crime scene unit had already gathered the woman's head and samples of the dirt from around where David had found her. Once they had finished, it was like she hadn't been there at all.

But David could still see her pearly whites, glowing a kind-of radioactive white. While Brody refilled his Yeti tumbler, David thought for the briefest moment he saw her resting on the file cabinet behind the water cooler, eyes wide, smile wider.

David shook his head involuntarily, blinking his eyes a few times.

"You gonna be okay, boss?" Kelly asked. She gave him that concerned look, doing that thing where her eyes looked looked like an abandoned puppy.

David nodded.

"Maybe I'll stop by later and bring you some homemade chili? Been on the slow-cooker all day, I'd be happy to do it." Kelly had often dropped off dinner for David, especially after his wife passed three years back from cancer.

She was half his age. David knew she did it out of kindness, not out of romance. He appreciated having someone look out for him now that Debra was gone.

"You know, chili sounds great," David said. "Thank you, kiddo."

Kelly smiled and patted David on the shoulder. She ducked out the door. Brody stammered his goodbye and followed after her.

#

The darkness came early while David sat, trying to shake the woman's smile from his mind. Sitting in the dark, head hanging low, David sighed and felt an invisible weight drag him down. He looked around the room, the four walls decorated with inspirational posters that came with the temporary structure. Pictures of mountains. Puffy, cotton-like clouds. A photo of a track runner sprinting across the finish line, torn ends of tape on either side of his raised arms. The dying light of the evening had begun to cast the office in a swath of shadow.

Crinkle.

He looked around the room. Shadows and darkness to greet him. Nothing beyond that. He rose and started for the door.

"*I wanted it...*"

David froze and turned on his heels, doing a 360-degree scan of his surroundings. The fake wood-paneled walls grew darker with every minute and he could see dust dancing in the fading evening light beams from outside.

He was alone.

#

Back home, Waffles greeted David at the door per usual, and he scooped the tabby into his big hands and carried her to the kitchen. She purred and rubbed her face against his chest. David smiled, the first good feeling since he'd found the head. He genuinely loved coming home to the cat each night after work. A long day at the dump followed by an evening of watching *Shark Tank* with his cat until he fell asleep in his La-Z-Boy? That was all David hoped for.

He tore open a can of wet food and placed half onto a tiny white plate beside the pantry. He carefully wrapped the remaining half of the can in plastic wrap and couldn't shake the image of the woman's smile from his mind as he stretched the plastic across the top of the can, the meaty brown cat food looking almost vulgar after what he'd seen earlier that day.

"Gnarly," David said to himself as he placed the can in the fridge. It was largely empty other than a carton of coconut milk, some coffee creamer and a half-empty Chinese food container of pork lo mein he'd meant to toss in the trash two days earlier.

Waffles was busy with dinner and David stepped to his favorite spot in the house. The matching La-Z-Boys he bought for he and his wife Debra hadn't moved since she passed. David sometimes thought about shaking things up and sitting in his wife's old chair, but he never did. He could still see the indent of her and smiled to himself remembering her laugh when they watched Mel Brooks movies or a re-run of *All in the Family*.

Waffles would sit there sometimes, curling into a ball, but not often. It was as if the cat somehow knew the chair waited for someone else. Waited for Debra. David thought that maybe his wife was already sitting there. He wasn't a spiritual man, and he never talked to Brody at work about religious matters, even though he knew Brody was as hardcore a Bible-thumper as David ever knew.

"*When he touched me, it all went away...*"

David turned, expecting to see someone standing in the doorway beside him. The living room was just off the main foyer of the house, and he imagined someone had snuck in after he got home. But there was no one.

His heart beat fast, a small pain in his chest. Getting too old for that level of excitement.

"This is it, Waffles," David said, loud enough for the cat to hear him in the kitchen. "I'm officially losing my marbles."

Waffles stopped eating and looked at him, as if saying *Yeah, but as long as you keep feeding me, we're good.*

He shook his head and flipped on the television. His fingers found the small remote attached to the La-Z-Boy and with the light press of a button, the legs of the chair began to rise. Soon, he was in his favorite position. Mark Cuban and the rest of the Sharks were bidding on a wicker furniture business and soon, David was asleep.

\#

In darkness, teeth.

Wide.

White.

Smiling.

David knew it was a dream. But the crinkling of the cellophane bag made David's skin crawl.

"You want him to touch you, too," the woman said. The smile remained. "When he touches you, it all goes away. He fills you with a beautiful, warm glow."

In the dream, David suddenly realized that he, too, was just a head, floating in oily darkness, staring at the woman, her translucent death-shroud beginning to slip from her face as she spoke.

Crinkle.

"It's like falling in love for the first time," she said. David remembered her eyes in the bag. They were wide. As if staring at the most beautiful thing she'd ever seen, not wanting to blink, wanting to drink in whatever it was she stared at so much that she somehow...allowed herself to be...

"Given a gift," she finished.

David stared at the woman. Her smeared lipstick. The light trails of eye makeup down her cheeks.

The bloody viscera that dangled from where her neck should be.

#

The doorbell bolted David awake, and he dropped the remote. The plastic clattering of the clicker almost shocked him more than the chime that continued in the house. Shaking the cobwebs loose, he remembered that Kelly would be stopping by with the chili. He looked over at Debra's chair and thought for a moment he saw her impression shift. He shook his head, realizing that it was nothing more than the glow of the television reflecting off the fabric.

"Coming, Kel," David shouted as he hit the button to lower the La-Z-Boy legs, then rose and stepped toward the door. Waffles was asleep on the upstairs landing when he entered the foyer. David flipped the light on outside on the porch. He opened the door. "Thanks again for stopping by, Kelly, it's awful nice of ya' to –"

There was no one there.

The light breeze of a strangely warm fall night greeted him. Sighing, he stuck his head out the door and looked around. All of his neighbors seemed to be home. The neighborhood looked painfully normal as it always did.

David thought maybe he was hearing things, that the bell didn't ring, but when he closed the door and took a step toward the living room, he froze when the doorbell sounded a second time.

"Sonofab–" he muttered, turning around and storming quickly to the door. Some kids playing ding-dong ditch were going to get a piece of his mind. Pulling it open, he stepped out onto the porch, expecting to hear the tell-tale sign of kids messing around. He thought maybe he could spot them in the bushes off to the side of the house, but there was no one there. "Listen, if anyone's out there, cut the bullshit, okay?"

"*You have to want it...*" the woman's voice sighed off to his right. He turned and stared. Bushes and trees dividing his property from his neighbor's.

"Shut up," he grunted, more annoyed than scared, turning back to the door and stepping into the house. He slammed the door hard and felt bad when he saw Waffles jolt awake in fright. "Aww, I'm sorry, sweetie. Go back to sleep."

The cat stretched and yawned, flashing her sharp teeth. Waffles shook her head and tucked herself back into her paws.

"That's a girl," David smiled, turning back to the living room. When his eyes fell on the television, he froze.

It was the woman from the dump.

But, all of her. Her entire body. Not just a head in a bag. The news was reporting the discovery and showing pictures from when she was alive. She wore the uniform of the local supermarket and David wondered if he'd maybe passed her by hundreds of times during his weekly shopping, as barebones as it often was.

She was young. Nineteen. A student at the local university, according to the report. David stepped closer and sat slowly in his La-Z-Boy, unable to take his eyes off the screen. The news displayed her name: Suzie Bennett.

"*He comes from inside...*" the voice whispered. This time, David didn't turn. It sounded as if the woman was speaking to him directly from the television. She wasn't a "woman" anymore. She had a name. Suzie. Nineteen-year-old Suzie.

"Just a kid," David sighed.

"*I knew what I wanted...*" Another whisper. So close to David's ear, the hair on his arms stood up and a tickle ran down the back of his neck. Only Debra ever got so close to him that he'd feel that way.

"Stop it," David shrugged, brushing the nothing that was around him away from his ear. "Just stop."

"*It comes from desire...*" the voice said. It sounded all around him. From every corner of the room.

David sat and looked at his wife's chair. He was often overcome with great feelings of sadness when alone in the house. The home that he and Debra worked hard for. Worked hard to enjoy the few memories they made over the years. The trip to Venice two years before she got sick. Their honeymoon to Cozumel. Their first night in the house. Making love by candlelight because the power company hadn't turned on the juice yet.

These thoughts, these memories, played over and over in David's mind, night to night the past three years. In those moments of despair, he felt a great darkness come over him, countless times, a voice calling to him, sounding far off, sounding so distant that it almost didn't seem real and yet now, by the light of the television in his own living room, David was hearing the voice as if it were right beside him.

"*He knows what you want...*"

"He can't," David said, eyes welling up with tears.

David turned and saw a shape in the corner of the living room. The light from the television flickered, casting a gray-cone outward but beyond that, David knew what he was staring at.

"Debra?" he whimpered, his emotions overwhelming him.

Rolling off the chair, on his knees, he crawled toward the shape in the corner. The blotch of shadow that somehow became an approximation of Debra. She was there. She wasn't there. David couldn't take his eyes off the shadow as it took a slow step toward him.

"Please," he said, staring into the darkness. Her shape was all he could see, there were no discernible features. Just a black, deep expanse where form should be.

He extended his hand and slowly, the shadow reached out to him.

As his hand grazed the shadow's, he became overwhelmed with emotion. There was a tightness in his throat, and he swallowed hard, pushing the emotion back down, deeper. Hoping to conquer it. His eyes went wide and he couldn't help but smile as he saw Debra take form before him.

#

The following morning, Kelly arrived, a large Tupperware container under her arm. She locked her car and walked up the path to David's front door. She rang the bell, then knocked when no one answered. On instinct, she tried the knob.

Kelly spotted Waffles on the steps, staring at her. "Hi kitty," Kelly said as she entered the house. Hearing the television, Kelly turned and her eyes went wide when she saw what was left of David. The scream tore from her throat and she dropped the chili, which exploded all over the wood flooring of the foyer in an eruption of red, meaty deliciousness.

David's head.

Wrapped in plastic.

And he was smiling.

About the Author

Robert P. Ottone is the Bram Stoker Award®-winning author of *The Triangle*. His other works include *Her Infernal Name & Other Nightmares* (an honorable mention in *The Best Horror of the Year, Volume 13*) as well as the suburban folk horror novel *The Vile Thing We Created*.

His short stories have appeared in various anthologies as well as online. He's also the publisher and owner of Spooky House Press.

He can be found online at SpookyHousePress.com or on Twitter/IG: @RobertOttone

He delights in the creepy and views bagels solely as a cream cheese delivery device.

Twitter: @RobertOttone
IG: @RobertOttone